Dead in a Ditch

Heather Lynn Osting

This is a work of fiction. Names, characters, businesses, places, events and incidents are either the products of the author's imagination or used in a fictitious manner. Any resemblance to actual persons, living or dead, or actual events is purely coincidental.

Dedication:

For Jerimy, who is truly my better half.
A man who not only makes me a better person by knowing him
but who makes the world a better place, just by being in it. No one is a dream come true quite like you…and nobody makes my dreams come true quite the way you do.
<3

And

To Rachel: My cousin, my friend, my editor and one of my very first partners in crime. Without you this book may not have ever come to be.
Thank you for your support, for "talking me through it'", and for all that you do and for all that you are.
<3

~hl~

INTRO:

My Father always said that one day they'd find me dead in a ditch. That I was a stupid girl and it would get me killed one day. Today has the potential to be that day.

Chapter 1

I awoke to the feeling of the sun beating down on my face. It was that golden ball of light that I loved and adored my entire life, which was with me on this day. Despite the fact that I was a redhead whose dermatologist vehemently instructed avoiding exposure, I could not help the natural high the sun had the ability to provide.

Normally opening one's eyes to sunshine would have been a much welcomed view, however I knew this time would be different. As I prepared to peel my eyes open, all of my senses decided to come alive. It was like my body was awakening from a deep slumber, only this slumber was not of the comfy, well-rested variety. My mouth was the first part of my body that my mind gave notice to. I tried to swallow but instead found a burning feeling inside my throat. My tongue was not just stuck to the roof of my mouth, but also swollen at the sides where my teeth were clenched down upon it. Upon my jaw's release, I was not entirely certain my tongue would still be in one piece.

After my jaw got up the nerve to finally release its hold, I ran my swollen sorry excuse for a tongue across my lips to find them amazingly sharp, like shards of broken glass. They were dried and cracked and tasted like metal. They were more industrial than they were human.

As if that feeling was not scary enough, I started to give thought as to what the rest of my body would look and feel like. I was not sure I wanted to know where I was, or in what shape the rest of me was in. *Oh God, what if I open my eyes and realize I'm not dead, only to wish that I was?*

My father's words, "*We're going to find you dead in a ditch someday*," flooded through my mind. One thing I was sure of was that I was not dead, but the ditch part– that was yet to be determined.

As my mind began to slowly survey my body's damage, I felt a pang of relief to find that I was not paralyzed. The downside was that I could feel my leg broken and twisted behind me.

So far, the leg feels like the worst of it, until I feel my face. Or–should I say–*try* to feel my face. The very attempt at moving my arm to my face told me that my leg was not the worst thing that had happened to me. Broken ribs and bruised kidneys could not be ruled out at this point.

I went back to clenching my teeth just to muster the strength to move my fingers. Lord, how long have I been laying here, immobile, broken, and cooking in this blistering sunlight? How many chilling nights have I been freezing here in the pools of my own perspiration? My fingers continued to move, eerily at first like I had never moved them before in my life, and then more determined as I forced them to move with more purpose than before. I was no longer just seeing if they moved, I now need them to act like fingers to perform an actual human function.

It hurt like hell. The pain from the tips of my fingers became awake with the attempt at mobility. It shot through my palm, crashed into my wrist and then up my arm like a rocket…burning, spreading, infecting all the tissues like a cancerous torch, scorching, torturing, seeking…I cried out in pain!

Whoever said that childbirth was the worst pain known to women obviously had never found themselves in my shoes!

I needed to open my eyes. I needed to see what had become of me. I needed to see where it is that I had come to be. *Oh please, don't be a ditch!* I could not live with the knowledge that my father was right. Estranged for ten years, he insisted I was stupid for a great portion of my existence when he was in my life. Yeah, it would just be a great injustice for him to be right, especially about this! I can imagine his smug, *I knew this would happen*, face upon hearing the news of my death. I had to live, even if only to spite him.

Why exactly did he have to be here in my head with me now anyway? Is he really my go-to-guy for inspiration and strength? The irony of it all almost made me laugh. If it did not hurt so bad I might have, but I was afraid my lips would shatter.

My life had always been kind of ironic. I suppose "dead in a ditch" was entirely plausible. But the fact that the man who did so much damage to me mentally and occasionally beat the hell out of me physically is the voice in my head now–that was just my luck! When I do die, I really must talk to the powers that be about this sort of thing.

I sucked air into my lungs and the rush of the air burned my nose and throat. My brain told my eyelids to open but fear crippled me and I found myself trembling and squeezing them shut instead. My now wobbly, ineffective fingers clenched, and my fingernails—some of which were broken and jagged—stabbed into my palms. I began again... *Oh eyes, please, oh please open...don't let me be broken AND blind...*

And this time my eyelids began to pull across my eyes. They felt as though they were lined with sandpaper. They scraped and scratched my pupils as they retracted to their open position. *Holy Moses!* The sun was brighter than I remembered, forcing me to blink over and over in an attempt to adjust to the light. This simple task was awful the first time, so doing it again only made me want to just lay there and die instead of attempting to live for even one more awful moment!

That was the moment when the anger of the situation set in. Yep, just then, I became angry at my eyelids for being abusive to me, angry at my stupid arm that hurt me to move, livid at my leg for being broken, and just plain pissed at the sun for burning me to my core. I had so long ago suppressed my inherent red-headed temper; it was shocking that now of all times it had decided to re-emerge in my life. As if a temper tantrum was going to help me now…but hey – in moments of misery, they say that the best and the worst of us will come to the surface. I just wondered, *is anger a survival mechanism? Could my redheaded, pissy nature be my savior?*

So here I sat, blinking angrily on my back and staring up into a sky that looks like any sky in the world. I could be in Paris, or I could be in Poughkeepsie. Either way, the sky was no help to me. I was going to have to get up, sit up, or otherwise elevate myself to improve my view. That was when I realized that all my effort thus far had brought me dangerously close to unconsciousness. Suddenly it was hard to stay awake. My head was throbbing, my eyes were burning and every ounce of my body was saying, *we've had enough, close your eyes Viv…be a dear and close your hazel eyes and forget about this for a while.*

I was not going to lie, not to myself, not now…I wanted to sleep! I wanted to sleep and wake up to have found this all just another one of the nightmares I used to have–you know the ones where you wake up in a panic and that wave of ecstasy comes over you when you realize that it is not real. When you realize you are not surrounded by broken flesh, just fluffy pillows; that the darkness was not you slipping into the seventh circle of hell, it was just your drawn blinds and navy blue bedding wrapping you in the darkness. Oh, what I would not have given for my pillow and blanket right now. Just to feel something soft that smells like home…HOME. I just wanted to go home. Tears welled up in my eyes and my throat tightened when I thought about that place.

Home to some is where you hang your hat. Home to me is where it all happens. Home is a four wall's embrace. It is shelter from the storm, it is a retreat, it is a womb, and it is truly where the heart is. Oh how my heart longed to be there now.

I could not give in to my pain, I had to get up. I could not just lay here and die. I have a dog and a flower bed at home that desperately needs mulch and weeding. If I died, my family would go through my personal belongings. My mom would find out that her precious daughter has a "goodie drawer" in her nightstand…*ewwwwww!* My mom can't know that! If I did not die here and now, then I would die later of embarrassment.

It was with that in mind that I used every bit of my strength, grit, anger, and homesickness to constrict my abs into sitting up. I thought the attempt was going to make my eyeballs pop out of their sockets due to the pressure it put on my head to try and lift myself. But despite how they felt, they stayed intact. Unfortunately though, all the strength I had only mustered enough leverage to lift me about a half an inch off the ground. And that half an inch in the shape I was in felt like a half a mile.

Insurmountable defeat washed over me as the song "*Big Girls Don't Cry*" by that Black Eyed Peas girl Fergie popped into my head. I absolutely *must* be delirious! First my crappy dad is in my head and now FERGIE? *Screw you Fergie!* I would like to see you black-eyed-pea yourself out of this mess! Oh cool–the anger's back. I should try to get up again before I really lose it.

This time I decided to roll. If I could roll onto my side that would have provided me with the perspective I needed. Just seeing the ground around me would help...I thought. I counted to three and then threw myself into motion. I assumed it would hurt, but my assumption was nothing compared to the pain that exploded throughout me. Cuts and contusions, breaks and scrapes, it all screamed and hissed at once in one giant wounded whelp. Nonetheless, it worked and there I was on my side.

I noticed sandy dirt, little tufts of grass, gravel, and rocks. So I ruled out the everglades. I was definitely not in the everglades. If I had been, I think the mosquitoes would have carried me off by now. Well, that ruled out one location, now only four hundred billion others to go! I tried harder to focus, to use my wits to come up with a better conclusion than, "not the everglades", but the terrain had my mind racing. I'm a Midwestern girl, born and raised in Ohio, so I don't exactly know what other parts of the country look like. Not all of them anyway–and besides, places can be deceiving.

Anyone who has ever stood in downtown Manhattan would never think in a million years that farmland and countryside was just a hop, skip, and a jump away. But Upstate New York is far from the mainstream hustle and bustle of the "Big Apple". I did not appear to be in a desert, but vegetation is definitely sparse here, wherever "here" was. My eyes searched for civilization—roads, houses, cars, hell– even a cow might be nice, but I see nothing but trees off in the distance and no signs of life other than my own.

I was not exactly a picture of "life" at this point, but I figured so long as I was breathing, I still count. I was half expecting there to be vultures circling over me, waiting to pick my bones...at least that was what you always see in the movies. Or buzzards. They are a whole other creature, you know. If you have ever seen one up close, you are bound to have a reaction to it. You would not know whether to fear them or loathe them, but you will not feel good upon locking eyes with one. That much I can promise you.

They used to perch, at least fifteen or twenty of them, all together there in a section of trees on the edge of the town where I grew up. A section of town where there was a hill called *Devil's Hill*. Even more paradoxical, there was a church perched at the foot of Devil's Hill. You would swear that those damned buzzards were the guardians of hell itself when you would see them in the trees— big, black, and watchful. So yeah, I am glad there are no buzzards. Maybe I am not nearly as dead as I am supposed to be, for I am certain that by someone's approximation I am presumed to be dead. Maybe there was something to the saying *only the good die young*, for I am only in my twenties, and young enough to fit the bill, just not dead enough to be good I guess.

So with a bum leg, half-starved and banged up like I was, I knew standing up and dusting myself off was not going to be an option. I knew there was only one way I was going to get to wherever it was I was going, and that was going to be by crawling.

By this point, the pain was all consuming, and while normally I think this kind of thing would cripple you, it only angered me. The more it hurt, the angrier I got, until I was on my stomach crawling in a direction I was not sure of and cursing like a sailor through gritted teeth. I was mobile. I was slow. So slow that I was probably leaving a mucus trail behind me–but I was on my way to somewhere.

I am not sure how far I got, or if it had been hours or days, but I was still not a corpse. This was progressive news under the circumstances. However, the sky had gotten dark and I sensed the rain was about to start. Guess that rules out the desert. It does not rain much in the desert. *Only three hundred ninety-nine billion nine hundred and ninety nine other locales to rule out now*, I muttered. Optimism is hard to come by these days. The anger is now clinging to me like the earth stuck to my dried blood and skin, and it seems to be my only real motivation. Anger, a lifetime trying to control it, and out here it is a lifeline. It is my constant companion.

The rain waits for no man or woman, it seems. It poured from the sky and over me like a river from heaven. I slid more so than crawled my way across the ground and thought of myself as a greased pig, slip sliding my way through the mud. Oh, if my college professors could see me now. How impressed those scholars would be! But now that I was chilled from the downpour, I was picking up steam as my body faced much less resistance than before. I drank from a puddle a few feet back and my lips felt less like there were clothes pins pinching them. That was a relief. I was cold, but thankful for the rain. I must keep on going, must keep…on…

In sets delirium as I thought I saw lights on the now darkened horizon. I can't tell if they are pole lights, headlights, or fire flies, but regardless, I'm crawling ever so slowly toward them. My arms were no longer feeling like arms, but more like wooden planks that someone shoved into my arm sockets. They hurt, but pain is a funny thing once you accept that it's not going away, and NOT going to get better. So my wooden planks continued on, toward the light, toward anything, anyone.

Time has no meaning anymore, and I am not even sure that what I am crawling toward are lights. I was not entirely sure that the sun had not burnt holes into my retinas. Maybe I was crawling towards holes in my retinas. Which made me wonder what holes in one's retinas would look like through the hole stricken eye—would they be bright spots, dark spots, or would I be blind altogether?

It was that mental conversation that came to mind as I woke to find my head stuck under something, something big and metal. I thought I had crawled into a culvert pipe until I heard voices. I thought I must be dreaming, because the voices were speaking in…*ummmm*, what language is that? Spanish, yeah, it's Spanish. But not like sultry, sexy Spanish that those gorgeous Latino women speak. It was more like speedy Gonzales was running around on the other side of this metal obstruction that seemed to have me pinned in my place.

It was hurried, urgent and forceful. It sounded to me like a swarm of angry Spanish bees buzzing about–but then again–I was delusional, it might actually be a swarm of angry Spanish bees. The funny thing is that it would not make this nightmare any worse or any more real. Spanish Bees and holey retinas seemed logical to me at this point.

Just then the swarm descended upon me. They tugged at my pant leg and the metal giant moved within an inch of me. *Wait metal thing, come back!* I thought to myself. It was the first and only solid object I had found in what seemed like my entire life. I could not bear losing it now. It was my shelter, my oasis, and now it was moving. *So much for solidity*, I thought. The swarm hovered above me, now landing on my back and arms. They were tugging and prodding me, as if there were honey for them to find. I think my sweetness had expired along with my seemingly decaying body. *Let the honey bees take what's left of me*, I thought. Spanish honey bees would not sound like the worst fate a girl could have.

At that point the bees began to roll me over and began saying, *Senora? Senora?* I did not open my eyes, but I felt my lips whisper, honey.

I was not sure if I was dead and ascending into heaven, or if I was dreaming, but my mind finally took me somewhere that I actually wanted to be. Faces of friends and family flashed by along with my favorite sounds: a Harley Davidson Motorcycle's engine, the roar of the river flowing over the German Dam in center of the Auglaize River, and birds on a summer morning in my back yard. My favorite smells swirled around me: fresh cut hay in the field, bed sheets dried on the clothes line, the smell of the man I loved…Oh, it was intoxicating. I was drunk on the goodness of all of these memories and sensations my brain was offering me in my unconscious state. If this was Heaven, I could not be happier to be here.

It continued and I saw flashes of the man I loved, and when I say loved, it was because there was only one man who fit the bill. I have lusted after, crushed on, been addicted to, been abused by, but never *loved* before I met Knox. From the moment I laid eyes on him I knew that the sun could rise and set, and I would not even notice while he was in sight.

Naturally he was exactly the polar opposite of what my mom would have wanted for me. He was the type of guy who I could never take to my office parties with my fancy businessmen bosses, and the women who are married to fancy businessman types. No, Knox was the kind of guy who looked good in your bed, around a campfire with a guitar in his hands, or on top of you…but to imagine him elsewhere was a little more difficult.

Looking back to when we first met, only a short time ago, I now realized that so much had changed. I was young and impressionable and wanting to break free of all that had been expected of me. No more parents monitoring my every move and now legal to drink—it was a recipe for danger, which is exactly what I wanted to taste. Not that I ever lived a sheltered life, but I was stifled by my mother's insistent religious views, closed-mindedness, and judgmental attitude towards the creatures in this life who enticed me and inspired my rebellious spirit.

Some are born to lead, others to follow, and some just wander, meander, spiral, teeter...and have no clear direct path in life. I never knew what I wanted to be when I grew up; I only knew what I did not want to be, and that was my mother. I did not want to find myself looking down on people who still had a little spirit left in them, not quite yet stomped out by the boot heels of modern day conformity.

So you can imagine my excitement when I planned to attend my first "biker rally". Black Swamp, it was a bad girl's paradise. Ever since I was old enough to know what it was, I wanted to go. Black Swamp was a biker's party outside of Van Wert, Ohio. It was in the middle of nowhere, but in the heart of it all.

Black Swamp was infamous for naked people, bands, beer drinking, bikes as far as the eye could see, tattoo contests, a pond shaped like the Harley Davidson Emblem, Easy Rider Magazine, and every other seedy thing you can imagine. It was everything and anything you never wanted anywhere near your daughter.

You can imagine how my mother's jaw dropped when I was around nine, telling people that someday I would go to Black Swamp. She was so embarrassed and would scramble nervously to tell people, "She doesn't even know what Black Swamp is, don't listen to her!" But I did know about Black Swamp and nothing was going to keep me from going there someday.

As luck would have it, that day had finally arrived—and it could not have come soon enough. I made arrangements to go out there with some of my biker enthusiast cousins, and I took a vacation day from work. Naturally everyone thought I was crazy, because no matter how badass I thought that I was, I was just as white-bread, small town as any girl who lived. My spirit, it knew no reason. It only knew that limits and boundaries did not mean much in the grand scheme of things.

What a glorious day it was when I arrived at the gate. I paid my admittance and in I went, swallowed up and into biker culture. Standing there with my pale skin, blazing red wild hair, black boots, and cut off shorts wearing an old and tattered Harley t-shirt...I can only imagine how wide-eyed I must have looked to those hardened bikers. Maybe my outfit fit the part, but the look on my face could not have.

My cousin Matt nudged me in the ribcage and said, "Viv, we've got to get a move on if we're going to get camp set up before dark."

I blinked my eyes, closed my dropped jaw and followed obediently as instructed. Black Swamp at that time was a mowed wheat field by day and a biker fest by night. We made our way across the grounds and found a spot to begin setting up our tents. Bikes and bikers continued to file in, one after another. The loud roars coming from their bikes' pipes made me forget what I was doing long enough to bask in the glory of the moment.

Sunshine, screaming bikes, hammers pounding metal stakes into the ground, the smell of campfire smoke and black powder exploding...it was amazing! There was an electric feeling in the air, the feeling that something was about to happen. Maybe good, maybe bad, but it was unmistakably in the air and painted on the faces of every last person that crossed through those Black Swamp-ground gates.

Let the games begin!

The place erupted into festivities: biker games, naked biker chicks engaging in lewd acts (and not in the customary dark corner), stripper poles, fried food, beer bellies, and orgies as far as the eye could see. I had never seen a real life orgy before, but when I did see one unfolding before my very eyes by the pond, my cousin warned me that if I kept staring, it was only a matter of time before they invited me to join in.

I blushed and also felt nauseous at the thought. The man who very much resembled Santa Claus was leaning back on a floating raft, while one of his lady friends bobbed up and down with her face on his manhood. The water splashed in her face as she caused a wake with her bare breasts slapping the water and the tops of Santa's legs. But Santa did not notice that, as he was wrist deep inside a brunette girl who was sprawled out beside him, her head back, face up, biting her lip one minute and moaning the next. Obviously she was enjoying herself in a very, very public way.

Another female swam up and began to pet the hair of the woman, whose mouth was full of Santa's staff, and they began to take turns licking, kissing, and caressing Santa and then each other. *Doing that in this dirty water is hardly sanitary!* I thought to myself. While I wanted to be wild and free, I guess there was a part of me that was not an idiot. Urinary tract infections, group sex in public, blowing Santa and then smiling for a photo op sans a few teeth—yeah, I guess you could say I was never going to be quite that wild!

Before I was invited to be their next playmate in the muddy water, I made my exit. I was not near finished exploring this new territory full of wonder and mayhem.

As I made my way through the biker camp, I walked up near a group of vendors.

They were all lined up in rows, some selling food, some ass-less chaps, and others offering spare bike parts and nipple clamps. I browsed the selection and took a deep breath in when I landed myself near the leather booth. Why is it that the smell of leather can turn an average woman into a sexually charged vixen on the prowl? I instantly felt my insides awaken to the idea.

What the orgy did not awaken, the leather did. I pulled a cold beer out of the back pocket of my cutoffs and slid it into my can coozie. I thought perhaps I could numb my desires with the cold liquid.

I kept walking, wandering, and weaving in and out of the way of bikers and biker bitches. I stopped to watch the sky divers navigate their way into camp. I bought a cheeseburger and was just about to take a big bite of its greasy goodness when I saw a man standing a few yards away, staring at me. He was staring so intently that I felt his eyes burrow right into my soul. At first the piercing stare made me unable to breathe, move, or even blink my eyes.

It was like he had control over me from the instant he laid eyes on me. His eyes were unlike anything I had ever seen before. They were not the dark eyes I normally found myself attracted to; they were light, like the color of amber, almost golden. He wore a bandanna around his head, his hair seemingly kept short underneath. His skin was perfectly sun kissed, his ears were pierced, and a little tuft of hair grew under his lip. He sported tattoos on his arm, neck, wrist, and likely under his clothing as well. He was absolutely entrancing. I tried to look away, but just as I was about to break our intense stare, he half-smiled at me.

Then I realized why. There I was standing in the middle of a crowd that was parting and sweeping around me with an uneaten cheeseburger two inches away from my mouth. I suppose I looked fairly silly frozen there like that, so without breaking my stare I took a big, dramatic bite of my burger. I half-smiled back with my cheeks stuffed to the gills with bread, meat, mustard, and pickles. I looked like a wannabe biker chipmunk. *Sexy!* I thought to myself.

He must have thought so too, because he looked away casually, as if we had never locked eyes in the first place. I suppose I can't blame him for his lack of interest in me.

After all, I was not particularly amazing in any way. I had pale skin, instead of bronzed like the other girls here. There were a generous amount of freckles on my shoulders, and I was round around the edges. I had big boobs that I never thought of as quite the asset that others seemed to see them as. But the one thing I had noticed that set me apart from the other girls here was the fact that my boobs were still where God had put them.

All that bra wearing I had committed to doing apparently kept "my girls" up, where biker women's seem to sway to and fro down below where mine were perched. Some were so unattractive that they reminded me of tennis balls stuffed into tube socks. Not a great look for any lady, if you know what I'm saying.

I have been cursed from the sixth grade on with D sized breasts, which has taught me a lot about gravity and the dangers of running and jumping. I never wanted to wind up looking like a pair of tube socks.

As I pondered my own inadequacies as a woman, I returned my gaze to where the handsome stranger stood only to find that he was gone. Just like that, it was as if he never existed in the first place. For a moment I wondered if my loins had imagined him, high on leather and red meat. Maybe he had been a hallucination? Regardless, I found myself surprisingly disappointed. I wanted him to have been real, here and now in this unreal place.

The rest of the night was spent looking into the faces of the strangers I passed. I was searching for those golden eyes that had stared into me, but unfortunately bloodshot or sunglass-clad eyes were all that stared back. He's far too incredible to be interested in me anyway, I thought while pouting where I stood. I shrugged and took my last swig of beer. *Ahhh!*

"*Hey you!*" someone said within ear shot, breaking my pout and quest to stumble across my hallucination once more. I turned to my right to see a vendor hollering toward me. I stared at the guy as he stared back at me.

"Ya deaf er sumthin?" he said breaking our stare.

I yelled back, "NO," offended by his assumption that I had some sort of disability.

"What do you want?" I said, and he replied, "Come over here for a minute."

Coolly I said, "Why would I want to do that?", still angry at him for asking me if I was deaf.

He said back, "Because I need to see you up close m'darlin."

I looked at him now skeptically and said, "I ain't nobody's darling, least of all yours!"

He smiled wide at my sassiness and said, "Sorry doll, didn't mean to offend you, but I have a business proposition for you if you just come over here for a second. And besides, what have you got to lose?"

I walked over towards him, scanning his vendor booth to see what it was he was in the business of doing, but I did not see exactly what he was selling. As I approached, his dark eyes never left my chest. It felt like he had just raped me with his eyeballs.

I crossed my arms across my chest upon stopping in front of him and said, "Can I help you?"

Then he looked me in the eye and said, "Baby, I think we can help each other. I'm an artist, you see, and I desperately need a canvas."

Not being aware of what kind of artist this man was I said, "How exactly am I supposed to help you with that?"

He said, "Your tits, baby doll...they could be my greatest work of art."

I cringed and crinkled my nose at the thought of being fondled by *Mr. Body Art's* big, dark, sweaty hands. "Are you messing with me?" I spit at him.

"No, I wouldn't shit a shitter. I do body paint and you'd be an outstanding walking, talking, bouncing advertisement. No charge doll, I'll paint you for free, just come in and place that fine ass of yours in my chair and let me work my magic."

I have to wonder why guys like him think my ass is fine. It was always the ones I find grotesque who think I am hot. I swear that no amount of compliments from a man of his caliber will ever fill one's self confidence bucket. Here I am, longing for someone entirely out of my league, and then there's THIS GUY! Being "hot" to the likes of him just depresses me. Is this the best I can do? Have my options reduced to this clown? *Just freaking great!*

He interrupted my inner whining. "I'll try not to enjoy it, I promise!"

He must have noticed that *ain't no fucking way* look in my eyes.

Naturally I was flustered, and in an attempt to avoid him finding out that I am actually not a badass biker chick, I blushed and barely blurted out, "I…I, um, yeah, um, no, I couldn't!"

"It's hot out here babe, don't you want to shed outta that hot ole black shirt of yours and let the sun glisten on those gorgeous titties?"

Offended again by his vulgarity in talking about "my girls" I said, "No, actually I don't wish for that, have you seen me? I'm Casper the ghost white over here and the sun is not my friend. And while you might think that exposing my "girls" to the world is a super hot idea, all I can think of is the blistering sunburn that would befall me!"

He heard me, and then raised an eyebrow. "No problem doll. How about you come over here and let me rub some sunscreen on you. I'll do you from head to toe and especially there!" as he pointed to my chest.

I blushed again. *Damnit, what's the matter with me? This blushing shit's for losers! I gotta learn how to not let it give me away*! I said to myself. That was when I heard a chuckle from behind me. I turned to find my golden-eyed, tattooed hallucination standing in very close proximity to me. He was so close that I could feel the heat coming off of his skin, and could smell the alcohol on his breath as it encompassed my face. It was sweet, mouthwateringly-sweet.

As I once more locked eyes with my hallucination, I found myself startled when

Mr. Body Art called to me again and said, "So, what's it gonna be? Are you in, or are you out?"

I was afraid to respond in fear of losing sight and smell of my hallucination once again. Before I had the chance to react, the golden-eyed stranger answered for me.

"Hey man, you harassing my old lady? I know her rack's eye catching, but they are very much spoken for and enjoyed by me, so piss off would ya?" Then he draped his arm around my shoulder letting his palm fall square onto my right breast, and he gave it a firm cupping as he pulled me away from the vendor's booth.

I was in shock. I was saved from a pervert by a guy whose name I did not even know but who just felt me up! It was a good thing he was handsome, because it was a ballsy move on his part that could have gone very wrong—had I been a real biker bitch as opposed to little old me. I was surprised when he did not remove his arm from my shoulders, even when we were out of sight of the *Body Art man*. I have to admit, it was more than a little awkward considering the fact that the man groping me was a total stranger. We continued to walk on in total silence until we were out of sight from the crowds.

Finally, after what seemed like a lifetime, he responded, "Knox".

"Huh?"

He said again, "Knox!"

I replied confused, "What the hell's Knox supposed to mean?"

He said, "It's my name, the name's Knox…and just who might you be?"

I was embarrassed for not grasping the fact that he was introducing himself, but seriously, whose name is Knox? How was I supposed to know?

I stopped walking, pulled out from under his arm and introduced myself. "Viv, Vivienne to be precise," I said as I extended my hand for him to shake.

He said, "Miss Vivienne, this introduction is a bit formal for the likes of Black Swamp don't you think?"

I looked around to my left and my right and thought–yeah, I suppose this might be a bit unorthodox for where I was, but weren't introductions fairly universal? It was not like I had kissed both his cheeks and introduced myself in French. This was still America, and last I checked a handshake was a fully acceptable way of making introductions.

He took my hand, only because I refused to budge on my formal introduction, but then he pulled it down and used it as a clutch to move my body towards his.

He pulled me in close and warned, "Vivienne, what are you doing here in a place like this? You don't belong here. Your kind can get hurt in places like this. You don't know the first thing about making your way in the world, do you?"

I pulled my hand away from him abruptly. "You don't know the first damned thing about me! Don't fucking assume you know me! You don't know me!"

I turned and stormed away.

"Just because you have eyes like that doesn't mean they see!" I spat back towards him in the midst of my hasty retreat.

I did not want to look at him, or have him see me look back as I walked away, but I could not help it. I looked back to see him standing there–his face not giving a single clue as to what he was thinking. One thing was for certain, he was not stopping me from walking away. Our parting ways were for the best– yes, I was certain of it. What a presumptuous bastard! *First the vendor asshole and now this guy? Christ, are all men this egotistical?*

I decided to head back to camp. I had enough wandering for one afternoon, and I was ready to be with faces I knew. Once back at camp, we cooked a pot of chili at our little community of tents. There was a large cast iron pot positioned over a fire filled with red meat, beans, peppers, and onions. The smell of the chili spice wafted through the country air. We ate and drank while telling stories of people we knew, places we had been, and rides we had taken.

I had not been around the world, so I could not regale tales of my travels, but I was wise to the world for my age. While I had not partaken in all the things I knew, I always had an awareness of what was going on around me because I listened to others intently—soaking it all in, learning and growing into whoever it was I would one day be.

My mind wandered to the bizarre meeting and introduction with Knox earlier. I thought about him touching me intimately and deliberately, then scolding me like a child for even being here–and again my blood began to run hot. Redheaded temper flare-ups are common but mostly un-welcome. I tried not to think about him, but it was hard not to. His words kept stinging me, long after they had been said. Why did I care what he thought of me anyway? Who was he to me? Nobody! That's who!

It was time to get some sleep. The events of today were sure to be insignificant by morning. I went into my tent and contemplated zipping it shut, but decided to allow it to flap open in the low breeze that had been blowing around camp in the darkness. So with a foggy beer-fueled head, I laid flat on my stomach and quickly drifted into unconsciousness.

Chapter 2

When I awoke, I was no longer in my tent at Black Swamp. I was lying on my back staring up at stainless-steel pots and pans hanging overhead. The view was much different than I remembered, especially because now I could only see out of one eye. I brought my hand up to meet my face, and it was the first clear view I remember of my battered fingers.

My fingers were disgusting–black, purple, and yellowing. I laid my fingers on my face to see if I still had a nose and if my wounded eye was shut–or perhaps missing. I felt around and found that everything seemed to be where it was supposed to be, albeit swollen. My lips tasted funny, not unlike bacon grease. This discovery made my stomach suddenly come alive. It forced me to irrationally contemplate devouring my lips right off my face, but I figured I looked bad enough as it was.

I don't remember a time when I have been hungrier in my life. I slowly sat up through the pain and was immediately swarmed by three dark- skinned, Spanish-speaking men, all yelling at me and flailing their arms emphatically. I didn't know what to do or what to think. All I could think was *How in the hell did I wind up in Mexico? I don't even have a passport!*

A little, dark-haired girl walked into the room. She looked quite afraid of my grotesque face but still managed to feign a smile. I tried weakly to smile back but was not sure if my face was moving in the appropriate direction. The one thing I was sure of was how horrifying I must have looked next to this angelic, little girl. The stark contrast of my pale skin taken over by deep colored bruises had to appear monstrous.

She then spoke in her perfect, little-girl voice.

"Hola, do you know where you are?"

I was so happy to hear English I nearly started to cry.

"No, I honestly do not."

She came closer and peered up at me. "We won't hurt you. We didn't do this to you. We found you under our dumpster this way."

The little girl then focused on one of the Mexican men, who was speaking rapidly in Spanish, gesturing toward me. "Yesterday we fixed you up best we could," the little girl repeated in English. "Your leg's probably broken according to Jose. He knows a little about medicine. He's a vet assistant back home. He also said that your abdomen is very swollen and he thinks you may have some internal bleeding. Oh, and your stomach–you were stabbed. Whoever stabbed you obviously wasn't very good at it as the wounds appeared superficial." The little girl then looked at Jose, or who I think Jose is, and says "superficiales?" Jose nods and she continued, "Yeah, superficial, it didn't hit anything important inside you. He stitched you up. It's not pretty, but it'll hold you together until you get to wherever it is you're going."

I looked to Jose and smiled at him with a lump in my throat as I weakly repeated, "Gracias".

I was immediately grateful for their help. I hoped that he could read that in my sincere thank you. He nodded to me but remained stoic in his acceptance of my gratitude.

"Isn't anyone looking for you? Shouldn't you be somewhere?" the little girl asked.

My head was spinning, and sitting up was a foreign concept at this point. It was a lot of information to have thrown at me by such a young girl, so I did my best to try to process everything.

I collected my thoughts and said to her, "Thank you for taking me in and doing what you could for me. I'm from America. My name's Vivienne. How far from the border am I?"

She looked at me very strangely. "The border of what?"

I was taken back. "Where exactly am I?"

She said, "Mamacita, I don't know where you're supposed to be or where you think you are, but you are in Illinois. You are just outside of Chicago."

Chicago? I'm near Chicago? Oh, dear Lord in heaven, I am only four hours from home. But how in the hell did I wind up in Chicago? The idea that I could be home in half a day's time made me light up! I would have bounced off the table I was on, had it not hurt so much. But then I asked, "Didn't you call the police when you found me? Why didn't anyone take me to a hospital?"

She pondered my questions momentarily and then thoughtfully replied. "Here on the farm, we take care of our own. Some of us don't have our papers. We don't attract attention to ourselves if we can avoid it. I mean, our employers know we're not all legal, so they too said it was better you recover here with us."

"They are real good people, the Lloyd's. They own the entire farm. They have a market too. My family has worked for them for many years. They examined you themselves and said to wait until you came to before we called anyone. Miguel can drive you to town or to the hospital if you like?"

"We just couldn't leave you there under the dumpster looking like you did, err, um, do."

Then it dawned on me that this little girl was wise beyond her years. I could not help but ask, "How old are you anyway? Better yet, *who* are you?"

She looked around the room at the three men who were staring intently at me, looking a little nervous. She said, "I'm eleven, almost twelve. I know, I'm short for my age." "And we"..., she pointed to herself and the men standing around us, "...are just migrant workers, and I'm Mia. We all work and live here on the farm."

Confused, I asked the girl for clarification. "Let me get this straight. We are on a farm, outside of Chicago?"

"Yes. Illinois is in the Midwest you know. Lots of rural communities surround big cities."

Again I am amazed at being schooled by an eleven year old. "Are you sure you're only eleven?"

When the men began to realize that I was not going to scream my head off, they started to look more at ease. Mia gave them a look that said, *she's cool, guys*, and I watched as one by one they took their leave from us. One put on gardening gloves and returned to loading potting soil into large buckets while the other two began pruning a table full of plants, flowers, and transferable bushes alike.

My eleven year old Mexican Angel, Mia, then helped me to slowly navigate over to her humble living quarters. She introduced me to a group of women who spoke about as much English as I do Spanish–which is not much–but they were hospitable nonetheless. They helped get me cleaned up and made me feel welcome and cared for.

"Are you hungry, senora?" Mia translated to me for one of the women in the room.

"Yes, very!" I said.

"How are your lips, are you able to eat?"

I put my finger to my lips and felt them. "Better," I responded, suddenly aware of the fact that my lips once felt like shards of glass, and now felt softer and suppler.

"My Madre did that. Back home, in Mexico, it can get very dry. We use bacon grease. It works better than anything. This is my Madre, Sophia," Mia said as her mother stepped out of the crowd of women and over to stand in front of me.

"Pleasure to meet you," I said.

She pointed to her lips and then to mine, before she said something in Spanish that I could not make out.

Mia laughed and said, "She said your lips were beyond the help of modern medicine!"

The other women laughed at this as well, and I wondered if that was really what she had said.

"Would you like a burrito?" she asked as she was suddenly surrounded by women with their hands ready to assemble a plate for me.

"YES!" I answered as quickly as possible. I loved Mexican food. Being in this kitchen reminded me of my favorite Mexican restaurant back home. *Banditos*, I loved that place. Just another thing from home that made my mind flood with memories of my life, a life that I was missing every moment I was away from home.

The women did not take long to fold and craft a gigantic flour tortilla. I watched in anticipation as they filled it with amazing fixings: rice, black beans, grilled chicken, guacamole, and sour cream! Oh it was heavenly! I knew just how weak I had become when it took all that I had left in my arms to lift the burrito to my mouth. It felt like it weighed ten pounds! From the size of it, I wondered if maybe it did weigh ten pounds. After only eating half of it, I was forced to set the rest down on my plate. I grew increasingly tired that even my chewing became laborious.

Mia noticed and said to me, "Come".

I left my food behind and followed her out of the kitchen. My limp was getting increasingly severe as I hobbled along slowly and painfully behind Mia.

She led me down a hallway and into a small room. It was minimal in design, a functional bathroom at best. The room consisted of a stand up shower stall with a concrete slab for a floor, a dingy little sink, and a toilet. It was without frilly towels, or plush rugs for your feet. It was a room that held no warmth. Well, until she turned the shower on, and I saw steam roll out from the sides of the plastic shower curtain.

Once I was left alone I wasted no time to strip out of my clothes, clothes that I recently noticed did not belong to me. I was not sure where they had come from. They were blood-stained and dirty, and they smelled like death. I was happy to shed them, and let them land in a heap on the floor. I was disgusted by the idea of getting clean, then having to put them back on afterward. Hopefully Mia had an older sister that I could borrow some clothes from.

Once I was naked, I realized that my body was bandaged everywhere. My torso was wrapped, and my bum leg was tied to a wooden splint. It took me so long to unwrap my wounds that I was not sure I would have any strength left to stand up for a shower.

I could not walk without my splint, so I hopped one-legged across the floor and nearly fell several times before making it into the shower. I hated how everything I now did felt like a chore.

After I managed to get into the shower, I slowly began my shower routine. It almost felt like something that I had done in a different life. I picked up the bottle of shampoo and squeezed the usually generous amount into my hand. As I lathered my hair with the lemon-scented shampoo, the water cascaded down over my head, helping to untangle my hair. It soothed some of my aching muscles, while stinging my cuts and scrapes. I closed my eyes and refused to evaluate the rest of my body. I did not want to see how badly I had been made to look. Seeing my leg when I took the splint off was grotesque enough. I did not have the stomach to inspect the rest of me.

My stomach burned like fire when I applied soap to it. When I ran my hand across my midsection, I could feel that scabs were covering my entire stomach. Part of me screamed to look down and see them, but the part of me that was trying to hold myself together kept me from looking down.

My body started to become weak as I nearly fell over, running into one of the shower partition walls. I stood there leaning into the wall for support for what felt like forever, letting the now lukewarm water wash over me. This was not the Ritz Carlton, but it was far more hospitable than where I awoke two days ago. Or was it four? It was all such a blur. I seemed to have gaps in my memory that I just could not seem to fill, regardless of how hard I tried. I wanted to go home. And that became my mission in this new and strange life –to get home.

After my shower, I pulled the shower curtain aside and reached for the towel I had hung outside the stall. I dried my face and wrapped the towel around my body. I saw a folded set of clothes on the toilet seat, which I believed were left there for me. Mia must have snuck in here while I was not looking. She left clothes, fresh gauze, medical tape, and vet wrap.

The clothes consisted of a pair of jeans, slightly tattered and worn, a white wife beater tank top, and a green mesh baseball cap with the Mexican flag on the front.

It was not exactly an outfit I would have picked out for myself, but anything was better than the disgusting pile of clothes on the floor that I had been wearing.

Before I could dress, I had to redress my wounds. Mia's medical drop included rolls of vet wrap, which was commonly used to wrap the ankles of racehorses. But I didn't care; it was perfect for me to wrap my torso with. After several revolutions, my body began to resemble a mummy. By the time I had reaffixed the splint to my leg and wrapped myself up tight, I practically was a mummy! When I was finally ready for clothing, I slipped them on carefully so that I did not hurt myself. I was amazed at how the clothes felt. Crisp and clean, like nothing I had ever felt before—or at least nothing I had ever appreciated before like I did now.

This new ensemble simply did what clothes do, they covered me up. As a woman, you spend your whole life carrying a mirror, looking for a mirror, and constantly wanting to check your reflection to make sure you are looking your best. When you look your worst, mirrors are not something you seek out. Their absence is welcomed. That was exactly how I felt on this day.

When I reemerged from the bathroom, little Mia was leaning up against the wall outside the hallway, patiently waiting for me.

"From you?" I asked as I tugged on the neck of my tank top.

"Yes, from all of us. We'll burn your other ones, they stink!"

"Probably a good idea," I said.

Mia giggled as I hobbled after her down the hallway. She would look back at me, giggle, look forward once more, and then repeat.

"What? What's so funny?" I finally asked curiously.

"You walk like a zombie!"

"I feel like a zombie, but I look like a mummy!" I said, agreeing with her assessment.

"You need crutches. You really shouldn't be trying to walk on that leg. It'll never get better, you know," she said, looking down accessing my splint and bandage work.

"What I really need is to get going. I need to get home," I said.

Mia walked me down the hallway and out the front door to Miguel, who was patiently waiting for me alongside a truck.

"This is Miguel. He'll take you into town. It's ok, Vivienne, he will take care of you. Where do you want him to take you? Bus stop? Train station?" she inquired.

"Bus stop, I guess."

Mia told Miguel my destination in Spanish, he nodded to the little girl, and then walked straight for me. Instinctively I flinched, as if his movement had put me in danger, but Miguel just picked me up and carried me around the truck. He sat me on the front passenger seat and closed the door behind me.

The gesture was sweet, coming from a man who was nearly a stranger. It was strange being so close to a man. Being carried is quite an intimate thing if you think about it–surrendering your mobility to another. Once safely inside the truck, Miguel hopped up into the cab next to me and started the engine.

Mia had not left my side since she introduced herself to me, aside from when I took a shower. Now, as I waited to depart, she was standing next to the truck looking so small and sad. She knew I was about to leave her behind, and she sincerely looked disappointed in my decision to go. I told her goodbye, and she smiled through her disappointment and said, "Adios mi amiga".

Mia, she was without a doubt an angel. I was sad to have to say goodbye to her too, but I had to go. I had a life to get back to, and I was in serious need of some pain meds!

Miguel put the old Ford into drive and we began our departure. I waved farewell to Mia and watched as she ran as fast as her little legs would carry her chasing after us. Before long, she was just a shadow, lost in a cloud of dust behind the truck. Miguel took me into town and dropped me off at the closest Greyhound Terminal.

As he helped me out of the truck he said, "Buena suerte. Ser seguro."

I was not sure what that meant, but I had the feeling he sincerely meant whatever it was that he said. Suddenly, I was sad to see Miguel go. I had an irrational reaction to throw myself into his arms and not let him leave, but instinctively, I knew I was just trying to cling to the only person that was showing me kindness at this time. He reached out his hand with a small amount of cash to cover my bus fare. I waved at him as he drove away, and then I hurried to the ticket booth...or at least attempted to hurry.

I had never ridden a bus before, other than the yellow school bus that used to pick me and my sisters up for school, so I was not entirely sure how the process worked. I purchased a ticket and welcomed the *Psshhhhhttt Woosh* noise that came as the driver closed the door behind me. As I made my way to a vacant seat, the bus began to move out of the station and towards my home.

I closed my eyes and pulled my ball cap over my hideous appearance. My hat had the Mexican flag on it, my jeans were two inches too short, and my white tank top did little to hide my injuries from those around me. I felt very exposed here. My outfit was not nearly as odd as the fact that I was dressed like a Mexican boy and also resembled a movie extra on the set of a horror film written for flesh eating zombies– my character playing one of the eat*ing*, as opposed to the eat*en*!

I noticed that the people around me looked apprehensive when I boarded the bus. Nobody kept their eyes on me for more than a few seconds at a time, to avoid the appearance of being rude or intrusive. We were definitely in the Midwest. Midwesterners were all about NOT being rude. I knew, however, that they were likely dying inside to know what had happened to me. Midwesterners are also as nosey of a bunch as they come. Anything out of the norm, especially those of a scandalous and seedy sort, are sure to cause an uproar in a small Midwestern town. But hey, at least Midwesterners are not rude. They may be gossipy and closed-minded, but they are not rude.

As the mile markers began to flash by my eyes grew increasingly heavy, so I laid my head against the window and dozed off while my breath fogged up the glass.

Chapter 3

When I awoke, I was back in my tent at Black Swamp. I was comfortably sleeping and softly snoring when I found myself waking up due to the feeling of something clasping around my ankle. It constricted in an instant, and I could not deny the feeling that someone was in the tent with me. Before I could assess the situation something clasped around the other ankle with the same feeling as the first—at first tight and pinching, and then tugging. I was afraid to open my eyes, so I opened only one, peeking discreetly around the small canvas space until I saw someone there beside me. I was instantly aware that he had a knife clenched between his teeth.

I could see his beard, long and dark, shadowing his face–and he was not alone. I heard rustling outside my tent on all sides. There must have been three or four of them. By this point they had tied my legs and my wrists together, and that was when he rolled me over.

He put his face right up to mine. "Girl, If you scream I'll slit you from here to here!" he said as he clasped my neck and then put his hand down my pants, poking me to show just where he intended to stop severing me. "And if you do decide to scream, which I hope you do, I'll gut you right here and right now. Either way, I'll enjoy myself. The question is, will you? Do you want to die?" He laughed in a way that let me know that he was not afraid of getting caught here in my tent. He feared nothing, least of all me.

I did not dare to scream, for he seemed very sincere in his want for my blood. He had the look in his eyes that I was no more precious of a life to him, as were cattle in the stockyards about to be shipped for slaughter. To him, I wasn't "Miss Vivienne"…I was stock. I could be bought, sold, or disposed of at will. I was stock he was going to collect whether I liked it or not. And with a jerk, I was ripped from my tent and drug across the ground until my little campsite was long gone.

The fresh cut wheat was so sharp that I could feel it piercing my skin, ripping it away one little wheat stalk at a time. My legs, arms, and shoulders took the majority of it, but my face had not been exempt from the assault. When I started to feel sticky, I knew the blood was flowing. Maybe that was a good thing. Maybe a blood trail would save me–maybe someone would come for me, rescue me, and save me.

But no one came for me. No valiant rescue attempt was taken on my behalf.
One minute I was just a redheaded motorcycle enthusiast, the next I had become the property of the devil himself. The back of the black leather club vest he proudly wore read *MotorCity Motorcycle Club*. Just like that, like an item on a grocery list, I had been acquired.

Chapter 4

Startled by a loud crunch, I awoke to find I was no longer alone in my bus seat. I pulled up the bill of my hat and looked at what, or who, had just plunked down on the seat next to me. It was a young guy chomping on an apple, sporting a Mohawk, and proudly displaying an array of boldly colored cartoon-esque tattoos peeking out from underneath his clothing.
He did not wait long to open his mouth. "So, you fall face first into some cement or what?"

Shocked by his blunt and inquisitive nature I said, "I beg your pardon?"

"You don't have to beg baby, I'm right here aren't I?" He laughed, amused with himself while I crinkled my forehead at the absurdity of the conversation. My facial expressions were a painful reminder that my face did in fact look like I had dived face first into a swimming pool absent of water.

I sighed and said to my new travel mate, "No, I did not fall face first into concrete, but thanks for asking!" I could not avoid my sarcastic overtone, and while he continued to munch on his apple, I watched my sarcasm go right over his head. He seemed oblivious to the fact that his questioning was not polite, and even more so, unwelcomed. But I would be a fool to think this would be where our conversation stopped–no…I could not have lucked out in any such way.

He continued on. "So what's your deal then? Got yourself some bastard boyfriend who uses your face like a punching bag?"

"NO!" I don't have a bastard boyfriend, I don't have any boyfriend, or any one really!" Knox's face flashed into my head at the thought of a significant other. How significant could I have ever been to him for me to be sitting here now? How could he have done this to me? I should be dead, and he probably believes me to be just that, while he's somewhere out there going about his life as if my rotting corpse tossed into a field does not cause him not to be able to sleep at night! I hope his fate is that of mine. I hope he reaps what he sows– *Bastard*! How could I have been more wrong about anyone? How could I have loved someone like him? He was a monster...a yellow eyed *MONSTER*.

Then, I heard, "A Monster energy drink? Nope, I don't have one. Don't worry, we have a scheduled stop coming up so maybe you could get one then."

Disoriented I said, "What?"

Apple guy replied, "You said you wanted a Monster. Didn't ya?"

"No, I said he was a monster!"

"Oh, so you do have yourself a mean old man who bounces your face off concrete! I knew it! I tend to have a way of reading people."

"Oh, is that so? Well, let me let you in on a little secret champ. I don't have an old man or a bastard boyfriend! A couple days ago I found myself looking like this, in the middle of nowhere. I crawled through hell until I ran my head into a dumpster and was rescued by Mexican bees...I mean, Mexicans. I'm not some white trash idiot who's taken one too many shots to the head to know what's good for her. I wasn't in an abusive relationship, someone tried to fucking kill me! Got it?"

Holy mother of God, I was angry! I was not bitter, it was too soon to be bitter, but I was mad as hell. This hostility was not entirely meant for apple boy here of course, it was meant for every filthy piece of shit who had laid their hands on me in the last month and a half. Unfortunately for apple boy, this happened to be my first chance to express it.

After some chewing and contemplation on his part, he swallowed and said, "Jesus lady, relax, I was just making conversation."

"Well, could you refrain from picking the most obvious fucking thing about me, and then grilling me about it?"

"Ok, OK! Wanna talk about your *feeeelings*?" He said with a snort and a laugh, "You apparently have a lot of those!"

It appeared that my new friend considered himself to be quite the comedian. His ability to not hate me for the seething, beat-to-hell ball of anger I was as I sat here beside him, well, it was kind of endearing. It had felt like forever since I could sit and have a conversation with someone who was not trying to kill me. Here on this bus we were without titles or ranks. There was nobody looking down at me or forcing me to look up to them. We were just two people talking.

It reminded me that I was free, and no longer held captive. I belonged to no one but myself again. I had not expected the twinge of sadness that accompanied this thought. How could there be any part of me left that still wanted to belong to him? I forced the thought out of my mind. I was full of conflicted feelings and emotions. Apply boy was my only chance at distraction from my current inner turmoil.

Apple boy and I spoke for better than an hour about this and that; we shared our interests in television, movies, music, and other pop culture. He had my complete attention until our bus passed a group of bikers on the highway—their dark leathers making them look as if they were one with their machines. A cold chill swept over me.

One of the absolute best sounds in the world used to be a roaring motorcycle. The noise was music to my ears, and now it served more as a warning shot, or an air-raid siren. It put me on alert with eyes wide and muscles ready to spring.

LB, my now friendly bus partner whose name I had recently been given, looked at me intently and said, "Are you ok? You kinda froze up over there, kid."

Him calling me kid was really quite comical, as he was likely not a day over nineteen. I turned my gaze from the bikers to face LB and said, "Sorry, I was just thinking about some things."

He nodded, smiled cheesily at me, threw his hands up in an act of surrender, and said "Hey, I ain't even going to ask!"

I greatly appreciated his submission. A six hour bus trip was hardly enough time to even begin to tell him what I had been through.

I knew I would eventually have some explaining to do, not just to a random stranger on a bus, but to everyone I knew– my family, friends, and the police. They all would have questions upon my return home.

Home! Oh, how I looked forward to getting there. I desperately hoped that I still had a home to return to.

Chapter 5

I was bleeding from being drug across the ground like a carcass after the hunt, when the man with the knife dragging me came to a halt. It was dark, and my face was in the dirt, so I could not see much. I heard low voices and saw a glimpse of light spread over me as they shined a flashlight from my head to my toes. I heard one man say, "Damn Rooster, we sent you out for grub, not girls! And especially not bloody ones!"

The man with the knife replied with, "Fuck you Izz! She's going to make the club a fortune! And that's not a dye job up top either, she's the real deal. I checked down below before I tied her legs together."

The two men discussed me as if I was not even there. I did not dare make a sound, because I was desperately trying to pretend that I was not a part of this conversation.

Their tone then started to sound urgent as Izz said to Rooster, "Fuck dude, you better get her outta here before Floyd finds out you snatched another one! He's going to be pissed! You know what he said about snatching up small town snatch!"

They both laughed at the euphemism.

Rooster said, "Yeah, he'll be pissed until I sit her in his lap. Then, he'll be sucking my balls thanking me!"

Seconds later, without any warning, I was yanked to my feet.

"What exactly are you going to do with her anyway?" Izz asked. "You can't hog tie her and haul her on your bike home you know!"

Rooster contemplated the idea for a moment. "Maybe I ought to bust her up a little so she won't be able to run off even if she did get free."
I could tell the idea excited him, mentally and physically. He started cracking his knuckles in anticipation.

Izz said, "You fucking retarded? Yeah, a chick all beat to hell on your bike won't be suspicious at all. Jesus, Rooster. I swear, once you smell a bitch's blood, you lose all fucking common sense! Wait, did you ever have any to begin with?"

Rooster stopped cracking his knuckles and looked hatefully at Izz. "Common sense is overrated, stark raving mad suits me better! So, *Mr. Common Sense*, what do you suggest I do with the bitch? Cuz I ain't leaving this one. This ain't going to be like Reno. That bitch was a skank anyway, and this is motherfucking money here. I ain't leaving her, although it would be a shame to have to kill her before I've had a chance to see what she's worth."

Izz takes in Rooster's response for a moment, then says, "Slap a helmet on her that she can't see out of, pack some heat, and if she gets stupid, fucking shoot her! You better hope she ain't some Senator's daughter, or has a dad that owns half of Ohio...cuz if you bring heat on the club, then she ain't money, she's the goddamn plague! Floyd won't be sucking your balls, he'll be cutting 'em off with a butter knife! Whatever you're doing, you better get to doing it. You're running outta night. The sun will be up in a couple hours, and you don't wanna be seen leaving here with her."

"So what if they do see me? I'm with the MCMC. I could fuck her on the registration table at the front gate on my way out and slit her throat while doing it. They wouldn't stop me! One look at my vest, and they'll see who I am and who I'm with. I'd be free and clear."

"Yeah, yeah...Roost, you're a real badass. We all know what you're capable of and that you've done what needed to be done for the club on every occasion. But how you enjoy the carnage? I'll never know. So just get the fuck out of here! I'll cover for you with Floyd. I'll tell him your ole lady has crabs again, and you needed to attend to her personal hygiene needs!"

"Blow me Izz!" was the last thing I heard before having a helmet with an opaque visor shoved violently over my head. Everything was muffled, including the sound of his bike kick-starting to life. I felt someone tugging at my arms and shoving them into a riding jacket. Then, I heard the zip as I was zipped into leather chaps to cover my bloodied legs. I was shoved onto a vibrating bike and instructed to, "Not be stupid or I'd get my pretty head blown off". The bike thrust forward as I imagined Black Swamp getting smaller and smaller behind me. I was on my way to hell, on the back of a demonic bike.

Chapter 6

"VAN WERT, OHIO. STOPPING AT THE VAN WERT STOP IN TWO MINUTES."

I awoke to find LB gone and the bus about to deliver me in Ohio. I wished I had not fallen asleep on LB, but he did leave a note that was shoved into my jeans pocket. I found it when I was walking down the aisle about to exit the bus. It simply said, "Take care of that face kid. Avoid concrete."

LB sure was a charmer. While our meeting was short, I was thankful for it–and to think I yelled at the poor guy. I really have to work on my anger management when I get home. Three steps down, now hobbling again with my bum leg, and I was back on familiar ground. I knew I could not walk the fifteen miles to my town. Hell, I could barely walk fifteen feet, so I went to the pay phone, used the spare change I had left from Miguel's bus fare money and called my mom.

The one person who would say "I told you so" was the one person I needed right now.

After a few rings she answered. "Hello?"
"Mom," I whispered.

"Who is this?" she asked.

"Mom, it's me Vivienne."

"Vivienne? *VIVIENNE!*" The phone sounded like it fell to the floor. After some fumbling and struggling to regain control, I heard my mom's voice come back to the line. "Vivienne? Oh my God, Vivienne, is it really you?"

"Yeah, Mom, it's me. I'm sorry…I'm sorry I haven't called, but I…I…"

She interrupted me. "Vivienne, where are you?"

"I'm in Van Wert at the bus stop. I need someone to come get me."
She said, "Stay on the line. I'm getting in the car now. I'm on my way. Vivienne, we thought you were dead!"

I hung my head, disappointed in myself. I said quietly to my mother, "Yeah...well, I almost was."

As I rested my head on the side of the phone booth I saw my reflection, not in the glass, but pinned to a bulletin board next to the public toilet door. It read: MISSING SINCE JULY 24TH. A big picture of my smiling face was underneath the bold lettering. My family did not think I ran away, they knew that I had been taken. They had not forgotten me, given up on me, or assumed I was just another rebel runaway. They had been looking for me the entire time.

I began to sob into the phone.

"Viv? Viv? What's wrong? Is there someone with you? Are you all right?"

"I'm...ok. Just please, come as quickly as you can."

I tried to compose myself to begin to express my gratitude to my mother for being the kind of mom who would never let me go without a fight, but before I could, there she was. Her pimped out orange PT Cruiser rolled up to the bus stop. The same PT Cruiser I used to make fun of by saying that her car looked like it was part of some "Fast and the Furious" street racing team. It was so not a mom mobile.

I smiled from ear to ear just seeing it again. My mom had indeed driven fast and furiously to get to me in such short order. I could see her dark-haired head peering to the left, then to the right, trying to locate me. She had kept me on the phone the entire way, and she said she was not letting me go for even a second. And she didn't.

I picked myself up off the phone booth's floor and pulled the Mexican flag hat off my weary head. I began to limp my way towards her, and like a flash, she was out of the car and running to reach me. She threw her tiny arms around me, and squeezed me making me nearly yelp in pain–but I could not tell her to stop. A hug was something fairy tales were made of, and even though it hurt, it healed too.

Without letting go of me, she gently ushered me into her car. She rushed around to the driver's side at a sprinter's pace, got in, and closed the door. She hit the automatic locks instantly and looked suspiciously on all sides of the vehicle, before she shifted into drive. She seemed different than I remembered. She was guarded and cautious. As desperate as she was to know what I had been through, she did not ask.

Meanwhile, I quietly tortured myself over what I must have put her through. Why couldn't I be more like my sisters? I knew I was never her favorite daughter, but now I was the one who has likely taken ten years off her life. A mother's love has got to be the strongest bond known to man, because while I stole ten years of her life, she would have given her entire life to of had mine restored.

I could see it in her eyes. She was trying to put on a brave face, but she was on the verge of falling to pieces. They would be happy and relieved pieces, by letting go of the façade of her unyielding faith and determination to find me. She was by definition a strong woman, but now she was made yet stronger by circumstance.

It was late and dark in the car. Thank God my mother could not see the full extent of my injuries. I knew that seeing me was a relief to her, but seeing me the way I was in the broad daylight might have been too much for her to take. It was better this way. It took her a while to speak. I could see that she was overwhelmed by all that she was feeling, so I sat quietly and let her collect her thoughts.

Once she did, the interrogation began.

First Question: "Are you ok? Do you need to go to the hospital?"

First Answer: "I'm mostly ok, but I think my leg is broken. I got a lot of cuts and scrapes and bruises too. The Mexicans tied a wooden plank to my leg to help me walk on it, and to keep it tight, but I'm fairly certain my leg could use some medical attention."

"I have had some stitches. Jose said I had a stab wound here." I motioned my hand towards my lower right abdomen, just over my hip bone. "But he didn't think it hit anything important," I explained.

"Vivienne, who in the world is Jose? Were you in the hospital already? Why didn't you call me?"

Her concern and worry was shifting to borderline pissed off and scorned.

"Mom, hold on. No, I wasn't in the hospital. Jose is a veterinarian technician who lives in Chicago. It's a long story. He and his people found me, patched me up, and put me on a bus headed for home."

"*His people*? Someone stabbed you? Why didn't this Jose person call the police or an ambulance? How irresponsible can this man be?"

She was livid at Jose, and I knew she was just blaming him because she did not know who else to scream at. So I just let her go for a second or two, then I finally said to her, "Mom, look, I'm sure this all doesn't make a lot of sense right now, but Jose didn't wrong me *OR* you. Don't hate the man who patched me up and sent me back to you. Ok?"

My mom sucked a big breath in and said, "Ok, ok…let's just get you to someone who works on people and not animals."

She tried to smile at me as she altered her course and made haste towards the nearest Medical Center.

I watched her as she flipped open her cell and dialed someone's number. She spoke into her phone very directly, "I have her. I'm taking her to the hospital now. She's in bad shape. Yeah, meet me there. No, no, she hasn't yet. I just got her. I will. I just want to make sure she's ok first. See you there." And with that, she flipped her phone shut and threw it into the console.

She seemed angry at whomever that was, and I could not help but ask, "Mom, who was that?"

"Detective Matthews." was her answer.

I was worried about her somber tone with him, so I immediately followed with, "Am I in trouble?"

Worried that she would upset me, she tried reassuring me by saying, "No, Viv, no, you're not in trouble, but there is a lot involved in the investigation of your disappearance. I've been working around the clock with the FBI, DEA and the ATF in recovering you."

"MOM? The FBI, the ATF, and the DEA? You called the DEA on me? I'm not involved with drugs...or firearms! And the FBI? Why would they give a shit about a stupid missing girl like me?"

My mom shot me a look of disdain, "What do you mean a stupid girl like you? You're my daughter! Did you think I wouldn't involve every single human ear that would listen to help me find you? And why do you think you're stupid? Why are you talking as if this is all your fault?"

"Because it is, Mom! I'm so sorry, I'm so sorry!" I cried forcing tears to stream down my puffy cheeks.

I was inconsolable the rest of the way to the hospital. I sat there in a puddle of tears with snot flowing from my nose until we pulled into the parking lot marked EMERGENCY.

I pulled myself together the best I could before exiting the vehicle. I received frightened looks from all sides of the hospital. The fluorescent lights were obviously not being kind to my appearance. It was the first time my mom got a decent look at me, and she gasped when she did. She tried to look reassuring, not to show her look of horror, but

I could see it. Just as I had seen it on every face I had come in contact with since I awoke on the farm outside of Chicago.

As I was loaded onto a gurney I said, "Don't worry, Mom. It only hurts 97% as bad as it looks. And hey, if you think I look bad now, you should have seen me a few days ago! I'm ready for my close-up now."

"VIVIENNE LYNN! Don't you crack jokes at a time like this! You're on a gurney for crying out loud!"

"Mother, a time like this is the perfect time to crack jokes. I'm home! Well, close enough anyway. " I shouted to my mom as they wheeled me through the double doors and into the emergency room. I was thankful for the white lights and white coats that now surrounded me. My body was finally in good hands.

After my initial emergency room examination, my next stop was x-ray. They strapped me up with the protective gear, and asked if there was any chance I could be pregnant before they began. The question caught me off guard and forced an image of Knox into my head. Seeing his face in my head hurt about as much as my injuries. I shook the vision from my mind and said to the technician, "Look at me. If I had been, do you think I still would be?"

The technician then said, "We better get you to the lab and check before we go any further." They wheeled me further yet, and a nice lady with curly blonde hair came out and spoke to me like I was nine years old.

"Ok, now Miss Vivienne, I'm going to draw some blood from you. I need to tie this around your arm and see if I can find us a good little vein. That way, we can make you all better."

Without even trying to be bitchy, I said, "Um, yeah...you're not taking my blood to make me all better, you're taking my blood to find out if I'm knocked up, if I have AIDS, or if I contracted some other horrible disease recently! Please don't speak to me as if you're the tooth fairy about to put something precious under my pillow!"

After blurting those harsh words at the lady with the lemon-meringue doll face, I thought about Izz and Rooster and how vulgar and offensive I thought they sounded.

Now, here I was, weeks later, and I was just as offensive as they were to me. *How's that for irony*! They had left their mark on me in every way, just as they had intended. I envisioned their smug smiles at the thought of ruining me and my integrity to the core.

Rooster's face never left my mind. Over the past few days, he has haunted me in the visions that I have had of my time spent with him. I can't tell the girl, with the perfect complexion and curly blonde ringlets, about the horrors of that time. She could not begin to understand my rude and bitchy reaction to her. To tell her, would be to rob her of her impression that the world is good– that man is good, that life is fair, and that good wins out over evil.

I will not rob her of what had been stolen from me.

Chapter 7

In the darkness, I continued to ride with Rooster. The vibration of the bike lulled me into an eerily catatonic state. Thoughts flowed through my mind...*What really can I do?* I could jump off, surely to my death. If the fall did not kill me, Rooster would just turn right around, hunt me down like a wild animal, and shoot me. My family would never know what happened to me. I was sure they would not be looking in any of the places Rooster would leave me—if he even left me in one piece.

I saw the lust for my blood in his eyes when I was taken. He was exactly the man he claimed to be—a ruthless, murderous, and mayhem loving outlaw. There was not anything that could stop him from following through with any of his threats. Frankly, nothing Rooster said was a threat. These threats were truly promises of what would happen if you disobeyed his orders.

Sadly, there seemed to be no escape for me. At least not off the back of this bike.

For now, I would obey and I would stay alive, because dying was not the end result I wanted. Not yet anyway. Rooster was hardly the kind of guy who was going to accommodate me in any way. There would be no kind words or pampered treatment at the end of this ride. I knew that any amount of whining would not be permitted in his presence. I did my best to mentally prepare myself for the physical and mental assault that I knew he had in store for me.

The hours passed by. I tried to keep track of how long we traveled, but minutes soon turned into hours. I rode quietly behind Rooster, blinded by the lined helmet– helplessly awaiting whatever form of hell that was waiting me.

By my estimation we had been traveling about five hours, give or take an hour, when Rooster rolled off the highway. I became aware of the slower traffic around us, and there were more frequent stops and starts. The air was noticeably less humid than Ohio in July. It seemed much cooler. We were in the city, and then shortly after, we were not. The noise of traffic then began to dwindle. It fell away behind us, until once again, it was just me, Rooster, and the bike...roaring across the asphalt.

Finally, we slowed to our final destination. Rooster shoved me off the bike, and I fell onto my right side. My helmet hit the ground first, and my neck felt like it snapped in two. My head throbbed from the fall and, my brain felt wobbly from the ride. My legs were stiff from riding so long that I could not straighten myself up to get to my feet. Rooster grabbed my helmet and began tugging.

"Ouch! STOP! You're going to rip my ears off!" I yelled at him.

He gave the helmet one more jerk, until it finally let loose and ripped a handful of my hair out with it. I still could not see from being in the dark for so long, but I could hear.

"Excuse me? Did you just yell at me?" Rooster screamed.

I thought for a split second that I had said it in my head. Apparently I did not because Rooster was about to put me in my place for it.
"I...I...uh, I didn't say anything," I stuttered.

"That's funny, because I distinctly remember hearing your cock sucking mouth telling me to stop. Now, a smart girl knows better than to tell a man his business. So either you are dumb, or you seem to think I give a fuck if I rip your ears off! So which is it? You some sort of retard, or do you think I care about hurting you?"

"No Sir, I'm not mentally challenged, and I'm painfully aware that you don't particularly care if you hurt me or not."

"Sir? HA! It's Sir now, is it? First you yell at me, and now you're calling me Sir? And I said retard, not mentally challenged! Does 'retard' offend you? How about nigger? What if I'd have said nigger? Would you be so proper as to say 'African American' back to me?"

With that, he smacked me on the side of the head and continued yelling.

"You ain't in no fancy school girlie. You're in the wild now. Out here we've got niggers, retards, and we've got whores— which is exactly what I'm gonna make of you.

You're going to be the best tail bought and sold in the state!"

"See, there are those nasty bitches down on the corners that trick out for drugs or money and are lucky to get ten bucks for giving head, but you–nah. You're gonna be a full service slut! You're gonna cost a pretty penny–and you're gonna make me a fortune."

He paused for a moment.

"Come to think of it, maybe I should start your education right now. You do look pretty fucking good on your knees."

I quickly looked down at the ground. Rooster found my distaste for him as quite the insult. He reached down, grabbed a fistful of hair, and forced me to look up at him. I closed my eyes, and he pulled my hair harder. I could feel the tears welling up under my closed lids and prayed they would not escape. Rooster would love to see me fearful and in pain. It would only excite him more to have that power over me. I kept my eyes closed, wishing for anything that could take me away from here.

Rooster towered over me, still gripping my hair tightly—and that was when I heard it, the sound of his zipper being unzipped. That was when my mouth did something unexpected. It spoke without my brain authorizing the act.

I was shocked when my lips began to move to give Rooster a warning. I said with my eyes wide open now, "Anything you put into my mouth won't be coming back out!"

Whap! Rooster's strike was quick, and it had the force to knock me into the dirt again. Like an idiot, I got up and not just to my knees this time. I rose all the way to my feet and said with contempt to the sorry excuse of a man in front of me, "That the best you got?"

I had no idea what I was doing, but I did know that I was about to get the beating of a lifetime. I held my jaw tight and prepared to take it full on.

A surprised look came across his face as he saw me standing there, brazen and unyielding.

"You've got a death wish? Would you like my fists more than my cock in your mouth? Oh, I promise you, you're going to learn to love both. When I'm done with you, you're going to beg for me, or beg for mercy–but either way–you're going to beg, bitch!"

At this point, I could not stop my mouth from moving as it now had a mind of its own. I snapped back at him, "That's where you're wrong! I don't, and I won't beg, not of you, not of anyone. You might as well just kill me now and be done with me! There will come a day, Rooster, when you'll wish you'd never laid eyes on me, let alone fists!"

That was the last thing I remember before it all went black. I realized, after that beating, that the only way I could avoid the pain that was coming my way was to be unconscious when it happened. I would be lucky if I did not suffer brain damage from all the blows my skull had been taking. For now though, in the darkness, I'm safe. My body's not, but my soul is. I'm safe. I'm safe.

Chapter 8

I awoke to the steady beeping of a heart monitor. I was in the hospital and very disoriented. My mom was stroking my hair to the rhythm of the monitor. "Yes, yes Viv, you're safe now, you're safe," she reassured me.

I felt startled by her touch, and she suspended her hand as I began to regain my bearings. I looked at my arms, hooked up to numerous tubes and wires, then looked up toward my mom.

She said to me in a low voice, "Viv, it's going to be all right. The doctors have been doing all that they can to get you fixed up."

I tried to think back to the last thing I could remember. She could tell I was struggling with my recollection.

"You passed out from exhaustion after your x-rays. They said you were severely dehydrated and malnourished. They have you hooked up to an IV now, so that should help you quite a bit. You were talking in your sleep saying, "I'm safe", over and over again. I was worried that you were having a nightmare, so I started to stroke your hair to reassure you that you are safe now. And you are Viv, nobody's going to hurt you here."

"I don't know that I have anything left to hurt, Mom. I feel empty. The only thing keeping me together is anger and confusion. I'm afraid to remember, and I'm afraid whatever I do remember I'll never be able to forget. What if I'm ruined?"

Just then, a few memories—though vague—began to come to me in pieces.

"Did they get my test results back? Am I pregnant?"

Upon hearing that question my mom started to cry. Huge tears poured out of her eyes, and she was visibly shaken.

"No, you're not pregnant. But after what you've been through, you may never be able to become pregnant."

She suddenly looked like she was the one who should be consoled.

"Mom, why are you crying? I'm not pregnant. This is good news, isn't it?"

"Yes, yes," she sniffed, as she wiped her sleeve across her face, smearing her mascara and drying her eyes a little. "But you may never be able to bear children, Vivienne. You may never have a family of your own now. I can't help but want that for you. Who's going to take care of you when I'm gone?"

"Mom? Where are you going?"

"When I die, Viv! I won't live forever, you know. I want you to have a family of your own someday. I want you to have people who will look out for you, and take care of you, and never let anything like this happen to you again! I will never forgive myself for letting this happen!"

"Mom, stop! You didn't do this to me. This isn't your fault! I was the one who put myself in the way of the bastards who did this, not you! Please don't blame yourself for this. I'm not a kid. I made my bed, and now here I am lying in it. Dad always said this would happen to me."

I crossed my arms angrily across my chest.

"If your father wasn't such an idiot, he would have protected you from life instead of provoking you into challenging it like a bull charging toward a semi-truck! You are such a Taylor, I swear. I wish you weren't, but you are who you are. Thank God the Taylors are a tough breed. And you're not taking the blame for this either! There were thousands of people at Black Swamp, and they all had a nice weekend and went back home. You didn't ask for this just by being there, so don't take this out on yourself and carry the burden alone. Your dad wasn't right about everything, because you aren't dead–you lived, Vivienne! You didn't die. You're here, and you were strong enough to find your way back. I can't imagine what you've been through. Do you want to tell me about it? Do you feel up to talking about it?"

"Mom, if it's all right with you, I just want to sleep for a little while. I feel sick to my stomach and I just want to rest. You can go home. You don't have to stay with me if you don't want to."

My mother frowned. "I'm not leaving you. I'm staying!"

"I kind of figured you'd say that." I said with a smile. "Ok, stay if you really want to. I love you Mom. Thank you for everything."

And with that, it was lights out.

Chapter 9

I was in hell, but at least I was in hell alone.

Rooster was no longer with me, and I found myself underground. I no longer wore the leather chaps they had forced me into. I was now re-dressed in my old cut off jean shorts, Harley T-shirt and boots–all of which were spattered with blood from my beating earlier. My body ached in a way that I had not felt in a long time. As a child, waking up after a physical beating was something that I had to learn to deal with, given the father that I had. I was blasted with pain as I began to turn my head to look around.

I could see sunshine streaking in through the planks above me, and I could see bits of the sky and trees. I seemed to be in a cage of sorts–an underground cage measuring about fifteen by six feet.

In the corner of the filthy cage, there was a cot and a blanket, both of which smelled like ass and was as dirty as the ground beneath me. I jumped to reach the horizontal wooden slats above me, and my fingers grazed the wood. *Ouch!* I realized I was about eight feet deep in the ground. To my dismay, the pit I was in looked secure on all accounts–definitely secure enough to hold the likes of me.

I tried to listen to find out if I was alone, but I did not hear anything. There were no voices or vehicle engines in the distance–only chirping birds and sounds of the wind blowing through the leaves on the trees.

When Rooster said I was in the wild now, did he mean the wilderness? Wherever I was, it was rural. I listened intently for passing cars, trains, anything…but there was nothing.

After a few hours of sitting on the dirty cot to gather my strength, I decided to try and escape. I believe all humans in a cage eventually contemplate escape, no matter what condition they are in. As a species, humans are always trying to escape confines. For some, it is responsibility they wish to escape, and for others, it is social expectations. Humans are born escape artists when it comes to the places and things we do not wish to endure. And I was no exception. I had endured as much of Rooster as I could bear. I knew that if I did not get the hell out of here soon, he was going to make good on all of his promises.

Mustering all of my grit, I leaped into the air and tried to push my fingers into the cracks of the planks. Instead, I rammed my fingers into one of the boards, and it felt like I had simultaneously broken three of them. My other hand managed to poke through, and I quickly grabbed hold. I found myself hanging there, a foot off the ground, looking very much like an orangutan hanging from a tree. I don't know why, but I was just irate with my latest injury. Swear words were ripping through me like I had invented them.

Eventually I resumed my escape attempt, and grabbed hold of the planks with both hands. After a few seconds I realized that these boards were not going anywhere. They were as secure as steel bars. *Damnit*! I thought angrily. Dismally I dropped back to the ground. I paced back and forth while examining the boards, trying to figure out a plan. I finally spotted two rusty hinges and jumped into the air to try the strength of the new door that I had found. Unfortunately, it held firm. Before I could let go and return to my caged frustration, shooting pain crushed through my fingers and down my arm.

Fuuuuck!

I looked up and saw Rooster smashing my fingers with his boot heel, grinning from ear to ear, knowing that he was showing me once again who was in charge. I did not cry out, I just bit down and hung on, awaiting his release. I was so pissed—he was crippling my one good hand.

"Aren't you going to tell me to stop?!" he taunted me.
"I know that hurts! Go ahead...cry out and tell me to stop—you know you want to!"

I kept my mouth shut. He lifted his heel, and I fell into a heap of pain on the dirt floor. I looked up to see that Rooster was not alone. Another dark-eyed man was standing next to him, peering down at me. He seemed to be tall, with long wavy hair, and a dark goatee. He was extremely handsome, but also very dangerous looking. His eyes looked neither kind nor murderous, and he was strangely intense. I looked at him for as long as I could before I felt that I had to look away.

Rooster looked at his comrade and said, "I told you she was a piece of work, didn't I?"

"Yeah...but I'm not sure she's the girl for you, Rooster. She looks like a pain in the ass!"

"Oh, I'll break her of that. She won't be so spunky when I have half the state of Michigan sticking their dicks in her!" Rooster announced with a cocky grin.

I was in Michigan. That stupid bastard just told me where I was. Of course this did not help me while I was locked in an underground cage, but it was a great feeling to have some sense of direction.

"You really think she's going to just be a good little girl and take it on the chin for you, Rooster? She looks like she wants to rip out your jugular with her teeth!" the new guy said with a laugh.

"Cal, any bitch can be broken. They're just like horses, you have to break their spirit–then you can ride them to your heart's content. Don't worry Cal, when I do, you'll be wanting a ride just like all the other pricks."

New guy's name is Cal, apparently. I'm in Michigan and being held by Rooster and Cal. This information combined with all of my non-intelligence amounts to a whole lot of nothing. I wanted to be the kind of girl who could put ideas and clues together and have it make a difference, but I was no Nancy Drew. No amount of knowledge about where I was and who had me was going to help me down here. A chainsaw–now that would help me. I sighed and tried to ignore my two captors above.

Cal then said to Rooster, "Dude, just because I have a dick doesn't mean I want to put it in your little pet there. I got an old lady who's on me night and day. I don't need to pay for pussy. You know that! Why are you trying to sell me on this shit?"

"Cal, you know I'd give you the club discount. Don't be like that, we're brothers. I'd never charge you full price for anything of mine. Hell, if you want, I'll even give you one on the house!"

"No thanks, Roost. I heard her tell you she was going to bite your dick off earlier. I don't think anything of mine will be getting near old Red here! Where'd you get her anyway?"

"I picked her up at Black Swamp, that biker rally in Ohio. I was bored, so I had to pick up something to play with."

"I told you not to go down there. I knew you couldn't keep yourself outta trouble. The Black Swamp boys don't let that shit fly there, it ain't Sturgis. You know Floyd's going to kill you for this right? There are rules for a reason."

"He'll forgive me when he finds out that I've saved her for him. I haven't laid a finger on her, and I won't spoil her before Floyd gets a taste."

"Haven't laid a finger on her, huh? Then why does she look like that? Rooster, that girl looks like a patchwork quilt of black and blue! Do you really think this little girl is going to give him the ride of his life? She's young, she's inexperienced, and she's all beat to hell! Look at her! Maybe bruises turn you on, but I don't want some bitch that looks like she sucks on hand grenades going down on me. Floyd won't either. But hey, good luck with that!" Cal laughed and started to walk away.

Rooster turned and walked to catch up to him. I heard them talking a little while longer, their voices growing fainter until I could no longer hear them at all.

I look like I sucked on hand grenades? Yikes, I must look worse than I thought!

As I sat in the pit with nothing but the cot, a smelly blanket, and my thoughts, I could not help but wonder when Floyd was coming back. According to my captors, I was safe until Floyd's return. Doom set in at the thought. I hope Floyd does not particularly like me. If he kills me before killing Rooster, well, as long as Rooster's dead, I will be a happy woman. I HATE him. I want him dead. And Cal was right, I would not mind ripping out his jugular with my teeth. If given the chance, I just might. I smiled at the thought. I was in the wild now and my mind was beginning to be primal... animalistic.

I was contemplating my dreadful future when I heard a bike start up and ride away. I heard footsteps and prepared to be jerked out of my hole to take another round of beatings, insults, and degradation. But instead, the footsteps stopped just above me and I saw not Rooster, but Cal.

I looked up at him, blinking into the direct sunlight that surrounded his head. He peered down at me with what appeared to be curiosity.

I did not dare speak to him, because honestly, what would I say?

"*Hey, uh, be a dear, just let me go, and we'll call it a day, eh?*"

Yeah, that was not going to happen, so I just looked at him silently.

After several uncomfortable minutes had passed, Cal finally spoke. "So, your karma's really got to suck for you to end up in this mess, huh? Who or what did you do to have this come your way?"

"So this is all my fault? I asked for this?"

"Didn't ya?" Cal said with a smile.

I could not tell if he was mocking me, if he was amused by my predicament, or if he was smiling because he was enjoying my company.

"NO! I didn't!" I said indignantly. "I don't think I've ever done anything to deserve what you assholes have done to me in the last twenty-four hours!"

"Well sure seems that way," he muttered.

"What do you know about karma anyway? You're a biker who kidnaps people. Do you worry about your karma coming back to bite you?"

"First of all, *missy*, I didn't kidnap you. Rooster did. Secondly, my karma's fine, just fine. Now Rooster, he'll surely burn in hell for all of his misdoings, but me, I'm just the babysitter."

"Oh, so you're babysitting me? Gee, do they also trust you with national security? I bet Washington's going to phone you any day now!"

"You're a hateful thing down there, aren't ya? You can hate me all you want Red–but it ain't gonna do you any good. I was going to get you something to eat, but since you seem to despise me, maybe you'd like for me to leave you to your thoughts."

He stood up from his crouch and began to walk away when I said, "Wait, no...I'm sorry. Don't leave."

I no longer heard footsteps coming nor going...did he leave? I had to admit, the conversation was a welcome change. A human being who was not shouting at me, hitting me, threatening to kill me, or fantasizing about selling me into white slavery was a welcome change of pace. "What is wrong with me? He was just being nice, and I was a total jerk," I quietly muttered to myself.

"You don't have to talk to yourself–I'm still here," he said as he wedged a piece of peanut butter bread and a can of coke down through the wooden slats. "Home cooking," he said and winked at me. "Made it myself."

I smiled back at him and jumped up to reach his offerings. My fingers *smooshed* the soft white bread, and my hands left dirty prints where I held the sandwich, but I did not care. I damn near shoved the entire thing in my mouth. I was starving. Getting the shit kicked out of you really works up an appetite.

"Now, I'm gonna need the coke can back. If Rooster finds out that I fed you, he'll be pissed. A pissed off sociopath ain't exactly something a guy needs riding around him on two wheels. Accidents happen easily when someone forces them to happen, if you know what I mean."

"Karma's a bitch like that, huh?" I smiled at him, between gooey bites. It felt nice to throw his karma crap back at him.

He took it in the spirit it was given, rolled his eyes at me, and said, "Nice comeback Red. Now don't get me wrong, I've known Rooster for a while now. He's a brother, and it's my duty to stand and die beside him if it came down to it. But his loyalties are to the club, and not to any one member. He'd kill me as quickly as he'd swat a mosquito if he thought I'd betrayed my brotherhood."

I guess I was not the only one Rooster liked to intimidate.

I listened to Cal talk as I zealously drank my soda and swallowed what was left of my sandwich. I was surprised that he was standing there telling me all of this while providing me with nourishment. Did he pity me, or was he giving me what would be my Last Supper? He must have figured he could say whatever he wanted, because I was not going to live through this to tell anyone. I knew at this point, I was probably as good as dead.

"Can I ask you a question?" I said as I polished off the last of my Coke.

"Sure, what ya got?"

"Is there any way out of this for me?"

He gave a sympathetic head tilt and said, "Sorry Red, but Rooster's not exactly the kind of guy whose dreams are dashed easily. If he thinks he's going to make you into the *great red-headed-whore of the Midwest*," he said with heavy sarcasm, "then he's going to die trying, or kill you for failing. I guess there's always the possibly that if

Floyd was to take a liking to you...then..." he trailed off in thought.

"Red, your only shot, as I see it, is if Floyd were to decide to keep you for himself, then he could put a stop to Rooster's business venture with you once and for all. Floyd is unforgiving when he's disobeyed, and Rooster did exactly what he was told not to do. Believe it or not, there are rules here, and we're an organization that abides by them. There's no room for defiance when the Prez puts something to the floor and it's approved."

I guess Floyd will be my savior or my demise, I thought to myself.

"Floyd's as honorable of an outlaw as a biker gets. He prides himself on being a family man, and even though his lifestyle ain't exactly legal, he's not a barbarian. Well, not a total barbarian. Hell, he's got a degree in Finance from the University of Michigan for Christ sakes."

I sat quietly and wondered why he was telling me the gang's life story as if I was a part of their group, but I knew better than to interrupt.

"I really shouldn't be telling you all of this, now should I?" Cal said as if reading my thoughts.

His need to talk superseded the fact that I was not an ally of the club, and that if things went south, I could bring a lot of heat not only to Rooster, but to the club as well.

He stood up once more and it looked like he was about to leave. "Coke can please," he said coolly, as he held out his hand. I stood up promptly and jumped to reach him. He quickly grabbed it out of my hand.

"This conversation never happened, you got that?" he looked at me seriously. "Don't mistake my kindness for weakness, because I assure you it's not."

And then, he was gone.

He gave me a lot to contemplate. Cal was not only easy on the eyes, but as it turned out he was surprisingly decent. He had a soul. If we had met under different circumstances, I think I would have liked him.

For the first time since I had been taken, I felt a shred of hope that maybe I would not be fucked to death by random strangers. I began to formulate my plan to find favor with this Floyd fella. Floyd. I had never met anyone by the name of Floyd. It would be my new favorite name if it saved me from a life of venereal diseases and horny men who were too ugly to get women without paying for them. The thought of sweaty, hairy old men crawling all over me, touching me, and putting their mouths on me made me feel nauseous. The idea caused me to double over, as I clutched my stomach and started to gag. I wanted to purge this feeling from my gut, but I could not allow myself to lose the only nourishment I had in me.

I swallowed my vomit, and with that I swallowed the idea that Floyd would find favor with me. I would make Floyd love me if it killed me, and then I would kill Rooster. That idea did not turn my stomach in the least. I started to smile at the very thought of his life being taken from him. Anger is a funny thing once you set it free. It can take you to a place that you never thought existed, and for me that was a very dark place.

I never wanted to murder someone before, and now the idea of death was my mission in life. What was happening to me? How could I go rogue this quickly? I grew up going to Sunday School. This was not supposed to happen to people like me. I should not even be here!

Chapter 10

I was back at the hospital again, surrounded by men I did not know. This was becoming a recurring theme of mine. First it was bikers, then Mexicans, and now these guys? I kept waking up from one nightmare, only to find myself in another.

I jumped up, startled, and felt a very strong urge to run. My mom came around from behind one of the men and immediately started shouting, "OUT! EVERYONE OUT! NOW! Can you see she's not ready for this?"

Men in suits and ties began to file out of my room. They were obviously disgruntled, and they griped to one another as they exited the room.

I looked to my mother with eyes searching for answers. One of the men laid his hand on my mother's shoulder.

"Josie, we're going to have to talk to her sometime. She may not be ready to deal with this for years. Our investigation grows colder every day, and we need answers."

"Mom? Who is he? Who is that?" I say as I point my finger at the blonde guy in the suit and tie.

"Vivienne, its time you meet Detective Matthews."

He walked slowly toward me and held out his hand.

I looked at him standing there attempting to shake my hand. For the first time since my abduction, I felt a weak laugh escape my lips.

My mom looked shocked. "Viv, honey, are you ok?"

They both looked at me, then at each other. I could tell they thought I had officially cracked, fell off the deep end, and was now visibly insane.

"No, no, mom, I'm sorry, I'm fine, I was just remembering something."

"That's good Vivienne, remembering is good." Detective Matthews said while still offering me his hand.

"Not for me. Remembering is not good. There's nothing good about these memories."

I took Detective Matthews' hand into mine and shook it unenthusiastically. Nothing seemed to work like it used to, and my hands were no exception.

"It's good to, um...meet you Detective," I managed to say.

His facial expression went from worried to all business.

Chapter 11

After Cal left me, I did not see him or anyone else for what seemed like weeks. I started to lose hope and felt as if this was going to be the end, until I saw a hand reach down with a sandwich and drink.

I felt more and more like as prisoner as the days turned into nights. I was kept from feeling completely hopeless by the food that was dropped through the wooden slats. As the sun went down each night, the cold forced me to curl up on the tiny cot with the rotten old blanket that I suspected had covered a corpse at some point. It was far from comfortable. It was cold and damp, and the noises all around me kept me awake. The birds that chirped during the daytime quickly transitioned into nocturnal noises that belonged to toads, crickets, bats, and owls. I wanted to sleep, but between the nightmares that I kept having and the nightmare I was living, I was not sure which I one I wanted to face.

The next day the sun came up far enough that it began to shine into my pit and onto my shivering body.

As I smiled into the warmth of the sun, a shiver ran through me when I heard a familiar yet frightening noise. There in the distance was the irrefutable rumble of bikes. My mind began racing upon the biker's return. How was I going to make Floyd take me as his own when I looked and smelled like a cavewoman? I began to comb through my hair with my fingers, and I rubbed my face clean with my shirt–anything to make myself look more presentable. Cal had told me it was a shot in the dark, but I knew that if I did not give it my best effort, the rest of my life would be lived in the dark.

The bikes grew louder the nearer they drew, and my heart raced faster and faster. The ground around me seemed to be vibrating as they all came to a stop. They roared in unison with one another until their owners shut them off, one by one, and kicked down their stands. I immediately heard talking and laughing. It sounded like wherever they had come from, had been a good trip. Then the voices trailed off into the distance.

A lone bike approached, and I suspected this bike belonged to Rooster. Like the rest, I heard the engine shut off. Then I heard one set of footsteps head off toward a destination, just like those before him.

I had hoped that Rooster would want to get me to Floyd right away, but apparently I was not the first order of club business. You would think that the whore thrown in the pit out back would be an issue that needed immediate attention, but that was not the case. Here I was, like a dog chained to a doghouse, and I was the least of my captor's worries. Of course, Cal and Rooster might have been the only ones who even knew I was here.

I sat down and waited, contemplating what would come next. Then I heard Cal's voice, along with another voice, that sounded vaguely familiar. As I heard them approach, I looked up to see who accompanied Cal when someone kicked dirt into my eyes, rendering me momentarily blind. I immediately put my head down and started rubbing my eyes vigorously. It hurt like hell, and everything was still blurry. I gave a second attempt at looking up, even though my eyes had not yet cleared, and I saw the garbled faces of two men. I knew one was Cal, because I remembered his voice from earlier, but the new guy was a mystery. Then I saw his eyes–his golden, amber eyes. His eyes were no longer indifferent like the last time I had seen them, this time they were ablaze.

My eyesight gradually adjusted and returned to normal. "Sorry about the dirt. What's up Red?" Cal said. "I see you didn't escape during the night. I was half-hoping to come out here and find you gone."

"No such luck. I tried, but was obviously unsuccessful."

I held up my three black and blue fingers that I had jammed into the plank on my left hand, and the four black and blue fingers on my right hand where Rooster had crushed them with his boot.

"Remember? You were there."

Cal ignored me and instead turned to the man I now recognized as Knox. "This here's Red. Well, that's what I call her. She answers to it, so I suppose it ain't the worst thing she's ever been called."

Knox nodded once, but never broke the gaze he had locked on me.

"I know this girl, Cal. You wanna tell me how she found her way all the way here from Ohio and into the fucking pit?"

He was visibly pissed.

Cal threw up his hands. "Hey buddy, don't go crazy on me!" he yelled. "I didn't have anything to do with this. You wanna bust someone's skull, you're gonna have to take it up with Rooster."

"Rooster? Rooster brought her here?"

Cal was starting to look worried and regretful for sharing Rooster's little secret.

"Knox, look, you know as well as I do, when Rooster sees something he wants, there's no talking him down. I guess he saw her down at Black Swamp, and he's convinced she's going to be a gold mine for him. He's already got dollar signs in his eyes."

"He's whoring her out?" Knox's words came so forcefully that Cal actually took a step back. "She turned any tricks yet, Cal?"

"No, she's been in here since he got back. She threatened to bite his junk off, and he hasn't come back here since."

"Has she eaten?" Knox asked. I shot Cal a look, not sure if our little secret would include Knox or not.

"Knox, man... you know me. I have a daughter. I wouldn't leave her out here to starve. I brought her a Coke and a sandwich her first day in the pit, and had a few of our members sneak her little bits from Momma's kitchen ever since. She at least had water every day and a bucket to pee in. Hell, if it wasn't for me, she'd have frozen to death. I'm the one who threw that blanket in there for her. Rooster said to let her suffer. He'll probably take a shot at me just for the blanket. Don't you go telling him I fed her, or I'll end up in the pit with her!"

Knox took a breath and said, "You know, there are worse things you could've done, Cal."

"Knox, I don't want nothing to do with the whore trade unless the whores are down for it. I ain't that guy. If the girls need some protection, someone to look out for them, and they wanna give us a share of their earnings…then I'm down for that. But sex slaves, kidnapping, taking girls from their homes and families and turning them into cum receptacles, I've never agreed with that. You know my stance on that part of the club!"

Knox just kept staring at me. I could not tell if he was angry at me for being in that pit, angry at Cal for not doing anything about it, or pissed at Rooster for putting me here. If it were my guess it would be all of the above. His stare was so intense, it was uncomfortable. I had no choice but to look away from Knox. I glanced over at Cal, who still looked at me sympathetically.

"So, what do you want to do here?" Cal asked. He was beginning to look increasingly uneasy.

"When's Rooster supposed to be back?"

Cal looked as though he did not want to answer but then painfully confessed. "He said he'd be back on Tuesday."

Knox looked away for a moment as if weighing his choices and then turned to Cal and said, "Cal, I want you to cut the lock, and you get her up and out of that hole now!"

Knox commanded Cal as if he was the general, and Cal was the lowly private. Cal took orders like a private too. I half expected him to say, "Yes Sir," as he headed off, presumably to get a pair of bolt cutters.

Once Cal was out of earshot, Knox's expression changed from pained to soothing. He squatted down closer to me. "Are you all right? Are you hurt?"

"Nothing some first aid wouldn't cure," I said.

"Has he…has he touched you?" Knox looked nauseated.

"Well, I didn't beat the hell out of myself." I said, and this time I smiled at him. I could not help but smile. I was just so stupidly happy to see Knox again. Never in my wildest dreams would I have expected to see him here, of all places! At this moment, Knox was my knight and shining armor. I had nearly forgotten that not so long ago I said I hated him. But I did not hate him now. Our last conversation back at Black Swamp that resulted in me storming off was meaningless as I stood helpless in this pit. He was getting me out of here! He was the rescuer that I wished had come for me when I was taken. Yeah, he was late. I could forgive his lateness, so long as he saved me now.

He did not smile at my small attempt at humor until I said, "No. Knox, he didn't touch me like that. He was about to, but he changed his mind."

"Did you really tell him you'd bite his dick off?" Knox's eyes flickered with interest.

"Uhhh…" I blushed at the thought. "Yeah, I told him if he put it in my mouth, it wouldn't come back out…something like that anyway. He was pulling my hair and using my face for a punching bag. I wasn't about to have to suck him off too! There's only so much a woman can take, ya know?"

"Who are you?" Knox said with a laugh. "That's not even logical! Nobody thinks like that. Normally, if a girl's getting beat half to death she'd surrender–she'd do what's asked to avoid the beating."

"The way I see it, even if I did as Rooster said, he'd still beat me senseless. So, I'd just as soon get the beating. Bruises heal, and you forget you ever had them. If someone rapes you and kills the beauty of what's inside you, now that shit's for life! No shrink in the world is going to give that part of you back again, no matter how much you pay them!"

Just then Cal returned with the bolt cutters. "Here," he said, as he handed them to Knox. "I can't cut her out of there. If Rooster finds out, I'm dead. You know that. This one's on you." Knox just glared at him, arms folded.

Cal thrust the bolt cutters at Knox. "Take em. Do what you have to, but I can't. I can't risk it. Sorry."

Knox grabbed the cutters and Cal turned and walked away, kicking up the dirt beneath his feet as he went.

In an instant the lock was cut, and Knox flung the hatch open to offer me his arm. When we had first met I had offered him my hand, a gesture that had him laughing at me. Now here he was offering me his. I didn't hesitate–I grabbed it like the lifeline that it was. He pulled me up, out, and to him.

Upon being sprung from the subterranean prison I had been confined to, I finally got a look at the surroundings I had only been able to hear and imagine up to this point. There was a large, rustic looking house off to the left. Behind it was a barn, painted brown in color, with a metal roof that was rusty in spots. There were several bikes parked up by the main building, maybe thirty or more. It was a rural, secluded area, and there were trees blocking the view of this place from the road. The entire area was heavily wooded–to the point that I could not see or hear any traffic going by, if there was any traffic at all.

"Come with me, I've got some things to figure out."

He led me toward the brown barn. Once inside, I saw that the barn was not a barn at all. There were living quarters inside, and they were nice.

"You live here?" I asked.

"Yeah, something like that," he grumbled. "Let's get you cleaned up."

He grabbed my hand, holding it in his own and quickly led me to the bathroom adjacent to what I assumed was his bedroom.

He pointed below the sink. "Towels are down there, the soap's over there and anything else you need should be in the medicine cabinet. Help yourself."

"Knox? I, uh...could you not leave me? Maybe stand outside the door while I shower?"

He smiled at me, and put his hands to my cheeks as he touched my cuts and scrapes with his fingers.

"All piss and vinegar one minute and sweet the next, huh?"

I could only nod at him, as I felt a lump in my throat making it impossible to say anything at all in response.

"Well, go ahead then…I'll be right here until you're done."

He pointed to a spot just outside the door. I left the door cracked as I went to the medicine cabinet and gathered a towel, soap, and shampoo.

I stripped out of my soiled clothes. I could not imagine how awful I must have smelled to the outside world right now. I imagine Knox did not find the smell all that appealing either since a shower was my first order of business after leaving the pit. I hated that he was seeing me like this. I was desperately hoping that he remembered how I looked when we first met, instead of the terrible sight that I was now. *Why am I thinking this way? Here I am kidnapped and far from home, and I am worried about what a guy thinks of me? I really need to get my head on straight if I am going to make it out of here alive*!

My shorts slid down my legs and landed around my feet. I kicked them away from me. My shirt was damp and dirty, and it found its way to the floor as well.

As I stepped into the shower I noticed Knox looking at me through the cracked door. He surveyed my legs first, and then his eyes traveled upward. He was taking his time. He evaluated the curves of my hips, and then smiled when he glanced above my belly button to find my arms crossed over my breasts. He was definitely amused. He smiled and looked down, embarrassed to be caught sneaking a peek at my naked body. I bit my lip nervously as I let my arms fall to my sides, no longer covering my breasts. I was allowing myself to be completely vulnerable in front of Knox, which was all the invitation he needed. He swung the door wide open and blew into the room like a tidal wave—not quite urgent or hurried, but strong and unstoppable. He pulled my body close to his and kissed me eagerly.

His hands stroked my face ever so gently, as his kisses became more and more urgent. I did not know what had come over me, but I had suddenly found myself very naked with a man I did not know. Instead of running for my life, as a sane person would do, I wrapped my legs around him and pulled him closer. I felt that for a brief moment, he may have reconsidered what was about to happen–but as quickly as the idea flashed across his face, the idea of being inside of me erased it. I tore at his shirt, which he quickly pulled up and off. Next his pants were around his ankles, and he was carrying me naked, wrapped around his waist, into the shower.

In that moment I was not thinking about consequences. I was not thinking about being good or getting home. All I knew was that if I was going to die, I wanted to die this happy, fulfilled, embraced, and tangled up with Knox.

Oh Lord, if I'm dreaming, I don't ever want to wake up. Let me be stuck in this moment forever. I realized that praying to God to let me fornicate forever with a man with whom I was not married to was not the most pious prayer ever prayed, and that God surely would not appreciate my request, but in this moment I could not help myself. After days spent in fear and in pain, this was as close to heaven as I was going to get. It seemed wrong not to thank God for sending me such a religious experience.

Knox touched me in places on my body that I did not know existed. I was young and inexperienced—as everyone seemed to be pointing out lately—but Knox took his time and made sure I enjoyed every second. Our bodies smashed together as the shower water streamed hot down both of us. I was not a virgin before being with Knox, but I might as well have been, because I had never experienced anything like this before. The connection and the intensity was life-changing. He altered me forever as our bodies touched and caressed. Having sex with Knox was not the same as being with a horny high school boyfriend in the back seat of a car. It was not innocent, but it was pure and there was pleasure to be found in every touch of his skin to mine. I was certain that I would never look at sex the same away again.

I felt my body tremble, and my legs around him quivered as I felt myself give way to orgasm. Knox felt my release, and he was able to let go with a final, deep, sensual thrust within me. I did not think for a second of him doing anything different.

He belonged inside of me–him, and him alone.

With my legs still wrapped around him and my back against the shower wall, he laid his head on my chest, catching his breath as he kissed the tops of my breasts between breaths.

How on earth had this happened? One minute I was caged in a pit, and the next I am having the hottest sexual experience of my life? And why did I feel like I had just crashed into my forever? I did not even know this man, and I might have just created a baby with him. I cannot believe that even for a second I did not think to say no! What the hell was the matter with me? My mother would be furious if she knew what I just did. It was funny how the thought of my mother could just pop up to kill the *amazingness* of it all. *Thanks Mom*, I thought to myself.

Knox began to stir, and I let my legs fall back to the tiled shower floor. He spun me around and began to lather me up. His dark, sun-kissed hands and my white skin were covered in suds. His lathering was just as titillating as having him inside of me.

Thoughts of my mother were erased once more, and it felt like electricity was being conducted between us. I felt a strong desire that was building and growing the more we touched. After he washed me from head to toe, he told me to finish without him. He said that he had something to do before it was too late.

With that said, he stepped out of the shower. I had seen a naked guy before, but nothing compared to seeing Knox in this way. His tattoos, tan lines, and scars were so appealing to me. He peeked at me through the cracked bathroom door and caught me looking out of the shower curtain, taking him in.

Once he was out of sight, I leaned back against the shower wall and let my whole body tremble as I stood there without him. I knew in that moment, from that day forward, I would never want to be separated from him again. I no longer longed for home like I once had, because in him, I felt like I found a new home. A home that could not replace the one I had lost, but one that would offer me things my old life couldn't.

Chapter 12

Detective Matthews was tall and blond, with an athletic build. He looked like he should have been an Ohio State Quarterback golden boy, not an FBI agent. I wondered if he was new to the job. He seemed fairly young, maybe in his early to mid-thirties.

See, I knew the FBI did not care about me–they sent in the new guy to appease my mother, I thought upon sizing him up.

My mother pulled up a chair alongside my bed, while Detective Matthews hovered over the other side. They both looked intensely at each other and then at me. Suddenly my skin began to crawl. I do not know why I had this immediate reaction, but I did. It was safe to say I was creeped out.

"What is it you want to know, Detective?" I said to him, to break the strange vibe I was getting from my mom and the Detective.

"Well, we need to know everything– names, dates, and events. Vivienne, we need to know everything from the time you were taken, to the time you called your mom from the bus stop."

"How much time do you have?" I said, staring blankly at him.

"I'm not going anywhere until I collect your full statement."

"He's a by the book kind of guy, isn't he mom?" I said mockingly as I angled my thumb in his direction. "A real straight arrow!"

I took a deep breath.

"Well, what do you know so far, Detective? I hate to bore you with details you already have."

"We know that you attended the Black Swamp Motorcycle Club Rally in Van Wert, Ohio on July 23 and 24th. We know you were reported missing from your tent by your cousin, Matthew. The Black Swamp club members performed a search of the grounds, including a dive team to check the pond on the premises. There was blood found at and around your tent's location, which first tipped us off to your possible abduction. Naturally, we lost your trail once you left the grounds. Please begin from there, Vivienne. And this conversation will be recorded. I have to make you aware of that."

"Um, ok...first, you really need to loosen your tie. You sure are wound tight, aren't you? Ok, ok...sorry, ok...I was taken by a member of the MotorCity Motorcycle club, named Rooster. There was another member of the club there at Black Swamp, who knew of my abduction. His name was Izz. Rooster came into my tent when I was sleeping, bound my ankles and wrists and drug me back to his campsite. From there, they loaded me onto his bike and then covered my face with a helmet, so that I couldn't see out. We left Black Swamp on a motorcycle. Rooster had me on the back of his bike."

"You didn't try to escape?"

"I couldn't see, and I was on the back of a speeding motorcycle! You don't think I wanted to? Do you think I went voluntarily? I didn't voluntarily go anywhere with that piece of shit! Why don't you go back to where ever it was you came from, if you're going to assume that I was some little tease begging to be kidnapped!"

"Whoa, Vivienne. I apologize if you thought I was insinuating that you were not abducted. I was only asking if any attempts to escape were made. I did not mean to upset you. That was not my intent. I want you to know that getting your account of what happened is not only going to help in your case, but in an ongoing investigation into the group we believe took you. So no, I do not believe you wanted to be kidnapped. Please continue. Where did they take you?"

"I don't know. It felt like a four or five hour drive into Michigan somewhere. They held me at some sort of clubhouse, or hideout outside of a city. I'm guessing Detroit? All I know is that it was secluded and remote. There was a cabin and a barn...and a pit."

"A pit?"

"Yes, they kept me in a pit in the ground."

My mom gasped and then turned her head so I was not able to see her facial expression.

"Go on..." Detective Matthews urged.

"Yeah, so I was in this pit, and Rooster told me that he intended to make me into a whore. He said that I'd be the most popular, high paid whore in the Midwest. Then, when he tried to break me in, I, uh..." I trailed off. "Mom, don't listen to this part."

She turned away.

"I told him I'd bite anything off he put in my mouth. He smacked me around me a bit and then threw me into the pit."

I played that part of the story over in my head, and I made sure to tell Detective Matthews that was when I tried to escape. I told him about nearly getting my fingers broken when Rooster caught me in my lame attempt at escape.

"Then what happened, Vivienne? Were there any other men there? If so, what were their names? What did they look like? Did they know you were there?"

Detective Matthews had more questions than gleaming white teeth it seemed. His teeth were very distracting, pearly white and perfectly aligned. He was so flawlessly put together that he was nearly pretty. It was really too bad that his personality was the equivalent of wheat toast without butter.

"Let's see...then I met Cal. He must have been some sort of clubhouse sitter or something, because he lived there but didn't attend the rally with the rest of the members. He was nice to me and gave me a sandwich and a soda. He made arrangements for people to feed me as I spent my time in the pit. He made me promise not to tell, though. He said Rooster would have his hide for it."

Detective Matthews did not mean to smile, but he did and jotted something down on his notepad. He must have thought it was nice of Cal to give me food.

It hurts me to think about him now. I never thought I would actually like one of my captors. I never thought I would care about what happened to any of them. I contemplated not telling Detective Matthews about Cal, but under the circumstances I figured it did not really matter now. Nothing I could say to the Detective could harm him after what had happened to him. Aside from Knox, he was my only comfort the entire time I was missing. I feared if I told anyone that, they would think that I had stayed on my own free will.

If I tell them about Knox, and about being his old lady, they will definitely think I was just a young, stupid girl in love with someone her mom did not approve of. They might say that I made the whole thing up just to cover myself for running away with a guy. Things would be a whole hell of a lot easier if this were all just some made up story, and I could just go back to being me. But that will never happen, and my scars are a constant reminder of that. The scars that are on me, in me, and all around me, deny me that luxury.

"Did you see Rooster again? Did he come back for you after he threw you into the pit for threatening to bite his genitals off?" Detective Matthews continued on with his questioning, forcing me to focus once again and come back to the here and now.

"Yeah, I saw him again all right–but this time I wasn't in the pit!" I answered.

"How did you escape, Vivienne?" My mom and the Detective intently waited for my answer.

"I was rescued."

"Rescued? Vivienne, you were found beaten and left for dead outside of Chicago! How is that being rescued?"

I looked at the Detective. "I was rescued, and then... I don't know, things must have gone wrong somewhere along the way...I don't know why he'd let me die."

"Who Vivienne? Who let you die?"

"Knox, my one true ally...he was supposed to save me. Or at least I thought he would, but he didn't."

Tears welled up in my eyes and my mom gave Detective Matthews the boot. She told him to go get a cup of coffee and to come back after I had a chance to rest. She thought it would be a good idea to see the doctor again for some additional test results before we went any further with the police investigation.

The Detective exited, and the nursing staff entered. They updated my chart and checked my fluids and my blood pressure.

I thought back to the last thing I remembered before waking up in that field in Chicago. The last memory I had was of Knox standing over me with a gun in the dark. His face was not loving and kind; it was regretful, shadowed, and ominous. Nothing seemed to make sense. I do not remember leaving with Knox to go to Chicago, and I do not remember what happened that would have Knox pointing a gun at me, instead of protecting me! What had I done? Why did he save me if he was just going to turn around and end me?

"Mom, did they check my head? Is there a chance that my head's messed up? Maybe I'm not remembering things correctly? There are these gaps in my memory." I rubbed my temples wishing and praying a simple massage would magically bring my memories back to me and fill in the blanks of my subconscious.

My mother's voice interrupted my temple rubbing when she answered my question. "They did an initial examination of you, but I'm not sure if that included a scan of your brain. I can ask the doctor to have a neurologist consult with him regarding your most recent concerns."

"Could you get someone? Please Mom, go find someone for me."

And with that, my mom left me unattended. I cried into my pillow at the thought of Knox abandoning me, wanting me dead like Rooster and all the others. After the time we spent together, how could I have been so wrong about him?

I stopped blubbering into my pillow when my nurse came in with a tray of food. As I awaited my mother's return with someone to examine my head, I ate my green jello, a fruit cup, pork chop, and soggy green beans. It was all gone, down into my gullet, before the nurse made it back to the nurse's station.

After I finished eating, I laid back, closed my eyes, and tried to remember what my mind seemed to be missing.

Chapter 13

I dried my hair with the towel as best as I could and put on the clothes that Knox had set out for me to wear. I did not know whose clothes they were, but since they fit me, they could not have been his. He was too tall and too built to have worn this medium-sized men's t-shirt.

The jeans were a little big on me. I had to tie them on with a piece of string found by the medicine cabinet and roll the bottoms up so that I could see my feet.

Knox came back after I had finished dressing. He said that he had spoken to Floyd and told him what Rooster did.

"Floyd's on the warpath and is looking to locate Rooster as we speak. The club's in the midst of something big right now, and if Rooster's personal motives screw things up, Floyd will see to it that Rooster is no longer capable of screwing any one, or anything. Floyd is considered fair by most people, but he's unforgiving if you cross him," Knox informed me.

"So what does this mean for me? What happens to me now?" I asked.

"I'm sorry, but you can't go home, Viv. Floyd won't allow it. I vouched for you though. I know it's not ideal here, but staying with me is the only way to keep you safe. I will figure something out to get you home, but for now you will be with me."

"Here" he said as he handed me a leather vest that read, "PROPERTY OF MCMC. KNOX."

I looked at the vest and them to him. "Are you kidding me?"

He looked offended. "Look, it's either that or you go back in the pit."

"I don't mean it like that…I just mean…don't you already have one? An old lady?" I asked.

"No, I don't. Why? Does that surprise you?" He snapped back at me.

"Um, well, because you...you are the epitome of appealing."

As soon as the words came out of my mouth, I wished I could have retracted them. Talk about sounding like a teenager with a school-girl crush! My cheeks flushed bright pink, and I looked down at my bare feet and wiggled my toes uncomfortably. *What a stupid thing to say! Ugh! What did I say THAT for? Of all the things I could of said, I go and say, "the epitome of appealing"?* It sounded like I had stolen the words from a romance novel, or from Fabio's famous little black book of lines to woo women with.

Before I could berate myself further, I saw the corners of his mouth curl up as he appeared unable to stop himself from smiling at me. He was visibly amused by my admission.

"The epitome of appealing, huh?" He said with his one eyebrow raised in an expression that was priceless. "Vivienne, I love that you seem to think you can see the good in me and that I have redeemable qualities, but I'm a dangerous member of a criminal biker gang. I just stole you from a psychotic brother of mine in order to keep him from turning you into a prized-hooker. What on earth is appealing about that? Your taste in men can't really be this bad, can it?"

"What's appealing? How about the part where you rescued me from that pit?" I responded. "Remember? You didn't have to...and I suspect now that you wish you hadn't."

"Vivienne, I don't regret it, if that's what you're thinking. This is my fault anyway."

"Your fault? How does anything that Rooster chooses to do happen to be your fault?" I asked emphatically.

Knox looked uncomfortable as he tried to process the situation. Instead, he avoided it entirely and said, "You hungry? You're probably starved. I can go to the clubhouse and get you something if you like."

"I am hungry and thirsty, too...but I don't want you to go out of your way..."

"It's not a problem. Momma's still in the kitchen, and I'm sure I could sweet talk her into fixing something up for me. She thinks I'm a gem. Her words, not mine," he said as he headed for the door.

Before he left, he turned to me. "I should have been in that tent with you that night at Black Swamp. Instead I watched you march off, all pissed, leaving you mad and unattended. One thing I learned a long time ago is that when you piss off a redhead, it's best to just let her walk away than to block her path. But in this case, I wish I would've blocked your path that day. I looked for you, and I walked everywhere hoping to find you again, but I didn't. I'm sorry Vivienne. I'm sorry that you have to get to know me this way."

He looked sincerely upset by the circumstances of our relationship...if that was what we had here, a relationship. I was not entirely sure what else to call it. But here I sat, wearing a leather vest that said that I was property of not only the club, but of Knox as well. I belonged to him and to him alone.

The only clubs I had ever belonged to were FFA, 4-H, and the National Honor Society. I had the feeling that being a member of those clubs were far less dangerous than what I had just entered into here.

When Knox walked out, he closed the door behind him and once again left me alone in his quiet and hopefully safe living quarters.

With nothing to do other than wait for his return, I had a chance to look around Knox's space and see the things he surrounded himself with.

His bed had efficient blankets on it, but nothing extravagant. A single white pillow was situated at the head of the bed. The walls around me were all wooden planks, stained dark and rich in color. A picture of the Harley Davidson emblem was framed and hung above his headboard. I climbed onto the bed and stood on his mattress to get a closer look. I noticed that it was not a print or a poster, but a drawing done by hand, and it was colored by hand as well. In the corner of the picture was a small letter k. I wondered if Knox had drawn this, and if he did, I wonder how long it had taken him. A picture of this size would take a considerable amount of time and detail. It was really well done, and the frame that held it there on the wall made it stand out to anyone who would have seen it.

There was no television in the room, but instead a stack of books on the nightstand next to his bed. The idea of him sitting out here alone, reading at night, changed my impression of him yet again.

"What?" he asked as he emerged from the doorway, finding me standing on his bed.

"Did you do this?" I said pointing to the drawing on the wall.

"Yeah, but it's not a big deal. I just wanted to spruce the place up, and that crap they sell at the store didn't appeal to me."

"It's really well done. Did you study art or have any kind of previous instruction?

"No, why do you ask?"

"Your lines are so good, and a picture as large as this would take some dedication to finish."

"It's not Picasso. It's really not that good, just something I do sometimes when I'm bored."

I then looked to the books. "You a reader?" I asked as I motioned to the books on the floor.

"Yeah, I like to read when I have time." he answered.

"I wouldn't have pegged you for a reader OR an artist." I confessed.

"Why not? Is it because I'm a Neanderthal biker type?"

"I didn't say that, you did. I don't think you're a Neanderthal at all, and I suspect that you're not just a biker either."

"What am I then?"

"You're a lot of things; the biker is just one part of you. When I saw you at Black Swamp, I knew you weren't like the others, and being in your room with you now, I know I'm right about that. I'm right, aren't I?" I asked him.

"I don't know what you mean. I'm just a biker, brother, and criminal, just like the rest." He said, while looking off in another direction, away from my intense stare.

"And I'm the tooth fairy." My eyes were set on him, and I held a determined look on my face as he looked up from the floor to meet my gaze.

"Here," he said, offering me a dish covered with a paper towel.

Under the towel was a generous portion of eggs, bacon, sausage-links, and buttered toast with what looked like raspberry jam. My mouth flooded with saliva as my taste buds anxiously waited to taste the spread.

"Hope milk's ok," he said as he set a large cup of it on the nightstand next to the bed, which I was awkwardly still standing on top of.

"Thanks," I said as I took the plate and began to lower myself back down to sit on the bed once again.

"Who's Momma?" I asked as I prepared to dive into my dinner.

"Oh, she's Hank's old lady. Hank died a few years back, so Momma went from his old lady, to den mother, so to speak. She doesn't know a life that doesn't include this club, so she stays here full time. She does the cooking, cleaning, and handling of club personal affairs when need be. She's kind of our *human resource personnel*, so to speak, as well as *hospitality manager, caterer, domestic servant*…and she's a hell of a mechanic!"

"A mechanic? You're kidding me!"

"Nope, I'm not kidding. There was no way the club would let her go when Hank died. She can turn a wrench better than half the guys here, as well as being handy with a frying pan. Momma's a dying breed. She has the ability to turn a blind eye to all things criminal, but lends an ear and a sound mind when needed. She is our rock, and many would not survive here without her. Not all of us here are as demented as Rooster, for some of us this life is all we know."

I did not understand how a woman could turn her back on some of the activities going on in this club, like for instance me being held captive in a pit in the back yard, but strangely, I could understand her want to help the people here. I was glad that the club had someone like her. A maternal figure was always needed, even in a place like this.

"Well, it's not something you'll see in a lot of other clubs, and she's not patched in as a full member–but no women are, and they never will be. Motorcycle clubs are a man's game."

"I hate that. I hate that women are excluded."

"Most women do. I'm not shocked that you hate it too. Now eat your food. You can worry about women's rights after you've regained some of your strength!" he ordered.

I did as he said and I ate until there was not anything left on the plate. I had to stop myself from licking the plate when I was finished. I had not known how hungry I was until the smell of that plate wafted into Knox's room. My animalistic instincts nearly had me attacking him. I wanted to take it from him faster than he could offer it to me. He was lucky he did not lose an arm or some fingers over the deal.

"Wow, I guess you were hungry!" he said when I handed him back the crumb-less plate.

"Yeah, I guess I was." I said as I reached for the glass of milk on the nightstand. I put my lips to the cup and drank the entire glass. Gulp after gulp, the white liquid disappeared behind my lips until there was not a drop left.

"And thirsty," he added with a laugh as I handed the glass back to him alongside the plate.

"I'll take these back to Momma in the morning."

He laid the plate, utensils, and glass aside and climbed into bed behind where I sat.

"C'mere," he said as he pulled me into him, down onto the bed.

It was a gentle, nurturing move, unlike the sexual, passionate one from earlier in the shower. Now, the flames were gone, and he was embracing me with the warm embers of our earlier fire. I felt comforted, and very tired. I tried to keep my eyes open. I tried to stay conscious with him, but one stroke of his hand on my head, wisping some stray hair back from my forehead, and I was done for. The waves of sleep overtook me, and I fell into an unstoppable slumber—one I had been in desperate need of since the night of my disappearance.

The next morning I awoke still in Knox's arms. I was certain I would wake up alone, like I regrettably had for a morning or two before this one, but he had not moved an inch. My head was still planted on his chest, tucked in with his arm down along my back, holding me in place.

I lifted my head only to realize that I had drooled all over Knox's shirt. *Oh, My, God! He's going to think I'm disgusting when he wakes up.* I contemplated ways to take off his shirt without him knowing but ruled it out as it was too risky. He would likely shoot me thinking I was robbing him or something.

I settled on the idea that drooling on him would surely put an end to any hot shower sex that may have been in our future. And hot shower sex was a sure way to erase my want to go home. So I had to find a way to keep that intact if I was going to have to stay here. I rationalized that drool was not that bad, but it was definitely among the top ten bodily fluids you would not want on you. *Could you be any more unattractive, Vivienne?* I said berating myself.

"What's the matter? You freaking out about the drool?" I heard Knox say from beneath me. "It happens." he said nonchalantly. "My Old Labrador Chance used to drool on me all the time when he was still alive…so I'm kinda used to it. Could be worse, you could snore, too."

He yawned and took his cell phone off the nightstand to look at the time. "Jesus! It's almost noon!" he exclaimed.

"Is that bad? Are you late for something?"

"No, I just can't believe we slept that long! I want to take you up to the clubhouse after a bit, introduce you to some people.

Don't be surprised if they don't exactly take to you right away. You being here isn't ideal for anyone, so try not to let it bother you."

I nodded my head in understanding, and Knox got up from the bed, stretched, and then bent to pick his black leather boots up off the floor. He groaned a little like he was sore.

"Are you hurt?" I asked.

"No, I'm just not a spring chicken anymore! Riding a motorcycle everywhere you go ain't exactly easy on the body. It can make you feel old before your time. And on top of that…my arm has been asleep for about nine hours from you laying on it, so I also have that working against me."

"I'm sorry. I didn't mean to make you uncomfortable," I said apologetically.

"Don't worry about it. Could be worse, you could have drooled on me too! Oh, wait– you did drool on me!" he chuckled and winked at me as he slid his feet into each of his boots.

My cheeks flushed red, full of embarrassment, and I looked down to try and avoid his teasing.

"Well, let's get this over with," I said.

I slipped into the jeans and T-shirt Knox had given me the day before and back into my black Harley Davidson Boots, which were the only apparel left on my body from the original outfit I had last worn in Ohio.

Knox grabbed my hand and led me out the door, into the daylight, and toward the clubhouse for my sure to be unwelcome meet and greet.

The introductions were forced and cold, a welcome that was anything but a welcome. I was met by watchful eyes and distrustful looks. It was safe to say that it did not go that well, and from that first meeting on, Knox kept me by his side most of the time. He did make one exception, when he would talk to Floyd, because I was not allowed in those corners of the club.

As time went on, I met some additional members. I smiled and was pleasant to them, although I really could not tell if they liked me or hated me. I did not know what role Rooster played here and what bonds he had made with the other members. Luckily, Cal continued to be courteous, joking with me about going from "pit girl" to "VP's old lady". He said it was quite the step up in the biker world. And apparently it was, as it was unheard of for the sex stock to be anything more than their title claimed. They were utterly disposable once they did not make the club a profit any longer. For the most part, everyone steered clear of me. They neither wanted to know me, nor allowed me to know them. I was essentially the club pariah.

      This made me more aware of what Knox must have put on the line by taking responsibility for me. If I spoke to the wrong person, if I ran away and rolled on him, he had everything to lose–and for what? He did not know me well enough to trust me. He was going on some other instinct that I just could not figure out. Does he share the same intense feelings for me that I so quickly developed for him? It seemed impossible to have fallen in love with someone I barely knew. How could I? I did not know a lot about love, I was hardly experienced at it….but nothing I had experienced before had ever felt anything like this.

Although I wanted desperately to contact my family, to let them know that I was safe, I knew that I could not foul up and get him killed. Not when he protected me with a fierce dedication that was unparalleled by anything I had ever known. I was raised by a man who did not protect me, but from whom I could have used protection *from*. I guess, in a way, Knox gave me a sense of protection and love that I had always longed for, and while I could not protect him, I *could* love him. It was that love that had me feeling resolute to adhere to his instructions. I would stay close to him. I would not make contact with the outside world. I would trust him to keep me safe. That was what he was asking of me, and I was going to give him that. While it was an unorthodox thing to do, to trust a man who was a brother-in-arms with the man who abducted me, I just had this gut feeling that if anyone could get me out of this alive, Knox could or he would die trying.

The days went by, as all of my days ran together after my abduction. I did not know if it was Sunday or Wednesday on any given day. Being here with the MCMC did not help with this, as bikers do not exactly have a set work week, and they do not adhere to anyone else's idea of one either. Knox said to me on one of those restless days, "Want to get out of here?"

"Sure, where to?" was my response.

"Away from here! I need a change of scenery," he said, looking disgruntled by his surroundings.

"I'm yours for the taking!" I said with a wink.

"You know, you really should be careful saying things like that. You seem to have a very unfortunate gift for being someone people want to take and not return," he said half-joking and half-serious.

"Are you talking about Rooster, or are you speaking for yourself?"

"Both I guess," he said as he grabbed my hand and led me out to his bike.

His bike was gorgeous, yet tough. It was an old FLH Harley Davidson, custom. Industrial metal grey in color, sporting forty thick spoke wheel tires, a wide masculine fuel tank and a black leather seat with flames stitched into it. The bike fit Knox well. It was not flashy, but nonetheless it was undeniably awesome.

"FLH?" I asked.

"In part, it's a Road King Front end. The rest is an FXRP.

"Yeah? What's an FXRP?"

"It's Harley Davidson's Low Rider police bike…I customized it myself. Lowered it, raked it, changed out the tank, custom fenders and wheels…"

"Nice." I said nodding my head with my eyes wide still taking in all his artistry in customizing it.

"You know about bikes?"

"A little."

"Who taught you about bikes?"

"Myself. I don't come from a long line of bikers. I, myself, was just born interested in them I guess."

"Huh. Do you ride?"

"Not yet, but I will someday. It's my dream to ride from Ohio out to the west coast on two wheels. If I did it now, I would only be able to afford to do it on a moped! I'm a Harley girl, on a moped budget!"

He and I laughed together at the visual image of me riding a moped across the United States.

Knox was still laughing when he swung his leg over the metal masterpiece and kick-started the engine. The bike vibrated and roared to life beneath him. He sat there, looking at me for a moment and then said, "You coming?"

That was my cue to hop on. I walked over to the bike and swung my leg across the black leather seat. I could feel the leather between my legs, still hot from the sun, as if being on the back of the bike with the man of my dreams was not hot enough. The leather upped the ante by making it just that much hotter. Between the heat, the smell of leather and gasoline, and the rumbling machine I sat upon, it was intoxicating. I was overwhelmed by my senses. When he released the clutch and rolled on the throttle, the passing breeze blew Knox's aftershave into my nostrils.

I closed my eyes and took a deep breath in, inhaling the essence of him deep into my lungs, while wishing to keep it there forever. I told myself to remember everything about this moment, because there was a very good possibility that a day or a moment such as this would not come along twice. I knew my days here were numbered. I knew that every minute with Knox could be my last.

We rode down the winding road, as I wrapped my arms around his waist. I did not need to hang on, I just wanted to. For the longest time we just rode, not speaking to one another, instead, we just listened to the engine fill the atmosphere with its wonderful rumbling.

The wind that blew into our faces removed the stagnant smell of suspicion the club had covered us with. Suddenly the mood was lighter, and we were truly alone together. There were no disapproving eyes or overly attentive ears of strangers here. It was just the two of us covered in sunshine and fresh air, on a bike that seemed like it could take us anywhere.

I laid my head on Knox's back, closed my eyes, and let the sun shine directly on my face with the warmth from the sun on one cheek and the warmth from his back on the other. It was blissful.

I felt him let off the throttle, and we began to slow. I opened my eyes and raised my head from his back to see why. We approached a bridge. It was a covered bridge, wooden and red. The river and the trees on each side of the bridge were gorgeous. They were so green and vibrant in contrast with the faded red hue of the bridge itself.

I had never seen a covered bridge in real life before, only in pictures and in the movies. After watching The *Bridges of Madison County* a million times, I was crazed with the idea of finding a love like that of Meryl Streep and Clint Eastwood's characters. The idea that my new found love would bring me to see a bridge like the one found in my favorite movie, was monumental.

He slowed to a stop and then let me climb off to explore. He sat for a moment on the bike, watching me as I walked off in awe.

I looked back to see if he would follow, but he just sat, with a slight smirk on his face. He motioned me with his head to go on, so I did.

The wooden design inside was immaculate, the boards crissed and crossed, bent and shaped to mold to man's purpose. It was truly a work of art and craftsmanship. The boards beneath my feet were solid and strong, but warm and inviting. The beams were thick and chocolate brown, with gigantic bolts piercing through them. They started at an arch that began on each side of the bridge at my feet. The arch went from ground level to a foot above my head and then back down again on the other side.

The bridge had a distinctive smell that filled my nose, it was neither good or bad, just distinct. I could not help but to climb up the side like a kid and peer out of one of the openings that looked down upon the river below.

I looked out from the opening next to the river and the trees and looked over to the bike, only to find that Knox was no longer on it. I looked to the left and the right, but did not see him until I pulled my head back inside the bridge. He was there behind me, placing his hands around my waist and lowering me back down to the ground where he stood.

"Do you like it?" he inquired.

"Yes! Very much so!" I replied.

"I come here sometimes when I need to get away. This bridge is pretty complex. I see it as solving a problem that once needed to be solved. They needed passage across the river, and someone took their problem and solved it with this bridge. It was something that wasn't easy, but with hard work and dedication, they took their problem and turned it into a beautiful handcrafted solution–this bridge. It's how you should get through ya know, creating a solution that not only solves the problem but is also something that others can enjoy."

I nodded, surprised by his thought process. I had not expected this from him. I did not really have many expectations or preconceived notions when it came to Knox, so damn near everything he said was shocking to me.

I took my eyes off of him long enough to look all around me and said, "I love it. Thank you for bringing me here."

"My world's an ugly one, Vivienne. I wanted you to see that there's still beauty in the world...you know, outside of the club."

"I don't know how I'll get you back, but don't lose hope that I'll get you out of this, back home to your family, your friends and back to a life that's beautiful, or at least one that can be again."

I thought about what he was saying to me. I could not help but feel that he was telling me that I did not belong here, just like everyone else in the club. I frowned when I realized that he, too, did not want me here. It was not that I did not want to return home, but in truth I was willing to sacrifice home to find out where this was going. *I always let my hormones get the best of me! How could I be so stupid as to believe that I could find love here, in this place, under these circumstances, and with Knox?*

"What's wrong? Was it something I said?" He asked me when he saw my smile fade away.

I looked at my feet for lack of ability to look him in the eye. I did not want him to see the tears that had welled up there. His words stung me, again, unexpectedly.

"It's nothing..." I said as I shook my head, forcing my eyeballs to absorb big, child-like tears.

"I've upset you," he said, as he got up from his leaning position alongside one of the wooden walls. He walked over to me, put his finger to my chin, and pulled my face up to meet his.

"What is it?" He demanded. "I'm not a mind reader. Please tell me what I said to upset you."

"You don't want me either...nobody wants me!" I said as the tears rolled down my cheeks.

He had a strange expression on his face as he watched me intently.

"You think I don't want you? You think what...that I don't enjoy you being here?"

I nodded against the pressure of his finger still holding my chin up towards him.

"Vivienne, you're the best thing to come along since I've been here. You're like cool water on a hot day. I'm only sorry that you're here under the conditions that you are. You deserve better than sleeping in a barn. You deserve better than to be torn away from your family and everything that you know. Don't you see, you're too good for this life, this place...me!"

"Too good for you?" I said with a near shriek.

"Naturally, that is the part you'd focus on," he said with a smile.

"I'm not anything special. I'm just a girl. Why would that make me too good for you?"

"Because you don't know who or what I am, Viv. You don't know someone who can give you stability, and someone who can keep you away from guys like me."

"I don't need a guardian, and I don't need to be sheltered. I haven't always lived a life that was all roses. You don't know me, or what I've seen and been through, Knox. I'm not a princess, and I'm not some precious, delicate flower. I've not had the most perfect life. This life of yours isn't any better or worse than my old life, it's just different."

"Does your old life include drug dealers, murderers, and rapists?"

"My old life had me getting abducted by Rooster, didn't it? That wasn't your doing."

"No, but he's an element of MY life, not yours."

"But I'm here now, and I'm with you," I said, trying to persuade him to live in the moment with me, under the wooden roof of this amazing bridge as the water rushed below our feet. I was scared too, but I was willing to take this chance with him, on his terms.

"You can't stay here. I know you think I'm a good guy, and you think that I'm different than the others here, but I'm not much better. My life here doesn't allow me the luxury of giving my heart to someone."

That part stung, to hear him say he could not give his heart to me. I removed my chin from his finger and looked off in another direction. I was about to walk away when he yelled.

"Damnit! There's not much I can do about it now. You've already gone and stole it from me. From the moment I saw you wandering around Black Swamp, smiling at me with a cheeseburger stuffed into your cheeks, I knew I was in trouble!

I was all ears then.

"Viv, I'd never choose to fall in love with someone knowing the life I lead. I didn't give you my heart—you fucking stole it from me. While it's inconvenient and probably destined to fail, I can't say that I wished you hadn't. You make my days better. Hell, you make my fucked up life better!"

Love? Did he just admit that he loves me?

He smiled wryly at me and said, "Sorry about the language. It's a biker thing," and with that he shrugged, looking somewhat embarrassed.

I felt a big smile explode across my face, and he shook his head at me.

You sure are easy to please, you know that? Take a girl to a bridge in the middle of nowhere, curse at her some, and she loves it! Who knew that worked with the ladies?"

Before he could say another word, I kissed him. He picked me up and pressed my body up against his and then up against the side of the sheltered bridge. The water trickled by, as his kisses moved from my mouth, down my neck, and onto my shoulders. He was passionate, warm, and his touch felt like the perfect balance between lust and love.

While the rest of the world was at work, school, doing their laundry, or taking care of their children, Knox and I made love on the bridge. I have had sex before, but I had never made love to anyone. It felt different on a million levels. If it were true that I really did steal his heart, I was not ever going to give it back. Not ever.

After our lovemaking subsided, we both shed out of our clothes and jumped in the creek. We swam and we waded through the murky water. We talked and splashed one another. I must have thought a thousand times that afternoon of not going back to the clubhouse…we could just go, drive away, and disappear together. But while a scenario like that sounded wonderful in theory, I knew it was unrealistic. If my childhood taught me anything, it was that running away was not a long-term solution to a problem.

Eventually, after hours into our fieldtrip, we began to gather our clothes to head back. We did not want the afternoon's good feelings and light heartedness to end, but we knew that at this time we did not have a choice. Once dressed, we mounted the bike and headed back. When we returned, we returned to the same uneasy feeling, watchful eyes and distrustful looks that had us wanting to escape in the first place.

Days passed, and Knox continued to keep me by his side at all times. I was only left alone when he handled club business with Floyd behind closed doors. During those times, I kept to myself. I did not want any trouble with any members of the club. Judging by the looks I received from them, they did not want anything to do with me either. As soon as I made eye contact with any of them, they quickly looked elsewhere or sometimes even removed themselves from the room so I could not interact with them. When I was with Knox, I continued to meet new members as they would come and go—but like the others, they kept their distance.

Cal, on the other hand, was becoming a friend, and often times found himself joking with me. Really, he was the only one who even spoke to me, outside of Knox and Momma.

I did not know what Knox had put on the line to keep me here as his old lady, but I got the feeling that it was a risky move. It was a move that was making him about as unpopular as me.

In the moments that he was away from me, I would daydream about being back at the bridge. It was the only time I had with him when we were just two people—a man and a woman—who were truly able to enjoy one another without all of the pressure, worry, and danger of our current situation.

For that moment on the bridge, Knox was not a biker and I was not a hostage. For an instant, he was not a brother in an army of criminals, and I was not a girl with a target on her back. I could not figure out how someone like him, someone decent, ever got caught up in all of this. I know he had said he was not any better than his brothers—that I did not know the kind of life he led—but from one day to the next, I saw only honor, loyalty, thoughtfulness, and bravery in everything he did. Of course I was biased, considering that I was sleeping with him. And yet I continued to wonder...what could have happened in Knox's life that would lead him here?

Rooster remains missing to which I am grateful. He had not returned since word was put out that Floyd was looking for him. Thank God he put me in the pit at the clubhouse instead of somewhere else where no one would have ever found me. Now, instead of sleeping in a pit, frozen, cold, and starving, I retire each night lying next to Knox in an actual bed. I awake each morning to find myself tangled up in the sheets with messy hair from the night's passions while Jude surprises me with coffee.

Since that first night, I refrained from drooling on Knox, but you can imagine my surprise when I first heard Knox snore. I would not have pegged him for a snorer, but he was. It struck me as hilarious that after our first night he said it was a good thing he did not snore, only to discover that he did! It did not occur to me to be bothered by it, though. Nothing about Knox bothered me. He was not perfect by any means, but his imperfections were endearing to me as opposed to annoying. It makes me wonder what he thinks of me? He seemed to be very interested in me physically, and he once said that I had stolen his heart–but since then, he has not said much else. I have no clue what goes through his head at any given moment, and I know better than to ask. It is clear that no conversation is ever truly private in an organization like the one on all sides of us. While I am no longer a hostage of Rooster's and have been rescued by Knox, I am a hostage of my situation and of this club. Even if Knox was not verbalizing these things, I knew the seriousness of my situation through the constant look of worry on his face.

As much as I want to belong to him, it was apparent that I would never belong in this world of his. I am and will always be an outsider. Could I change? Could I become what he needed me to be in order to stay here with him? I am sure I could have tried–

but regardless of how hard I tried, nobody here was about to let me forget who I was and how I came to be here. To them, I remained a gigantic liability, and because of me, every member was more at risk.

It was only natural to treat every minute with Knox like it was my last. Somehow, while he seemed to be perfectly secure in the idea that I was temporarily saved, I knew in my heart that I would not be safe here–not now, not ever.

He tried to comfort me by telling me not to worry–that the club members' resentment towards me was all in my head. He told me that because of what I had been through, I was traumatized into being paranoid and distrustful. I am not sure why he thought it would comfort me to remember being traumatized, but he was bound and determined to convince me not to worry. It was hard not to be concerned when his behaviors kept giving him away. He knew I was right, for he rarely left me alone or unattended. If I had nothing to fear, why was I constantly being watched over?

And it was not just Knox doing the guarding. If he had duties or errands that he could not involve me in, he had Cal stand guard over me. I was hardly worthy of a loyal guardian, but Cal never seemed to grow weary of babysitting me. However, after that day that Cal would not cut the lock to free me, I knew that if it came down to him being the only one standing between me and someone coming to hurt me, he would not stand in the way for long. He might die for his brothers, but he was not about to die for me. I was after all an outsider, and no one dies for anyone less than their family.

There were times that I missed my old life and would contemplate escape. I did not know what would put Knox more at risk–me being here, or me leaving. I would assume the latter. If I left, would Floyd set out to have me killed? Could Floyd risk what I might already know about the inner workings of this organization? Would Knox be killed for my dishonor to the club? These were the questions that had me cemented to this place, for without knowing the outcome I was better off staying put.

I was enjoying my time spent with Knox; even though I was always in a state of worry...my time was running out. In short, I did not know what to do. It was not like I could just go and ask Floyd. *Hey…um Mr. Floyd, I mean sir, I just wanted to clear up a few things about me being here. You see, I think Knox and I are in love and we would like some time to figure this out. Also, can you call off Rooster so I can stop worrying about getting myself and Knox killed. Oh, and by the way, can I give my mom a call and tell her where I am, and assure her that I was not brutally beaten and murdered since my abduction.* That was never going to happen!

I had only seen the back of him once the entire time that I had been here. He was an elusive creature, and he was completely off limits to me.

He had wavy salt and pepper hair that was long enough to pull into a pony tail at the base of his neck. He was broad shouldered, and his legs were sturdy and long. He was a tall man, and his waist stopped about where my shoulders were. He had quite the presence about him, because nobody got within three feet of him unless he commanded someone to intrude upon his personal space. When he moved, people moved to accommodate him. When he spoke, people shut up to listen.

It was not a coincidence that he was in the position he was in. He did not need to bully and control people the way Rooster did, for he had more than proved himself in the circles of this world–that was evident. I never saw his face, but you did not need to see it in order to know all of this. It was an unmistakable fact that Floyd, the President of the Motor City Motor Cycle Club, was not a man you ever crossed and lived to tell the tale.

Three weeks after being pulled out of the pit, I was turned over to Cal once again. He said to Knox as he reported for duty, "I'm here to babysit your brat again. Jesus, Knox, if she ain't left your ass by now, I don't think she's ever gonna. Look at her, she's all hearts and cupids for you!"

Knox shot daggers at Cal with his eyes. All it took was one look and Cal apologized. "Geez man...sorry!"

Knox prepared to leave. "Viv, be good, I'll be back in a few hours. I have to go on a run with Floyd, Rod, Ace and a couple of the others."

Cal's eyes got wide and then he quickly looked away to hide his reaction. I of course noticed, and fully intended to question him about it as soon as Knox was out of earshot.

I decided to try asking Knox first. If he would not tell me, then I would bug Cal to death about it until he caved.

"Knox, what kind of run are you going on this time?"

I knew I was on a need-to-know basis when it came to things relating to the club, but if Knox was going on a ride that would have him leaving me and not coming back, I was going to throw a fit. He could not leave me behind and not come back for me. I had enough issues without adding abandonment to the list.

"Viv, relax, I'm coming back. You get worked up too easily!"

Telling a woman to relax is one of the most infuriating things a man can tell a woman in response to her doubts. Relaxing implies that a woman is overreacting. If there was even a chance that harm would come

Knox's way, it was not an overreaction for me to worry about him. When a person runs in the circles that he does, and lives a lifestyle that imposes great risks, even a minuscule chance can escalate to a great chance in the blink of an eye.

"Knox, don't go!"

I know I sounded pathetic and weak in my pleading–but worse yet, I knew that no amount of pleading could make him stay. My stomach was filled with butterflies and my pale complexion got a shade whiter.

Knox grabbed my face in his hands and said, "Viv, seriously, it'll be fine. I always come back. You're going to get gray hair if you freak out every time I walk out the door. And I like your hair red. I'm not ready for my old lady to look like my grandma!"

I smiled at him unwillingly.

"That's my girl…that's more like it. Now keep that smile on until I get back. Cal, take care of her like she were your own. Actually, no…take care of her as if she were mine! She is mine, you know, and she better be in the same condition I left her in too. Any gray hair and I'm holding you personally responsible!"

I could tell he was playing up the lightness of the mood surrounding the run that he was about to embark on. I knew he was trying to give me a false and hopeful sense of reassurance. But while he was a man of few words, I could tell he was hiding something from me. I was not an idiot about everything.

He kissed me and then turned to meet Rod, who was waiting at the door for him. Then he was gone. Rod paused to look at me before following Knox out the door. His look sent chills through me, and I immediately feared for Knox's safety. One by one, I could feel the gray hairs coming in. His words, *"everything's fine, Viv"*, were not going to pacify me this time. He had to know that shit does not work on a woman in love. Did love even matter in a place like this and in times like these?

Cal looked worried. "Hey Red, wanna throw some darts?"

I shrugged my shoulders and said, "Sure. Right after you tell me what's going on with this run! What do you know? You have to tell me!"

"Vivienne, first of all, you know I can't tell you anything, and even if I did know something–which I don't–I'm as unimportant around here as you are a pain in the ass! I'm on a need to know basis here, too."

I began to pout and plopped down on a bar stool.

"C'mon, pouting won't do you any good here!" Cal said as he handed me a fistful of darts.

I stood up and looked at him unenthusiastically as we both took turns trying to throw through our worry. Cal tried to pretend that this was just another one of his babysitting jobs, nothing more, and nothing less.

He was fairly convincing when he said, "You know what we need?"

He put up a finger to tell me to wait a minute, and he left the room. He came back moments later with a six pack of Budweiser and a bag of Pretzel Rods.

"Look what I found in the kitchen!" he said, smiling from ear to ear. "Beer makes everything better," he said as he snapped open a can and gave it to me.

"Thanks," I said as I tore open the bag of pretzels.

"Maybe you'll play better drunk!" he said, reminding me that he was beating me relentlessly, like he always did when we threw darts. I do not know why I kept agreeing to play. I never seemed to get any better, no matter how many times he beat me. I questioned whether alcohol would help my game.

I tried not to whine about losing to him constantly, since he was the only person around here who would even look at me, let alone entertain me while Knox went on these runs.

As I sipped my beer, Cal took his turn throwing, and I thought about the fact that I loved a man I knew very little about. There was a possibility that I could be pregnant with his kid, and here he was out on a run doing something I was not supposed to know anything about! Relationships do not make a damn bit of sense sometimes. Not in this life, or in any other. The act of loving someone is completely illogical. It is painful at times, but it can be the absolute easiest thing to find yourself doing without even knowing you are doing it.

"I win!" Cal announced.

"Shocker," I said sarcastically.

"Two out of three?"

"I don't know. Do you want to switch to Checkers?"

"Checkers? Are you kidding me?" He looked offended. "Do I look like a checker player to you? Am I eighty years old sitting in a park across the street from my retirement community?"

"Um, no," I answered.

"I may be a babysitter, but I'm not a damned checker player. I swear, babysitting you is ruining my reputation around here. I gotta find a new gig!"

He winked at me when he said it, so I knew he was not nearly as miserable or offended as he wanted me to believe.

Who knew anyone would get so upset over being accused of playing checkers! "You have a bad checker experience you want to tell me about?" I asked.

He rolled his eyes at me. "Best two out of three, or what? Those are your options missy."

"Yeah, best two out of three," I said resignedly.

I got up from my stool, turned away from him and walked over to pull my darts out of the board. When I turned around, I saw Rooster thrusting a blade into Cal's right side. My nightmare began again.

"CAL! OH MY GOD, CAL!" Instead of fleeing like Knox would have liked, I ran and threw myself onto Rooster. I caught him before he could pull the blade out of Cal and bury it into me. All three of us fell to the ground. Cal was in a world of hurt, and blood spattered everywhere as Rooster left a gaping hole in his side. The wound was now opened as the knife was removed, and Cal was left lying, convulsing on the floor.

Rooster did not take long to overpower me. He was just too strong—and too evil—for me to be any real match. He hit me so hard that I thought my cheek was going to explode. The force knocked me back into a wall, and I slid down onto the floor with a thud. Everything was out of focus, fading in and out as I saw him hovering over Cal.

I wanted to scream, but I could not find my voice. I wanted to hurl my body into Rooster again, to distract him from Cal, but I could only watch as he stabbed him again and again. Cal's eyes were wide and then grew faint. My eyes filled with tears. He was fading away right before my eyes. Cal's eyes were on me, but I was not sure he saw me. In that moment I whispered, "I'm sorry," as Rooster pulled his blade out and wiped the blood onto Cal's shirt. Cal was lying on his stomach with his cheek pressed hard onto the concrete floor. His skin began losing its shade of honey brown. He was growing paler by the second as the blood trickled out and formed a pool at his side. I wished Rooster had killed me instead. I just could not watch this happen to Cal, I had to do something.

Rooster then turned his vengeance on me. As he began to walk toward me, I gripped the darts in my hand tightly. If he was going to lay his hands on me, I was going to make him bleed for it. I may not have been able to kill him–like I have so longed to do–but I wanted him to at least feel pain. Cal deserved for Rooster's blood to be spilled here too.

When Rooster drew near, I tightened my jaw and prepared to assault him. As soon as his feet came to a stop next to me, I took all three metal tipped darts and slammed them into Rooster's thigh. He did not see it coming that much was clear. The look on his face as they sank into his flesh was not the face of someone who thought pain could find its way to them.

I knew the darts would not do much in the way of stopping Rooster from killing me, but I needed him to know pain today. I needed him to feel pain and bleed just like Cal had. I wanted to show him that he was no different than us–that his blood and ours were both red, and that pain goes both ways.

"You fucking bitch!" he said as he examined what I had done to him. He pulled the darts out by grabbing all three at once, then yanking them out clean. "You want to know what that feels like?" he threatened. "How about we take turns. I took three, now you're going to take three!"

And with that, he jammed all three of them into my arm. I could feel them tearing through my bicep and wondered how many holes I would have in me when he was finished. He left the darts hanging in my arm and then grabbed me fiercely by my punctured arm.

"I'm going to have some fun with you yet! MOVE!"

He shoved me across the room to the exit, then threw me over his shoulder and hauled me out...out into the night.

I knew that this time, even if I was on the back of a speeding bike, I would jump off the first chance I got. However, this time Rooster was more prepared. He shoved me into the open driver's side door of a Chevy truck. He pushed me from the driver's side to the passenger side, then crawled in behind me and slammed the door.

"Where's your boy Knox when you need him? Did you really think I would just let you two ride off into the sunset together? Let me remind you that you are mine and not his! I found you first!"

His lips curled around the word "HIS" like there was some latent issue that I did not know about. From what I was gathering, there was a lot more going on between Knox and Rooster besides me. And to Rooster, this was not just a game, it was out and out war.

The locks and door handles had been removed from the passenger side door of the truck. There was no way for me to bail, aside from kicking out the window, which was nearly impossible. Rooster would have me subdued long before I could accomplish a feat like that.

We drove south, and eventually got onto the I80/90 toll road going west. I was not blind this time, and I was paying explicit attention to every detail along the way. He knew it would not matter, because he was not going to lose me again, and at the end of this road, he was probably going to kill me. He was very confident in that, I could tell. I wish he would have thrown me into the bed of the truck. From there I would have had a chance to signal for help or attempt to escape. But he was so close to me now that he knew my every move. I would not get anything past him while in here. I just needed to wait, and if I waited patiently and remained alert, an opportunity just might present itself to try to escape.

Rooster drove on for hours. Of course, he did not seem to need a break, or a coffee, or anything. As I was completely preoccupied with what I would do next, I noticed that he pulled out a little glass pipe from his coat pocket. It had a rounded, bulb-looking end with a hole in it. It resembled a test tube or a beaker from eighth grade science class. I watched as he drove with his knees and began heating the end of his test tube pipe with a lighter. He cracked his window as he smoked his pipe. I knew that it was not tobacco, but I could not quite figure out what it was. I just stared at him until he said, "Jesus, what the fuck you staring at?"

"Nothing," I said as I turned my head to look out the passenger window.

"Never seen someone do meth before?"

"Meth? Um, no, I haven't."

And I was not lying. I knew what meth was, but I had never been around it before now.

"You really don't know shit about life, you know that? Did you grow up under a fucking rock? Or did your dad keep you locked in a closet your whole life, afraid someone like me would come along and get in your panties, fuck you senseless, and have you screaming for more?"

"No, I doubt my dad cared enough about me for that. I wasn't locked in a closet, and I wasn't a rock dweller either. I just...I didn't grow up in the city, around drugs or addicts!"

"So what, you think I'm some sort of addict now? You think you're better than me? I ought to shove you out of this truck and watch that semi behind us grind you to pieces under his rig for saying shit like that! Wait til I'm done smoking here…and I just might."

I did not dare say anything in return. Besides, what does one say to a psycho high on meth? I could see his muscles flexing and his knuckles tightening, and I knew I was only moments away from some blows.

Then he screamed at me.

"WHAT THE FUCK DID YOU JUST SAY TO ME?"

"I didn't say anything! I swear!"

"You lying whore, you think I can't hear you. I can hear into your brain. I can hear your thoughts. I know that you think you're better than me!"

"I don't, I'm no better than anyone else. I didn't think that!"

"YES YOU DID! Your mouth is a filthy, lying, whoring mouth!"

He grabbed my face with one hand, squeezing my cheeks, and grinding them into my teeth. He grabbed a bottle of booze and started pouring it all around and into my mouth. I tried spitting it out, but it was in my nose, in my eyes, pouring down my chin, and all over me. My eyes were burning fiercely, as if someone had filled them with hot coals. "We gotta clean that whore mouth of yours! You need sterilized before we get there!"

"Get where?" I tried to say, but it sounded like I was talking under water.

"Where are we going?" I attempted to say again. That, too, was hardly recognizable. Then again, Rooster thought he could read my mind, so I half expected him to answer regardless of being able to understand my garbled words.

"Well, let's just say that Floyd's not getting first stab at you anymore! That fucker sold me out. If he wants to make an example out of me, well then I'm going to make an example out of YOU! As a bonus, I'm gonna make an example out of your pussy boyfriend Knox. You ain't his old lady, he's more like your little bitch boy. He ain't nuthin you know! He's not my VP, he's not a goddamn thing to me! But you…he thinks you're his sweetheart. HA! Wait til he sees you ain't nothing but a coked out whore who can't get enough of having my dick in your mouth! Think he'll want you then?"

I had no intentions to speak. It was as if the meth intensified Rooster's monstrous side. But worse yet, this wickedness was the only thing that I have seen put a smile on his face since our first encounter. He was high on not only methamphetamine but on pure evil.

He continued.

"I know you think he's coming for you, but he's not. Just like that little blonde in Reno. Knox was going to be her knight in shining armor, too. Fucking right he was! I fucked her and cut out her eyes before she got to see her prince rescue her. That fucking guy never even came for her. Some prince charming she picked for herself there. Stupid cunt. What's a'matter with you cunts anyway? Do you think you can just tease and tease and then control us? Do you think that you have any kind of power over us? You're all just pussy! Pink, wet, warm places to stick our dicks, and you're a fucking dime a dozen."

I thought about this girl in Reno, this girl who thought Knox would save her. Was Rooster right? Was I just another girl along the way for Knox? Is this what he does? Do he and Rooster battle over young, innocent girls until they kill each other, or the girl winds up dead? Was this all some horrible game? If so, how could I be so stupid to fall in love with him?

I felt as if I was in a house of horrors, and nothing was as it seemed. Just then, I wished that Rooster would push me out of the truck to be torn to bits beneath that semi's eighteen wheels.

Chapter 14

KNOX

That afternoon, Knox pulled up to the clubhouse alongside Rod and Ace. Floyd was on a private phone call outside, and he motioned to Knox, Rod, and Ace to go in. The smell of blood and sweat was in the air. Knox's nostrils flared as he walked deeper into the room, and he immediately began looking for the source. He noticed a boot sticking out from underneath the pool table and gave a warning look to Ace and Rod. Both men simultaneously drew their guns as Knox darted toward the pool table to identify the boot's owner.

"Secure the room!" Knox yelled. Rod and Ace began opening doors to clear the area, along with checking for additional casualties. After surveying the area, Rod and Ace ran outside to inform Floyd that there was a situation inside the clubhouse.

Knox found Cal lying halfway under the pool table and felt for a pulse. It looked like Cal had lost a lot of blood–there was little hope that he was alive. There was no way Cal could have survived this kind of bloodshed.

Knox started to feel a pang of grief, and then there it was–pulsing beneath Knox's fingers. He felt a tiny little bump of a heartbeat. Cal was alive! Knox did not waste any time getting to his feet to run for the first aid kit. He broke the lock and ran to Cal's side for a second time.

"First things first, Cal," Knox said urgently. "We have to get you to retain whatever blood you have left."

Knox grabbed the bottle of Quickclot from the first aid kit and ripped Cal's shirt open to assess the damages. Cal was completely unconscious. He would not feel the pain or burn of the Quickclot granules that Knox was about to pour into his open wounds. Knox wished he could call for an ambulance–to get help here fast–because he knew that would increase the chances of Cal staying alive. Unfortunately, he knew Floyd would never allow it, even if it would save

Cal's life. There were rules at the club. No ambulance would be called, regardless of the circumstance.

He worked quickly and methodically. After pouring the packets of Quickclot onto and into Cal's punctured skin, he carefully gauzed and taped him up. This was not the first time Knox had held a life in his hands, and it likely would not be the last.

Rod helped Knox lift Cal's limp body and the two men carried him outside, where Momma was waiting in the driver's seat of her van.

As the men loaded Cal into the van, Ace instructed Momma to drive like hell and get Cal to the hospital before it was too late. Knox wished he could take Cal to the hospital himself, but with Vivienne missing, and no idea of her whereabouts, he had to let Cal go without him. His eyes were wild, but he could not show how panicked he was over the girl, not to anyone—not yet. Knox had a reputation and he had credibility with his peers and with Floyd. He could not show his real emotions right now and destroy what he had worked so hard to build—he had to remain calm if he was going to have any chance at getting Vivienne back.

He stormed into the clubhouse and tried to re-create the scene. He started at the dart board, as he knew Cal and Viv were always playing darts. Sure enough, there were three darts into the board, but the other set was missing. There were smears of small, bloody, handprints where he had found Cal's body on the floor. Surely Viv did not do this to Cal. The thought did cross his mind. *What if I've been sleeping with the daughter of Satan this whole time*? He realized that he knew very little about Viv. What he felt for her was very real, but his time with her had been short. Had he rescued a cold blooded killer from Rooster, when it was Rooster who needed to be rescued from her?

Knox started to question his judgment, thinking back to all the time he had spent with Viv. He needed answers and he needed them NOW! And then, he saw the big, bloody footprints tracked across the room. The footprints were far too big to be Viv's. His attention was directed to the blood smeared on the wall and the splintered wood, where it appeared that someone's head had hit the baseboard. His heart sank as he touched the red hair that was stuck in the splintered wood trim.

How could he have been so wrong? Viv would never hurt Cal–she would never hurt anyone! His instincts were right about her. Knox immediately felt ashamed for letting his paranoia get the best of him. It was Rooster, and it had always been Rooster who was to blame. He was letting them all know that Rooster gets what Rooster wants. The fucking asshole had walked right in here and taken her...AGAIN!

He must have known that they would be on a run. Knox was sure he had been monitoring them since the time he left, unless he had someone to help him here on the inside. Knox looked around the room at the faces of the leather clad men stationed around the bloodied scene. Could it have been anyone else? Rod, Ace, Momma, or maybe even Izz? They call this a brotherhood, but maybe there is no one who is sacred in this place. Could there be any trust amongst vagrants, thieves, drug runners and pimps? It was probably ignorant to think that, but at times Knox wondered if the people here had any loyalty to give.

Just then, Knox felt his phone vibrate inside his pocket. He had instructed Momma to call him if she ran into any problems, and he worried that she had. As he looked down, he noticed there was a text message from a number he did not recognize. He hit ok to accept the message. When he saw the red hair pop up on the screen, he nearly smiled, until he scrolled down and saw Viv bound and gagged, lying on a bed, wearing nothing but blood splattered panties and restraints. He could not fight the rage that began to boil in his gut. There would be no reining it in, reputations and credibility will all be damned. Knox no longer cared what the Floyds of the world thought or what the Rods or Aces would do to him. He was officially on the warpath, one that began with him standing in a cooling pool of Cal's blood and would end with him stopping Rooster once and for all and Vivienne going home safe, back to where she belonged.

Thoughts of Reno crept back into Knox's subconscious. The hollow, eyeless sockets of that cute blond girl had haunted him for over a year. The girl had been a stranger to him. She held no special place in his heart, but he felt that he had failed her nonetheless. He was the one who should have reached her in time. He was the one who would have to face her parents one day and explain to them that his efforts were not enough. Rooster killed Elyse Goodman and did not bat an eye. He would kill Vivienne too–slowly, meticulously, and without any regard for human life. Rooster would drain Vivienne of all signs of life.

Knox did not know where he had taken her or where to even begin. All he knew was that he was running out of time. He could not fail himself again–and he certainly could not fail Viv.

Knox drew a deep breath. He grabbed his phone and slowly dialed a number he knew that could cost him his life.

Chapter 15

VIV

I awoke to find myself sprawled out across a bed, tied up tight like a boat to a dock. The last thing I remembered was riding in Rooster's truck. He was telling me about that girl in Reno.

How the hell did he get me out of the truck and into a bed without my knowing?

"I shoved you into a suitcase."

I turned quickly to see Rooster standing in the doorway. "How did you…you answered me, but I didn't ask you a question?"

"Oh, for fuck's sake. I told you I could read your mind. By the way, you ain't as smart as you think you are. You're just a little bitch whose brain works just like all the other broads I've had."

At this point I was starting to think he really could read my mind, but waking up in my shoes would have anyone questioning their sanity. I began putting the pieces together to figure out how I had gotten here. I needed to think straight. I could not allow Rooster to get into my head–that latest comment was just lucky timing on his part.

Then it hit me. He could not read minds, he was just all hopped up on meth! Paranoid, high and euphoric are all side effects of methamphetamine usage. Rotten teeth, psychosis, aggression, and jaw clenching. Rooster fit the bill all right. I heard meth users can actually go into a schizophrenia-like psychosis after quitting that can last up to six months, and are resistant to any kind of treatment. I had read this once, but had never experienced it firsthand. It made sense, looking at Rooster's current round of hatred, violent personality, mood swings, and murderous contempt for others. My body chilled to think that his contempt for me was only the most recent assault on humankind.

I wonder now if they ever found the body of the blond girl whose eyes Rooster had cut out in Nevada. Did her parents search for her? Were there posters with her pretty face on them? Did someone create a tip line to call? I could not help but feel a kindred bond with this girl who I had never met. I wondered if Rooster looked at her the way he looked at me? Did she suffer? Did he shatter her from the inside out and offer her as a sacrifice to his insatiable hunger for carnage?

Did she cry at the end? I had cried for Cal as I watched his life slip away, but I had not cried for myself in all of this. I guess that was a result of my not-so-kind upbringing. I wondered if maybe I did have a death wish. Too many thoughts and questions were flooding my mind…Stop! Perhaps it was my fate to die in this way.

Maybe it was better that Rooster killed me instead of another girl–a sweeter girl–the kind of girl who would grow up, have babies, and become a Sunday school teacher one day. It would be all right with me if I went instead of someone like that. Someone better, someone more deserving, who would make the world a better place. Maybe there was still good in the world. Evil, like that in Rooster, does not take the best girls the world has to offer. He takes the Vivs of the world. The rebellious, unruly, obstinate, hard-headed, defiant, pains in the asses like me. Serves him right, I thought and laughed out loud.

Rooster shot me a look. "You losing it, bitch? Why are you laughing? You think this is funny? Do you think what I'm about to do to you is funny?"

He's going to kill me now, I imagined. I closed my eyes, then felt Rooster grab my left foot.

"You think you'll laugh when I cut your toes off one by one? How about when I cut you from ear to ear, making your mouth into a gigantic gaping hole in your face?" he threatened. "And by the way...your little bitch boy says hi!"

My eyes flashed open wide as I winced at the pain of him twisting the foot he still held in his hand.

"Knox?"

"Yeah, Knox!"

He pulled his cell phone out of his pocket and waved it around.

"How about we send him a video this time? You wanna? It'll be your big shining moment in the spotlight! Don't all you whores want to be famous?"

"Not particularly," I muttered to him. "Hey, what do you mean send him a video *this time*? What did we do last time?"

"Oh, I sent him a pretty picture of you all tied up and doped like you are."

"You drugged me? When? And with WHAT?"

"It's none of your business with what! But if ya really want to know, I stabbed you in the neck with a needle when you were looking out the window of the truck. How else you think I was going to shove your stupid ass in a suitcase so nobody would see you?"

"Did he respond to your text?" I inquired.

"He sure didn't. Not surprising though, I told you he was a pussy!"

"No he's not!" I shouted.

I had no idea why I was shouting at Rooster. No idea why I was defending Knox's honor, when I was not entirely certain how honorable he was anymore. Cal was dead, and Knox was not coming for me. Rooster was shooting me up with needles, and I was about to make my first half-naked video. That was my reality. *God, please don't ever let my mom see it. Please God, don't let my mom's final earthly memory of me be tied up here, nearly naked, bleeding, playing over and over again on CNN after I'm gone.* A mother would never recover from something like that.

My mom would be proud if she could hear me now; praying to God at what was surely the end of my life. I guess all that Sunday school she had forced me to sit through had sunk in. She would be happy to know that. If I made it to heaven—or wherever it is murdered girls go—I know my mom would arrive sooner or later. I would thank her for getting me in up there.

The phone in Rooster's clutched hand lit up. He seemed surprised, and he tried to hide it from me. Rooster became visibly angry–and I wanted to believe that was because the phone was being lit up by Knox. Maybe there would be a chance that I would not wind up raped, pillaged, and left for dead in the middle of nowhere...with Knox nowhere to be found.

Rooster went into the bathroom. We had to be in a hotel room. This did not look like someone's home. It smelled like a hotel room, and I could hear traffic just outside the window. It was with this realization that I decided to try my luck.

I started screaming at the top of my lungs, "HELP! HEEELP! SOMEONE PLEASE HELP! HELP MEEE!"

Rooster came busting through the door and hit me across the face so forcefully that it hurt my wrists where I was tied up, due to the force of the blow.

"You shut your mouth! You shut your god damned mouth or I'll cut your tongue out and make you swallow it!"

"Better yet, how 'bout we play some darts? You and your little buddy Cal liked to play darts...well, guess what? So do I, how about I go first?"

Rooster grabbed the bloodied set of darts that were lying on the nightstand from the clubhouse. He threw them at me hard enough that sometimes they stuck in me, and other times they just broke the skin, then fell out. I closed my eyes and prayed that Cal was a better dart thrower than Rooster. I kept imagining one of those darts sticking in my eyeball, rendering me blind. I could not bear the thought of not being able to see what was coming at me in the form of torture.

One dart did come close. It struck me just to the side of my eye and then tore down the side of my face toward my ear. Rooster laughed and said, "Almost got it that time!" When it was all said and done, I must have had more than fifty puncture wounds in me. Knee caps, shoulders, hips, breasts, forehead...no part of me was safe from this attack. The blood oozing out of each of the little red wounds must have made me look gruesome.

When I opened my eyes, he was sucking on that glass pipe again. When he finished, he shot me a frightening look. He then reached for something on the nightstand that was out of my view. When I saw the duct tape, I knew things were about to get even worse. He taped my mouth shut.

"I won't put anything in your mouth yet, but I am going to put something in you. You'll never forget how it feels to have Rooster inside of you."

Chapter 16

KNOX

Desperate and determined, Knox used the ace up his sleeve to gain the coordinates from where Rooster had sent the text from. He had information that Rooster was in the Chicago area, and Knox made haste in his departure from the clubhouse to where Vivienne had been taken.

The miles could not go by fast enough. He thought of all the times in his life he had done the right thing. He worked hard, he put himself through school, and he earned a degree. He landed a great career. But today, he had never felt further from that man, or that life.

Raised in Knoxville, Tennessee by his kind and thoughtful parents, Knox grew up with older and younger brothers whom he loved and adored. He knew the joys and sometimes hardships of being a middle child. His parents later divorced, but that only made him a stronger kid than before. He faced adversity, and he knew how to handle himself. He was not the type of guy who let people in. When his folks split up, he became a little guarded and cautious in letting people get close to him.

Hell, in this life–this biker life—the closest person to him was not his supposed mentor Floyd, it was Cal. Cal was his only real ally in all of this, and now he could very well be dead. Knox had gotten him into the club, and now it was Knox who felt responsible for what had become of him. Cal's daughter came to mind, and Knox could not bear the thought of seeing her stand at her daddy's funeral, so little and so alone without someone to guide and protect her. She would never get to know who her daddy was, how good he was, and how loyal and brave he had been. Knox knew that there would be consequences for protecting Vivienne and allowing her to stay. *How could he predict that those consequences would be so great?*

He did not give it enough thought. He was selfish in his decision to keep her close. And now he had to face the result of that decision. He had put Cal and everyone else close to him in harms way, and now he had to make it right. As crazy as it sounded, Knox knew that given the opportunity to make that decision a second time, knowing what he knew now, he still would have kept Vivienne with him—even knowing the high cost of that decision. He would do anything for the red-haired, hazel-eyed girl that he had fallen for while watching her eat a cheeseburger on that sunny day. She was completely oblivious to the fact that she was the most interesting female he had ever seen. He knew the moment he locked eyes with that girl that she was not just easy to look at, but she would be the match that set him on fire. She would be the warmth he needed on cold nights. She would be his.

Knox was not a murderer, but he wished he would have killed Rooster when he had been given the chance. Why didn't he? Sure, it would have ruined everything he had worked so hard for, but it would have been the lesser of two evils given the current circumstances. Rooster's death would have saved many lives, but it would not bring back the lives already taken.

Knox's phone vibrated in his pocket, and he flipped it open to receive Rooster's message.

"I can't decide which was more pleasurable–riding your old lady, or riding your motorcycle. They both make a lot of noise and make my balls swell with delight, but I'm going to go with your bike. It doesn't cry and beg for mercy when I ride it hard like your old lady does!"

Knox closed his phone. He felt as if a knife ripped through his chest. He could not breathe. He felt immediately sick, so he leaned his head towards the open window of his truck and let the wind hit him in the face until the nausea subsided. As quickly as the reflectors on the side of the road flew by him, so did the minutes that might cost Vivienne her life. In this moment, he had to hope and pray that she could somehow shelter herself, to be strong now like he knew her to be...at least until he could get there.

Knox's phone rang again. This time it was an incoming call, and he was quick to answer. He knew this phone call would not undo what had been done, but there was still hope that with a little help he might make it in time.

Chapter 17

VIV

When I awoke, I was back in the truck–no longer nearly naked—but in excruciating pain. I was far more banged up than I remembered. My body was aching all over from the dart holes and from Rooster violating me in a way that had not been done up to this point. Down by my hip bone, I could feel what felt like a heartbeat. I stuck my fingers in the waistband of my pants and felt the blood that was oozing out of me and soaking into my clothing, it hurt tremendously. I touched my fingers to the wound and found what felt like a stab wound. The bastard had stabbed me with a knife! I had no idea how deep the wound was and I was not strong enough to put my fingers inside of the gash to see. I kept one hand over the wound, applying pressure and hoping it would clot. In further examination of myself, I discovered my wrists were raw, swollen, and burning where I had been tied. My stomach strangely felt like fire ants were eating me alive. It burned as if he had poured acid on my midsection.

With one hand holding my stab wound, I used the other to lift up the shirt Rooster had dressed me in, a black Outlaw T-shirt, and saw by the help of a passing semi's headlights, that I had been carved like a pumpkin into a jack-o-lantern. He had carved his name into my stomach. The word "Rooster" was now bloodily carved into my flesh. *I must have passed out from the pain, surely I would remember this*!

A wave of awful memories hit me like a ton of bricks, and I shuddered. It was bad enough that I was sticky from the blood oozing out of me, but the sick bastard had covered me in his semen as well. He had rubbed it all over my wounds, saying it would help with infection. *He* was the infection in all of this; an infection that no amount of antibiotics would ever eradicate from my body.

This time with Rooster–this whole experience–was horrifying, painful, and unforgettable. Knox was gone, my body, soul, and insides were ruined, and I was covered in semen and blood. I released a small breath and out came the tears. The tears of what was now lost, and what was to come. They were the tears that Rooster had been waiting for. The tears that he knew would be my resignation of this life, my ultimate surrender to him.

The truck stopped, and he turned off the engine. It was pitch-black outside, and there was not anything around that I could see. There was no moonlight to illuminate a sign of our location. As Rooster opened the truck door and the dome light came on, I could see that his face held a new look. It was one that had him looking determined as opposed to demented. It was intense instead of insane.

He got out of the truck and left me there. Frantically, I felt around on the seat, on the floor, and behind the seat for something, anything to ward him off of me should he start in on me again. I had hoped to find a tire iron but was shocked to discover that the knife he had used on Cal was shoved down into the cushion.

There had been many times I had fantasized about killing Rooster, and now I may have finally found the chance. It was a tangible sign that I was not meant to die. Not like this.

I had been given the opportunity to take a life once before–my dad had given it to me a long time ago.

One night during one of my frequent "lessons", also known as "beatings", my father finally realized the hatred I had for him as it welled up inside of me with each pounding of his fist. My hatred for him grew and swelled. He saw it, smiled, and encouraged it. He taunted and provoked me, doing his damndest to make a monster of me. He wanted me to fight back, and he wanted me to be ugly, just like him.

That was when his eyes got wild, and he ran for the closet. He dodged the table and chairs that he knocked over during the onset of his rage. He moved so quickly away from me that it startled me. He reached the closet door, opened it, felt around on the top shelf within it, and came out with a gun. This was not just any gun, it was a revolver. He flipped it open, checked for bullets, and when he had verified it was ready to go, he came at me.

I thought, "OH MY GOD! MY DAD'S GOING TO KILL ME!" as he came steadily across the room in my direction. My eyes were wide, my throat was too tight to scream, and I was petrified. It was then that a powerful presence came over me. I stood my ground as part of me did not fear dying, while another part fell quiet at the realization that my time might be over, here on earth.

There were no words to describe the feelings that come over you when the man who brought you into this world was about to take you out of it.

And then, in a strange turn of events, he handed me the gun. At first, I did not put my hand out. I was in shock at what it meant. He yelled at me, "TAKE IT!" and instinctually, I did as I was told.

"Point it at me," he ordered.

And so I did.

"Shoot me!" he screamed.

Things were out of control. We were standing in a room full of overturned furniture, my own father screaming at me to shoot him, and I was holding a loaded gun. It was a scene I had never imagined my eyes would witness, and yet there I was, faced with this impossible scenario.

I stood there with my hands shaking and my mouth so dry that I could not even swallow. I squeaked out to my father, "What?" It had to be clear that he wanted me to shoot him. He had punished me. Why was he now giving me reins for retribution?

"PULL…THE…TRIGGER!" he said through gritted teeth and a locked jaw that was pulsing at half the speed of my heart.

"I'm not going to shoot you," I said to him.

"Why not? You hate me. Take a shot, or are you too *scarrrred* to?"

"I'm not scared," I lied. I was terrified of my father. "I'm NOT going to shoot you!" I screamed.

I thought about pulling the trigger in that moment. I could put a hole in his chest that would show he truly did not have a heart. I could shoot him and remove the man from my life once and for all. But those thoughts only lasted a split second, for I was not the monster he thought he had spawned. I would not, could not, kill a human being for their sins in this world.

But that was then, and this is now. I could not kill my father when given the chance, but I could and would do every single thing in my power to kill Rooster. Even if it meant both of us leaving this earth together, I was going to kill Rooster tonight. All the hate, all the rage, and all the pain I had felt in my life was feeding me now. It was pulsing within my veins. While I was not sure I would ever get the "good me" back, for this moment I had to let her slip away. I allowed that side of me to take shelter in the dark, like my mind had done not so long ago when Rooster dealt me that first beating. My goodness retreated now, and all that was left was the worst part, the darkest part of me. The part of me that was forced to grow into what my Father had long ago attempted to nurture…his evil…in me.

Rooster had parked behind a row of trees. That much I could see only because the headlights irradiated them as we slowly drove by moments ago. I took the knife that I retrieved from the truck seat and quickly shoved it down the front of my pants, careful not to cut myself. Oh the surprise he will get if he tries to molest me again! Strangely, the idea had me ecstatic. It was the only happiness that existed in this dark place.

The most devilish things flashed through my mind; castrating him the way he had mutilated me, or slitting his throat and watching the life drain out of him like he had done to Cal. Back in that hotel room, he took from me the only thing I had left. I had nothing to lose, no Knox to love, and no life worth living anymore. I was the walking dead, and Rooster was going to die trying to kill me. That much I knew.

He opened my door and yanked me out. He began to shove me into the darkness. At first my eyes did not adjust well, and I could not see an inch in front of my face, but as we walked on, I started to see that we were in the middle of a field. I had a feeling we were not in Michigan anymore.

"Keep going till I tell you to stop," Rooster said from behind me.

I walked on...and on...and on. I was exhausted and torn up. It seemed like we had easily walked a mile or better, in the dark. I wondered how far he was going to take me. Why are we walking? He could have just killed and buried me right next to the truck. Why all this effort now? He had not exactly been careful to hide his identity back at the hotel. He did not even steal a new vehicle. The truck he was driving was the one we drove away from the clubhouse in. He kept his cell phone on and with him, easily traceable if someone had wanted to locate his whereabouts, so I could not figure out why he was taking the time to walk me all this way. So they would not find me?

I wondered if the girl in Reno took a walk like this one, in the dark, alone and scared. Had Rooster carved her up like he did me? I wondered if Elyse Goodman would be there when I finally die. Do victims get to spend eternity together? Will we be stuck in Purgatory together forever as Rooster's captives?

Rooster finally said, "Stop." I was relieved to stop trying to shuffle my feet any further. All the walking had gotten my blood pumping and I could feel the blood from my stab wound now dripping into my shoe. I turned to look at him, and when I did, he punched me in the mouth. I fell to the ground and he jumped with both feet onto one of my legs. I felt it snap and give way under his weight as I curled into the fetal position to try to protect myself from the assault. He kicked me from all sides, until he was huffing and puffing for air. He was obviously working up a sweat and he paused for a moment to catch his breath. In that moment, I pulled the knife out of my pants and slashed wildly in his direction. I gashed deep into the flesh of his ankles. His strong legs went wobbly like jello, and he fell to the ground beside me. He cried out in pain as he felt the knife rip through him. When he fell, he was hurt, but he was far from dead. I may have just pissed him off.

He climbed on top of me and tried to wrestle the knife from my hand. I managed to stab him in the hand instead. He pulled away from me, but I was not about to let him get away, only to come back and kill me when he regained his strength. I drug myself across the ground, my leg too broken to try and stand. He crawled away from me, his legs as crippled as my own, with neither of us making much headway. He could not kick at me with his limp, floppy feet that were covered in blood. It was currently the only advantage I had against him.

I knew this would be my only opportunity to end Rooster's life, and ultimately save my own. I pulled myself slowly across the ground towards a slowing Rooster. When I caught up to him, I flung my arm with the knife in his direction again, not having any idea if I would actually hit him. I realized I had when I heard a *whoosh* escape his body, and his breathing took a massive turn for the worse. At that point, I was fairly certain that I had hit his ribcage and possibly punctured his lung.

Now in distress, Rooster had to realize that he was in trouble. I had a weapon, he had only one working lung, and legs he could not stand on, and I was not dying. That was when he tried to ward me off by throwing a knee at me that caught me square in the temple. That was a devastating blow. I fell face down in the dirt, unable to move, unable to go on. I did not have any strength left. I wanted so badly to see Rooster die, but now I had to lie here and die instead, which was what I fully intended on doing. I was bleeding out of every square inch of my body, through pin sized holes, a stab wound, and carved flesh. I had been assaulted to full capacity. I knew it was only a matter of time for me now. I saw Cal's life evaporate from his body, and in that moment, I could feel mine leaving too.

Chapter 18

KNOX

Upon being given the location of the latest transmission from Rooster's cell phone, Knox made his way into the country and found the Red Chevy Truck that Rooster had been known to drive when he was not on his bike. It was parked alongside a ditch by a row of trees. The keys were still in the ignition.

Knox grabbed a flashlight and began to scour the area for any sign of life. He finally found a footprint that he thought belonged to Rooster. He took off in the direction it led. It was dark, and Knox stopped dead in his tracks when he saw another pair of headlights pull up and stop where he had parked behind Rooster's pickup. He turned off his flashlight when he saw two men get out and head in his direction.

There was nowhere to hide, as now he was in an open field. If they had a flashlight, it would be only moments before they would catch up to him. He stood frozen for a moment but then decided to keep walking in the direction of the footprints that he had found. He hurried in the darkness, not knowing if he was even going in the right direction. He tripped, and the toes of his boots became lodged as he went down like a ton of bricks. When he rolled over, he put out his hand to feel what he had tripped on and he felt a warm body. He had tripped over some-*one*, not some-*thing*.

He could not turn on his light since that would give away his location, so he felt the body to determine if it was Vivienne who he had stumbled upon. However, the lump of flesh he discovered was far too hairy and bulky to be his girl. He realized he had run right into Rooster. All the way here, Knox had thought about what he would do if he actually found Rooster, but he had not anticipated finding him like this.

Knox wondered if Rooster had tried to sell Vivienne to an associate or a rival gang member, and they had killed him instead of paying for her. Just then, Knox heard footsteps approaching. He grabbed his 9mm and pointed it into the darkness.

"Who's there?" Knox said with authority.

He flipped on his flashlight to find Floyd and Ace standing there, guns drawn and looking surprised to find a gun pointed right back at them. They immediately put their weapons down.

"Knox, we followed you as soon as you left the clubhouse. Rooster wasn't only your problem, he was my problem too. I'm the one who's in charge of this operation, and I needed to see this through!" Floyd said, with his hand still gripping his gun.

Knox dropped his beam of light onto a now bloody lump of flesh that resembled Rooster.

Floyd looked down at Knox's feet and said, "This your doing?"

"No, I found him like this. I don't know what the hell happened to him."

"Where's the girl?" Ace asked.

"I don't know that either."

Floyd looked at Knox sternly. "Knox, I know you don't want to hear this, but I think this is out of our hands now. The girl's been beaten, witnessed a murder, has likely been raped, and who knows what else. We can't keep your little pet any longer. If she's not dead yet...then she needs to be. We won't survive after the fallout from all of this. Knox, you know as well as I do, should she make it to the authorities, our life as we know it is over!"

Knox's stomach twisted in knots after hearing Floyd's resolution. Knox knew that if Vivienne had survived Rooster, it would be a miracle–but for her to survive Rooster and Floyd–the odds of that were astronomical.

Floyd turned on his flashlight and surveyed the surrounding area. Not too far from where they stood, they saw a flash of red.

Fuck! Knox thought. Why did she have to be here, in the middle of nowhere, when Floyd is hell-bent on killing her? If she is not dead already, she will be soon.

The three men walked over to where Vivienne was lying broken on the ground. They stopped just short of stepping on her. Knox held his breath as he stood there, not knowing if she were dead or alive. By the looks of her, she should have been dead. Floyd rolled her onto her back, and all three of them looked at what was once a beautiful, vibrant, young girl. Blood was dripping from her nose, there were obvious gashes in her head, arms, and legs, and one of her legs was bent grotesquely.

Knox had to look away as Floyd bent down to see if she was breathing. He turned back to hear the verdict, only to find Floyd pointing his gun at Viv.

"WAIT! STOP! Is she even alive?"

Knox knelt down beside Viv. He pulled her close lovingly, but then quickly began checking for signs of life. Her body was warm, and he felt a slight pulse. He had no idea how to save her at this point, and his mind ran through everything he knew about keeping someone alive.

Knox knew there was only one thing he could do to give her a fighting chance.

He stood up and said, "She's as good as dead. I guess she was fun when she was in one piece—but look at her now, what a waste!"

He pulled up her shirt to expose her torso, and everyone fell silent as they read what Rooster had carved into her stomach. He did exactly what he had done to Elyse Goodman.

"Forever branded by the son-of-a-bitch," Knox muttered, sounding disgusted.

Floyd then offered, "Yeah...how could you ever go to bed with a woman who's been used and left to look like that! Put her out of her misery, Knox. It's the right thing to do for all our sakes. Besides, she doesn't deserve to suffer any longer. Say goodbye and then finish her."

Knox knelt down next to Vivienne once more, kissing her in the one spot she was not bleeding from, before he pulled out his gun. Her lips were so battered and swollen, he thought he would hurt her just to kiss her.

She opened her eyes, but did not speak. She just blinked and looked at him disbelievingly. Tears welled up in her eyes and streamed down the sides of her face, but she remained silent.

Floyd did not see that Vivienne was awake. "Knox, it's time! Finish her!"

Vivienne's eyes got wide, and she tensed up, obviously frightened by Floyd's words. She did not try to flee, and she did not attempt to fight him. She looked hard into his eyes, sending him a message of love and acknowledgment that it was time to say goodbye. She squeezed his hand and then squeezed her eyes shut, preparing to take the final blow that would end her life.

In the darkness, shots rang out. There were two quick shots, followed by one final shot that ripped through the air. Floyd looked at Knox, who was visibly upset.

After a moment, the men turned and began to walk back the way they had come. They stopped where Rooster lay and each took turns spitting on his corpse.

Ace looked at Knox and said, "I tell you one thing, man, I think it was your little lady who put a hurtin' on Rooster. I mean, she didn't take it lying down; she was a fighter to the very end. There's honor in that. Remember her like that."

Knox just nodded and walked on; while he appreciated the pep talk, there was no amount of memorializing that was going to make him feel better about what he had just done. It was done for his club, done for his brotherhood…done for show.

If he never did something horrible for show again, he would maybe stand a chance in finding some sort of peace in this life when all of this was over.

Once they were back at their vehicles, Floyd said, "Ace, take my car. I'm going to ride back with Knox. We have some things to discuss."

Ace nodded like a good soldier and caught the keys that Floyd tossed in his direction. Ace got in, started it up, and began to drive off leaving Floyd and Knox standing there, separated by the hood of Knox's truck.

Floyd had something on his mind, and it was not Rooster and Vivienne's death.

Knox had the impression that he was about to join Vivienne and Rooster–to die in this place. He reluctantly got into the vehicle and prepared for whatever it was Floyd was about to say.

"Knox, we've got a problem. It's important that we talk in private before I go before the club and explain to them that we have been infiltrated."

Knox nodded and hung his head, ready to admit defeat.

He looked at Floyd and said, "How do you want to handle this?"

"It won't be easy. Cal's hospital room is being guarded by Federal agents. We can't get near him."

Knox looked up, surprised. "Cal's alive? He survived? Are you shitting me?"

Floyd appeared aggravated. "Knox, sure, it's great he's alive–if he was a brother–

but he's not. He's a mole that's detrimental to the club as long as he's alive!"

"A mole? Are you sure? What did you have in mind? Do you want us to come into the Detroit Trauma center with guns blazing and start taking people out? You know as well as I do, the club wouldn't survive something like that either!"

Knox found it hard to put the vehicle into drive knowing Vivienne's body was not far from where he was parked. He was of no use to her now, and while her presence held him like gravity to the earth, he knew that the best thing he could do for her was to leave with Floyd. He was heading back to hell...Michigan. The word was out, and the jig was up. Cal was a Federal agent, and now he was marked for death.

"Floyd, you know, Cal couldn't have known much. I mean, this thing with Viv is the worst of what he could actually know firsthand. Hell, we left him as club sitter while we went to rallies. He swept floors and bartended events. He was hardly our head of security. Maybe we're not nearly as fucked as we could be."

"Knox, regardless of what he knows or doesn't know, doesn't it fucking blow your mind that there was a Federal agent–eating, sleeping, and shitting under our very noses, and we had no idea? What kind of operation are we running that this sort of thing could happen to us? Fuck!"

Floyd was getting visibly upset as each word flew out of his mouth. This was not good as far as Knox could see, but he had no choice but to continue driving. Floyd stared out the window angrily, and the wheels in his brain spun and churned as he stewed over their current predicament.

Chapter 19

VIV

An older gentleman in a white doctor's coat walked into the room carrying my chart.

He cleared his throat and said, "Hello Vivienne. My name is Dr. Bradshaw and I understand that you have been through quite the ordeal. I am head of neurosurgery here at St. Rita's Hospital, and your mother requested my services in reviewing your case. She briefly explained your current situation and the fact that you are not able to recollect specific memories. Can you please tell me a little more about what exactly you are experiencing in regards to your thoughts and memories? Are you having visions? Are you hearing voices at all? Any trouble distinguishing between what is real and what is fantasy?"

"Whoa doc, slow down. I barely remember my name at times, so those are a lot of questions to comprehend and answer!"

Dr. Bradshaw laughed. "Well, my dear, it appears that you have not forgotten your sense of humor. Take your time, Vivienne, because the answers to these questions will aid in my assessment of your recalcitrant memory problem. Let us start out with what seems to be most troubling to you."

"Well, doc, I feel like there are holes in my memory. I remember some things clear as day, and then I think about where I am now and those memories don't add up. Everything leading up to me waking up looking like this seems to be one giant abyss. I know that what I need to know is there, only locked behind a door that I cannot, for the life of me, open!"

"Well, your chart indicates that you had experienced several blows to the head. I can see that your body sustained physical injury of a violent nature. I can only assume that the physical assault you endured would not be limited to physical pain, but mental pain as well. I think an MRI should be conducted to rule out a possible subdural hematoma.

"English please, Doc?"

"Yes—of course. A subdural hematoma is bleeding on your brain.

Should an injury like this exist, it would give reason for your memory loss, or it could be…"

"What could it be? I need you to fill in the blank!"

"Vivienne, there is the possibility that due to the trauma you have experienced your mind has temporarily shut down in order to protect your psyche. Studies have shown that in situations similar to what you have been through, the victim's mind shuts down in order to block out the assault. There is the possibility that when your body could not take anymore, your mind shut down in order to protect you."

"Schedule the tests, Doc. I need to remember, so I can try to forget. I don't know how I can get back to any kind of normalcy if I don't know what happened to me."

The doctor left the room, and I sat back and waited for the nurse to come and retrieve me for my scheduled tests.

It did not take long before my stomach began to growl. I realized that it was just past one. I regretfully decided to order lunch from the hospital menu, as my mom had left for the time being. She had finally gone home to get a much needed shower and sleep in an actual bed for a couple of hours. I could not blame her–I had slept on that dirty cot in that pit, and I know from experience that roughing it can really make a person feel less than human. She did not smell like I had though, *thank God*!

I ordered a lunch from the hospital menu that consisted of macaroni and cheese, a roll, and a small salad. As an afterthought I added the fluffy, pink, parfait jello for desert. My mom had been thoughtful enough to bring my favorite drink, Big Red, to help wash down the awful hospital food.

I took the opportunity, while alone and eating, to try and recall the last thing I could remember before Knox had pointed his loaded gun at me and pulled the trigger.

I did not have long to reflect. Detective Matthews walked into the room, ready to talk. He offered the usual, "How are you feeling," banter that is customary in cases like mine, but I knew he could not wait to get down to business. To buy me some time, I decided to find out what the hell was up with him and my mom.

"So do you want to tell me why my mom seems ill at ease around you? And don't act like you don't know what I mean, because every time you two are within five feet of each other, the atmosphere in the room changes."

"Viv, I think we should really focus on what's important here and pick up where we left off."

"You tell me what I want to know, and I'll tell you what you want to know. How about that, Detective? Are you saying my mom's not important in all of this?"

"Viv, of course your mom's important. She's amazing and has been a real crusader in getting you back. She never believed for a second that you left willingly." Detective

Matthews smiled, then seemed to stare off momentarily. "She's a real trooper, there were so many nights we..." and then he stopped mid-sentence, like he was frozen in thought.

"There were so many nights you what, Detective?"

"We were just a good team from the very beginning. We fell into rhythm with one another the moment she walked through my office door. She and I made a good team, with respect to the case, and that's all. Now, can we get back to your side of this? Your mother said that you're having some problems with your memory? How confident are you in the details you've given me so far?"

"Detective Matthews, did you and my mom do it?" I laughed as I inquired.

"VIVIENNE! What kind of question is that?"
"A sincere one!"

I then lifted my gown up to my chest while keeping my lower half covered with the hospital blanket. I pulled at the bandages that covered my stomach.

"Vivienne, I don't think you should do that." He said as I began to peel the tape and gauze away. Once I had pulled the bandages clear of what they covered, I pointed to my stomach and showed him the carved, scabbing name that was etched into my skin. The name was ROOSTER, and it was as plain as day. The detective's eyes read shocked and mortified all at the same time.

"You want to know how my memory is? Well, for starters, I don't remember this." I looked down at my carved stomach. "THAT'S HOW MY MEMORY IS! How does someone survive being carved up like a thanksgiving turkey and not remember it? You would think something like that would stick out a bit in one's memory!"

"Actually Vivienne, in extreme abuse cases, it is common for the victims not to remember the worst days of their abuse. There's only so much a mind can endure before it checks out. It's called self-preservation; a survival technique, one that we all have and use in these extreme cases.

Soldiers who have been taken hostage in war situations often come home having lost long spans of time, in some cases *years*!"

"Are you trying to make me feel better detective, because if you are, you totally suck at it!"

The detective shook his head as he sat on the edge of my bed. He put his hand over mine. "Vivienne, you're going to get through this."

I looked at his normal looking hand lying over top of my black and blue hand, and I could not help myself, "Seriously, you have the hots for my mom, and now you're coming onto me?"

I tried to sound serious, but I had to smile at the now blushing, blond-haired man who looked far more awkward than a detective should.

This time, I did not need my mom to run the Detective off, I had done it myself. He stood up quickly and excused himself, claiming to have to make an important phone call.

I laughed as I watched him retreat from my room. It was good timing on his part, because just then the nurse showed up to take me for an MRI.

As she wheeled me slowly toward the elevator, we passed not just one, but three detectives, including one uniformed officer, sitting outside my hospital room. I wondered if they were there for information or protection. Was I *still* not out of the woods? Was it possible that I was still not safe?

I thought about that so intensely that I did not even realize I was being loaded into the big white tube to be scanned. They instructed me to lie very still, calm my mind, and focus on my breathing. Someone spoke to me through speakers on the left and on the right. I felt like I was in a coffin, a coffin with speakers and a light at the end of the tunnel near my feet.

It was impossible, however, to quiet my thoughts. I felt anxious and worried. I pictured the brain scan all lit up with the nervous neurons that were firing all at once. Suddenly, my brain was floating on a whole new frequency as the machine around me hummed to life.

Afterwards, when I was safely delivered to my room, I heard the men outside my room talking. I listened closely as I heard a name that caught my attention.

"Did you hear that Justin actually saw this Rooster nearly rape her?"

"Yeah, and he fed her too! I told you he didn't have the balls to pull off a bad-ass biker!" another said.

I could not just lie there and let this pass me by. I got out of the bed, grabbed the IV stand, and began to shuffle across the cold, hard floor toward the door. Halfway across the room, an alarm began wailing. I was yanked backwards as I realized I was hooked to many other wires. Before the nurse could bust me, I ripped the wires from where they were taped and secured to my body, in an attempt to dash towards the door. My leg was now in a hefty cast that made it impossible to move quickly and quietly. And the cast weighed a ton! It made a loud clunking noise as I tried to hurry across the room.

When I made it to the door I was met head-on by Rita. I knew her name because my nose was now two inches from her name badge. She was a gigantic, busty woman in her mid-forties, I guessed. If she were to have a nickname, it would be tons-of-fun, for obvious reasons, as she looked to be anything but fun. This was not the type of woman who took crap from anyone. I froze like a deer in headlights as I tried to figure out how I was going to get to the other side of her. Her body was positioned in front of the doorway.

I knew I was physically outmatched, so I figured that reasoning would be the only way around her. I started out by saying, "Hey Rita, how's it going? I was just taking a little spin on the legs. I was worried I was going to get bed sores from all of this lying around!"

"Is that so?" she said skeptically. "And you expect me to buy that?"
Damn she's good.

I decided to level with her. "Look, Rita. You're not going to find this as important as I do, and I know your first responsibility is to my physical health and well-being. I appreciate that, but I have to talk to the men in the hallway for a second. So, you can move out of my way and let me go, or you can tackle me to the ground, hogtie me, and drag me back to bed. Either way, one of us is not going to be happy. So can we work something out or what?"

Rita raised her eyebrow at me. "You really are a piece of work, aren't you?"

I smiled at her and shrugged my shoulders.

"I'm going to get you a wheelchair, turn off that alarm, and you're going to get yourself off your feet. Then, you can talk to the men in the hall. That's what's going to happen. Now get your butt back in the bed, and hang tight until I get back with the chair."

I sighed dramatically, very much like a teenager, and resigned to the fact that Rita looked like she could do more damage than Rooster, when it came to throwing a punch. I let her escort me back to bed. This standing up thing had actually made me feel very lightheaded, so I was easy to persuade.

She did as she promised, and before I could get comfortable, she was helping me out of bed and into a wheelchair. I felt kind of bad for thinking of her as "tons-of-fun" now. She was not so bad; she was a little militant, but decent nonetheless.

"I got this, Rita." I thrust my chair forward with a strong movement from my frail arms. And whoosh, just like that, I was mobile. I made it to the door and then down to where the men sat.

"You all have some explaining to do!"

They looked at me suspiciously.

"I mean, who the hell is Justin? Justin fed me? Justin's not cut out for the role of a biker? Who in the hell is Justin? In the entire time I spent with the MCMC, I never heard the name Justin."

The men shifted in their seats and tensed up from head to toe. They all took turns looking away from me. One of the uniformed officers hollered down the hall. "Shouldn't this patient be in bed? Nurse? Someone, we need a nurse over here!"

If I had been on my feet, I would have been tapping my toe impatiently, holding my hands on my hips in typical female fashion.

I said it again, this time more forcefully. "WHO THE HELL IS JUSTIN?"

"We could be fired for telling you. You're going to have to take it up with Detective Matthews," one of the older agents said.

"You really want me to tell Detective Matthews that you loose cannons out here were flapping your gums, two feet from my open door, about something I'm not supposed to know anything about? You really want me to ask Detective Matthews?"

One of the other men, who was wearing black rimmed glasses, replied, "It's classified, ma'am."

"How classified could it be when you are casually talking about it in a public hospital hallway, less than eight feet away from someone not privy to the classified information? With guys like you on the team, it's amazing that National Security can't be bought and sold on eBay!"

This pissed off the herd of men.

"You wait one damned minute!" one of the men came at me with a pointed finger and a hostile tone, "You're here now because of us, you're alive now because of us!"

"How do you figure? Where the hell were you when this was happening to me?"

I flipped up my gown, leaving myself sitting there in only my white cotton, hospital-issue panties, pointing to my stomach which was still un-bandaged from showing Detective Matthews my injury.

"Where were you when Rooster was carving me like a Halloween pumpkin and raping me?"

I stopped and fell stone silent.

"He raped me." I said to myself. "He raped me and carved me… and he smoked Meth…and there was a hotel. He shoved me in a suitcase, and, Oh my God, I killed him! I remember now, I remember…Oh my God, I killed him, I killed…GET DETECTIVE MATTHEWS! Tell him I remember!"

My head was spinning, and everything was coming back so fast. My stomach turned at the memories that came flooding into my mind. I was moments away from throwing up as I remembered all that Rooster had done to me. The pain, the helplessness, the wanting to die…I had wanted to remember, and now, I was empty.

One man immediately got up and walked away briskly, and one of the uniformed officers instinctively put his hand on his sidearm. The older agent, the one with the Boston accent, grabbed my chair and wheeled me back into my room and closed the door.

In mere moments, Detective Matthews came flying into my room. "What have we got? Thomas said she remembers?"

"I'm right here!" I said. "Don't ask him about me when I'm sitting right here! Ask ME! And hurry up, before I forget!"

"Ok Viv, what do you remember?"

"Rooster, I killed Rooster!"

"Yes Vivienne, we know."

"You know? You know that I'm a cold blooded murderer? Why aren't I in hand cuffs, wearing orange colored pajamas?"

"Vivienne, how hard *did* you hit your head? Why would we arrest you? You killed the man who tried to kill you in cold blood. You killed the man who abducted you, the man who beat you within an inch of your life. You killed the man who stabbed a federal undercover agent and nearly killed him."

"Who? Who's the federal agent? Were you guys coming for me? Did you almost get me back?"

"You would know him as Cal. His name is Justin Davis, of Kansas City, Missouri. He's been undercover with the Motor City Motorcycle Club for eighteen months. He was only a prospect, and we hoped he would be voted in–but things don't always work out as we would like. Rooster stabbed him that night he took you. That much we knew."

"Cal…I mean, Justin…he's alive?"

"Yes, he's alive. He lost a lot of blood, but he is still breathing. If he wouldn't have gotten to the hospital in time–if Knox hadn't found him and patched him up–it's likely he wouldn't have made it."

"KNOX!" I exclaimed. "Yes, yes, I remember now. Knox is the one who left me for dead! He was standing over me with a gun the night I killed Rooster–I remember that. At first I thought he was there to save me, but then he shot me!"

"You don't have any gunshot wounds, Vivienne. I think you might be mistaken. We found Rooster's body fifteen feet from where we believe you woke up. We located his truck and traced your footsteps back to where he took you that night. He had puncture wounds from the darts you stabbed him with at the clubhouse and a severed Achilles tendon. His cause of death was suffocation due to a collapsed lung, and he had severe internal bleeding. He had crawled fifteen feet from where you were found when he succumbed to his injuries. The knife that was used to kill Rooster was within reach of where you were found."

The events of that night played back in my head as Detective Matthews gave me the play by play. I remembered it just as he had recreated the crime scene. I was thankful that my memory finally seemed to be intact.

"What about Knox? He was there, and he left me there to die. He shot at me, I know it. I remember that vividly!"

I was starting to shake, tremble, and plead for him to listen.

"If Knox wants me dead, he'll see to it that I end up that way! Please, you HAVE to believe me!"

"Vivienne, it was Rooster. Rooster is the one who did this to you. I am not entirely sure what you remember, but Knox did not do this. Do you understand?"

He then motioned to the agent who was taking notes on his behalf.

"Maybe we should call the doctor. She's becoming hysterical. If she doesn't calm down we may need to sedate her."

"NO! I don't want to be drugged. Rooster drugged me without my consent and I won't let that happen again!"

"Maybe now's not the time...but do you remember what happened to you prior to going to the field?"

Just then my mom burst through the door.

"What in the hell do you think you're doing? I thought I told you when I left to let her do this in her own time!"

She was visibly pissed. The veins in her neck and forehead were bulging, and her eyes were red with fury.

"Josie, she called for me. She told me she remembered some things, and she thought she would give her statement before she forgot."

However intended, his excuse was not good enough for my mom.

She grabbed the detective by the shirt sleeve. "I need to see you in the hall!" she screamed, as she yanked him out of the room.

I yelled out towards the hallway from my bed, "No more secrets, please! Please don't talk about me—or about what's happened to me—in hushed tones in the hallway. Mom, I know you and the detective are knocking boots, or having some grand romance or whatever, and I just confessed to murder. I think we are beyond hushed tones and hallways, aren't we? And mom, I've learned that I have been raped violently. That's why I may not be able to have kids, isn't it? Rooster ruined my chances to have kids not because he stabbed me, but because he raped me in the way that he did."

"Vivienne, I'm so sorry. We'll get you the best psychiatric help available. It won't be easy and won't happen overnight, but we'll get you through this. I've been thinking, and I want you to sell your house and move in with me."

"Mom, I'm not selling my house! Anyway, won't that be awkward when you're sneaking Romeo out in the morning wearing the same clothes as the day before?" I pointed to Detective Matthews and my mom shot me a look—then shot her *supposed* lover a look as well.

"I don't want to sell my house, I don't want to move in with you, and I won't have kids from the sound of things. But it doesn't matter, who'll want me after all of this anyway? What kind of guy would even look at what's left of me? I have a goddamned rapist's named carved into my stomach and a shattered womb. Besides, after what Knox did to me, I don't know that I'll ever trust another man as long as I live."

Detective Matthews said, "I'm so sorry, Vivienne. I'm sorry we didn't get to you in time."

"Whatever, Derek! You know better than to say that around me!" my mother shouted.

I did not know who Derek was until I noticed who my mom's harsh words were directed. Apparently Detective Matthews' name was Derek.

"You wouldn't intervene! You wouldn't go in and get Vivienne when you had the chance! You left her there as bait for that bastard rapist, Rooster, to just take her!"

"Josie, she was with Justin. And Jude assured us she would be safe at the clubhouse. Jesus, Josie, it wasn't like we were reckless with your daughter's life! We had two agents around her at nearly all times! We couldn't risk our entire five year, undercover operation because your daughter got into the middle of it. We were trying to bring down a band of criminals, which was not an easy task."

"What about that blonde in Reno? The one whose eyes got cut out?" I interjected.

Detective Matthews, aka Derek, said, "You know about that?"

"Rooster told me he killed her, raped her, and cut her eyes out. I think he planned on doing the same to me as he had done to her. So why didn't you stop him then? If you'd have stopped him then—Cal, I mean Justin–wouldn't have gotten stabbed, and I wouldn't have been taken by that bastard Rooster!" I spat his name with complete disgust.

"First of all, we didn't have enough information on what actually happened to Elyse Goodman. Our man on the inside believed it was Rooster, and he had been the last one to be seen with Elyse, but otherwise, we didn't have any other information. He hadn't even confessed Elyse's murder to anyone before now."

"I'm sorry, I'm confused. Did I miss something? You said Cal was just a prospect–that he wasn't even a part of the club when Elyse was murdered in Reno."

"It wasn't Justin who was on the inside, it was Jude. The same insider we had watching over you, Vivienne."

"Who…who? Who is Jude?"

"Agent Jude West. He and Agent Justin Davis have been doing undercover work with the MCMC. We couldn't tell you about Jude and risk his cover being blown. We can't risk one of our own. The only reason we told you about Justin was because his cover has been blown. He's out, and the MCMC knows he's an agent. This is far from over for Agent Davis. He's not safe as long as he's in Detroit. He's being transferred to an undisclosed medical center as we speak. We can't take any chance of retribution or an attempt by the club to silence him."

"What's Jude's cover name? Is it Knox? Is Agent West...is he Knox, Detective Matthews?" I demanded to know. I would have stomped my foot if I had been standing and not currently in a full leg cast.

"I'm sorry, Vivienne. You already know far too much for your own good. I can't tell you any more than that. The cover operatives are absolutely classified while they are undercover. I cannot breach confidentiality while an investigation is pending."

"Can you answer this? Does the club know I'm alive? Does Agent West...Jude...whatever his name is—does he know I'm alive? Does Floyd?"

"Vivienne, it is our understanding that the club believes you to be dead. Currently, Agent West doesn't even know you're alive. We have not heard from him since the night Rooster abducted you from Detective Davis' watch at the clubhouse."

"How do you even know that he's ok? How do you know he's still alive and that the MCMC hasn't found out that he's an agent? What are you doing to keep Knox safe?"

"Vivienne, what makes you believe this Knox character is our insider? I have not breached confidentiality and named our agent. So why are you assuming it's this Knox you've mentioned? As a matter of fact, I distinctly remember you telling me that it was Knox who shot at you and left you for dead, and that he was a murderer, just like Rooster. Do you think a Federal agent would allow that to happen?"

"He allowed it to happen to Elyse Goodman! Maybe you people allow a few to be killed along the way so you've got 'em by the balls when you finally do pull the plug and make your arrests!"

"It doesn't work that way, Viv. I assure you, our agents do NOT partake in first hand criminal activity. Our agents are there to observe and report, not to commit crimes."

"Bullshit! You don't get deep into an organization like the Motor City Motorcycle Club by observing! Gangs don't work that way. If this agent has been with them for years, he's more than proved himself a worthy and active member of the club. Blood's been shed by your agent–don't kid yourself. I know–I was there. I saw them with my own eyes. I heard them talking! How do you know your agent hasn't crossed over? How do you know that he's not playing BOTH sides of this now?"

Detective Matthews was getting more and more agitated by my line of questioning.

He quickly flipped open his cell. "I've got to take this," he said as he hurried out of the room. His entourage of suits followed.

Only my mother was left in the room. I looked at her through narrowed eyes. "You've got some explaining to do. The Detective...you're doing my Detective!"

"Vivienne Lynn! I'm not doing your detective! Well..." she trailed off. "We almost did, and I think he'd like to, but we haven't yet," she admitted quietly. "The night I found out that he was withholding your whereabouts from me, I threatened to castrate him in his sleep if he didn't tell me where you were. He kept saying that you were safe, and that I had no need to worry. Needless to say, since that night our relationship has taken a turn for the platonic…I guess he didn't want to fall asleep next to me and find out that I wasn't bluffing about the castration thing,"

She blushed.

"You know how protective men are over their testicles."

No wonder my mom always acted so odd around the Detective. She was pissed at him, yet so hot for him at the same time!

"I want to castrate him now! He won't tell me whether Agent West is Knox!"

"Vivienne, why is that so important for you to know? What does this Knox mean to you?"

"Mom, I can't explain it right now. I don't know if I'd do it justice if I tried. He's the one who saved me. He's the one who rescued me from that pit. If he hadn't…hell, I might still be down there. Mom, I don't know how to say this, but I think I love him. I love Knox. I know it doesn't make sense. I know it's absolutely impossible to fall in love with someone you don't even know–someone you've only spent a handful of days with–and someone you thought may have fired shots at you, but I have. It's totally illogical and slightly insane, but I really need to know if he harbors any of the same feelings for me."

"If he's not Knox—if he's Jude–there are two possibilities: one, he was only doing his job. It was his JOB to protect me, and I was just another part of the job. Or two, the man I fell in love with isn't an outlaw biker, he's not a criminal or a drug running murderer, but just a guy who fell in love with a girl. I'd sleep better at night knowing I didn't love the man who tried to kill me. Do you have any idea how insane it is to think you are in love someone who tried to kill you?"

"Yes, I do," she said. "Your father!"

"It really does a number on you, doesn't it?" I related. "I'd like to think that somehow, in all of this, I'm a better judge of character than that. I'm not the type of girl who doesn't know a murderer from a hero."

My mom nodded sympathetically along side of me, knowing all too well how I must have felt in that moment.

"I don't know much, but I know you, Vivienne. I don't believe you'd love someone who had it in them to lay a finger on you, a finger that was not done so with love. You know because of your father's lack of adoration, that love doesn't come through clenched fists and hurtful words. Have faith in that, Viv, have faith in that."

Chapter 20

KNOX

Floyd was keeping a very tight rein on all members of the MCMC, especially his inner circle. Knox had not been let out of his sight since he locked eyes with Floyd over Rooster's dead body, a dead body that Knox had never been so happy to see. If Knox were a more twisted individual, he might have taken a picture of it with his cell phone and later taped it into a scrapbook of his favorite memories.

All his years in the club had officially warped his sense of humor. He felt a sense of accomplishment upon seeing Rooster's body lying there. Not that it was his accomplishment–it was Vivienne's. It was difficult to think of her, and it made his gut twist into a spasm. He hated himself for leaving her there, broken and barely alive. He had thought about killing Floyd and Ace, and then rescuing her from her certain fate...but hindsight is 20/20.

Knox imagined Vivienne's mother, likely with red hair and hazel eyes that looked like Vivienne's, and of the tears that would pour out of them when she found out that her daughter was gone. He closed his eyes and imagined the coroner zipping the bag over Vivienne's closed eyes and her silent, still body. Jesus, *I'm a morose son-of-a-bitch these days*! he thought.

"Knox, I don't think a nap is what we need right now."

Floyd interrupted Knox's morbidity and forced him to open his eyes and return to the tense, closed doors strategy session he was privy to, along with his fellow brothers.

"The way I see it, we only have one shot at this. Rod's old lady works at the hospital, and she said that we should move quickly. She is unsure of where he is in his recovery, which means he would be able to leave at any time. If we don't go after him now, we aren't going to get another chance. He'll be in a relocation program, and we'll never get to kill the bastard!" Ace said, frustrated.

Floyd raised an eyebrow at Ace. "We all know time is of the essence here, but we can't just go in balls to the wall and think we're invincible either. It has to be an inside thing. It has to look like an accident...like Cal took a turn for the worse. We can't assassinate him and think that we'll come out smelling like roses. That would be a suicide mission. Right now the place is crawling with Feds. If we even ride our bikes by the hospital, they'll come busting out the hospital doors with a SWAT team!"

"Rod, your old lady...can she get us in there? Can she get us some credentials or something to get past security? Knox and I can't do it. We need someone who's not associated with the club to go in there. Who do we know that's good for the job? For starters, I want you to call your woman and find out what she can do." Floyd commanded Rod.

"Knox, you're awfully quiet. What do you think? You're the VP here, so what's your plan of attack? Ever since we got back from Chi-town, you've been acting like you ain't even here. Are you still out in that fucking field with that dead girl and Rooster? You better fucking snap to it, because now is not the time to put your head in the sand. If the Feds want to bring the heat to us, we need to strike back, and let them know that we don't just *think* we are above the law, we *are* above the law!"

Knox nodded. "You're right, Floyd. Sorry, man. You know I'm on board. I think I know who we should get for the hospital job...Rosey."

"Who the hell's Rosey?" Floyd asked suspiciously.

"He's that sandman out of Tucson. You remember we met him in Reno last summer. Rooster introduced us to him at that titty bar off Highway 395."

"You really think it's a good idea to get one of Rooster's associates involved with the club now? After what happened in Reno?" Floyd was obviously questioning Knox's judgment.

"Hey, man—then get someone else. It doesn't make any difference to me. All I know is that Rooster vouched for the guy and swore he'd never botched a job. Rooster knew lethal when he saw it. I bet any of his associates would be as highly recommended as they come for this line of work. But feel free to get whoever you want!"

Knox was pissy. He did not appreciate having his judgment questioned in front of his brothers. Floyd's distrust was starting to really hit a nerve.

Floyd flew off the handle. "Well it better make a fucking difference to you! It's not just the club that's going down for this Knox, if it goes down, we all go down. You won't be missing that little redhead when you're someone's prison bitch! Where does your loyalty lie these days, Knox?"

"Are you calling me some sort of traitor, Floyd?"

Knox stood up, ready for a fight.

"Why don't you just say what's on your mind? You think because I'm the one who brought Cal into the club to pledge, that I knew he was a Fed? Is that it? Are you fucking blaming me for this? I know that's it–

just fucking say it! You want my blood for it? Come and get it!"

Floyd stood up from his seat slowly. All the men at the table pushed their seats back but continued to stay seated. Tension filled the room.

Floyd looked up with a furious and deadly look in his eye. "How about we put your little theory to the test then...either you kill Cal, or I kill you. You want to prove your loyalty to the club, then YOU do the job! Take the Fed out!"

"That's fucking insane, Floyd! They see me down there and they'll kill me. You fucking know that, too! If the Feds don't arrest me or kill me, then you will? Is that how we prove our loyalty?"

"Then I suggest you put your head in on how to carry this one out, Knox. It's Cal's life or yours–you decide!" Floyd's tone was unyielding and final.

Nobody said a word, but a couple of the guys shot Knox looks of concern.

Knox left the room and slammed the door on his way out. He heard Floyd tell Rod to see it through. So I kill Cal, or Rod kills me, and if Rod does not kill me, then I will get hauled in by the Feds. What kind of options are those? Knox thought to himself. This is bullshit.

Knox contemplated how he might carry this out and how it would all go down. Regardless of how he worked it, this was not going to end well. He knew that between Rod and his girlfriend at the hospital, he would have eyes on him, and anything he tried to sneak by, would be caught. Plus, Cal would know him the instant he walked in the door.

He sat and stared off while loading rounds, one by one, into multiple clips for his weapons. Weapons he wished he would have never used. He knew what it was like to take a life of another, and the idea that now it was his life or someone else's did not sit well with him. But he knew that getting into a club like the MCMC required blood to be shed and lives to be lost. Why he willingly signed up for this case seemed like a question he just could not answer anymore. He knew that Vivienne's death made everything look different than it had before. Losing something he loved had made him question his love for anything and anyone.

How can a man love the brother who could go from family to foe with just a flick of Floyd's tongue? Brother was a term he now loathed. *Fuck family, and fuck Floyd too*! He thought to himself.

With that in mind, he went out to the barn, grabbed what was important and left what was not. He loaded up his gear and left the only home he had known for the past five years. He drove off not knowing if he would ever come back or if he would live to see any of his supposed family again, but nonetheless, he headed into town. He was on a mission to get closer to the hospital, closer to the end, and closer to Cal, his only true brother in all of this.

Chapter 21

VIV

My mom snoozed in the chair across the room, but otherwise my room was empty. I saw guards pacing urgently outside my door, and it was unsettling.

Just then the phone rang.

"Hello?" I said into the receiver.

"Hello, is this Vivienne Taylor?"

"Yes, speaking. Who is this?" I inquired.

"This is Adrienne Westchester from News Channel 35. We've been following your case since your disappearance earlier this summer, and we're doing a story on your homecoming. We would like to send a reporter down to get your statement on the facts of your case."

Just then, Detective Matthews flung open the door. "HANG UP THE PHONE NOW, VIV! Someone's tipped off the press. We have to move you, and we have to move you now! HANG UP THE PHONE!" I did as he asked and I killed the line between me and Miss Adrienne Westchester.

My mom flew around the room in a blur, making appropriations for my departure. Within a half hour, I was on the roof of St. Rita's Hospital being taken in the Life Flight helicopter to an 'undisclosed location'.

Before I knew it, I was in Washington DC at a Medical Center on an army base. *Fort McNair*, was the name I saw on everything, as they wheeled me to my new resting place in a tiny room, behind a canvas sheet that separated me from the other half of the room. This hospital did not look to be the height of medical sophistication, and I found myself kind of hoping Rita would walk around the corner to be the one to take care of me. Rita would have looked right at home here, as militant as she was. I laughed at the thought.

From the other side of the privacy sheet, I could hear a heart monitor beeping. I wondered if I was sharing the room with someone–and if my roommate were in as much danger as I found myself to be.

Now that the story of my survival had leaked, the MCMC would surely know that there were loose ends that needed tied up. The only one I really stood to ruin was Knox, as he was the one who ultimately left me to die. Rooster was already dead, and Knox had made sure I did not know anything about their "secret runs" and other criminal activity. *I hardly feel like a star witness for the prosecution*, I muttered.

"You're not, but I am." I heard from behind the curtain.

"Excuse me?" I said to the mystery man behind the curtain.

"Red, is that you?"

"CAL! Oh, my God–Cal, is that you?" I swung my cast and other leg out of bed, and yanked my tubes and wires with me across the room. Once more I was traveling on my broken leg. If Rita were here, she would have killed me.

I flung the curtain back and looked right at Cal.

"Wow, Red, you look like shit!"

I could not help myself—I nearly jumped in bed with him just to give him a hug.

"Cal, I can't believe it! I can't believe you're alive–alive, and here with me!"

"It's Justin, Red. Cal was just my rad biker name," he said with a laugh. "Did you really buy me being a ruthless biker type? Tell the truth!"

"Well, you were incredibly different from what I'd known of Rooster's hospitality, if that's what you mean!"

"Red, I'm so sorry about what happened. I turned my back for a second, and he came out of nowhere. I am so sorry!"

"Hey, I'm sorry that I didn't kick the shit out of him when he was stabbing you. I was so worried for you!"

"I saw you stab the bastard with those darts. I gotta tell you, that was pretty badass! Ever think about a career in law enforcement?" he said with a wink and a smile.

"Yeah, well, he got his revenge for that. He took turns throwing darts into the air and watching them land here, and here…and yeah, there…" I said as I pointed out the little scabs that had now formed over my puncture wounds. "Oh…and then there's this."

I lifted my gown and showed him my mid-section.

Justin did not flinch like everyone else had. Instead, he reached out and caressed my wound, feeling it with his fingers softly, before looking up at me.

"How is it you are here with me, hugging me, when this is what happened to you?"

"Only the good die young, I guess." I did not know what to say, because I honestly did not know how I had survived the torture and resulting injuries. How both Cal and I had survived a man like Rooster was beyond any logic or reasoning.

"He'll find out, you know," Justin said to me in a hushed voice.

"Who, Floyd? I know. That's why they moved me all the way down here with you." I said, slightly annoyed and yet slightly cheerful at the same time.

"No, not Floyd—Knox. He's the only reason I'm alive today. If he hadn't patched me up and had Momma take me to the hospital, I wouldn't be here. Floyd would have left me to die. He's a smart man when it comes to the club and bloodied club members draw attention. If Knox wouldn't have made the call to save me, they'd have left me to bleed out. I was pretty close to doing just that when he found me. I vaguely remember him being there…things are still kind of blurry when I think back to that night. But one thing I remember clearly is that Knox is the reason I'm alive. I owe him my life."

"Justin, is Knox Jude? Is he…is he a federal agent, too?"

Justin took his time and looked all around the small room before he pulled me in close and whispered into my ear, "Yes Vivienne. He is."

My eyes welled up with tears, and I remembered.

"I was instructed that under no circumstances should I tell you, but damnit Viv, we've been in the trenches together. I know you and Jude did more than *pretend* to have a relationship. Vivienne, he's been riding with the MCMC for so long now, and I've never seen him get close to anyone during that time. Sure, Floyd thinks they are close, but he was doing more than his job with you, Viv. If you wouldn't have killed Rooster, he would have done it himself, Federal agent or not. He probably doesn't even know everything that Rooster put you through."

Justin shook his head in both disbelief and disappointment.

"I can't help but play it all back–that night–and I can't help but think that I should have been more watchful. I gave Knox my word that I'd look after you, and I couldn't have failed him more. He was worried about you getting grey hairs, and I left you to get stabbed, raped, and used as a dart board! I'll never forgive myself for letting you get hurt like that."

"Well, you better start trying, because I never blamed you. There is so much blame going around in my circles, and there isn't any left for you to own. My mom, me, you...I don't blame anyone but the one person who's truly at fault–Rooster. I hope he burns in hell!"

"In that case, Viv, it's good to see that you're not bitter!" Justin said with a sarcastic smirk.

"Nothing years and years of therapy won't fix and maybe a good plastic surgeon," I said, smiling, still resting my hand on my jack-o-lantern stomach.

Chapter 22

KNOX

Knox drove slowly on his way to the hospital. At this point, he was in no rush to get killed or to kill the man he not so long ago worked so hard to save. As he drove, Vivienne was in the forefront of his thoughts. In his mind, her smiling face was now free of all the cuts and bruises that she inherited from spending time with Rooster. She was riding alongside him, happy and content. That was how it should have been, in a world separate from his own.

What he would not give right now to be free of danger, to be just two people with something to smile about, and something to enjoy together. *Why do we meet the people we are to love the most, under THE WORST possible circumstances*? He wondered if he were cursed–cursed for being a living, walking, talking lie. Someone who had spent the last five years not being true to himself, to the force, or to the club. To be who he was expected to be, was to be no one person at all. How could he love Vivienne when he was three men, all three of whom were flawed horribly? Not that she was any kind of perfect creature, as he remembered fondly of her cheeks shoved full of that fat cheeseburger back at Black Swamp.

    He laughed at the painfully sweet thought of her, still full of life, cursing and crashing her way through like she had a way of doing. He felt as though he had known her his entire life. Maybe he had waited his entire life to meet someone like her, someone who made him want to be a better person. The kind of person who knew who he was, and the kind of man who would not get her killed. He was a failure. He knew it. He was a failure as a biker, as a Federal officer of the law, and as a man. It was his job, not just as an officer of the law to protect those who could not protect themselves, but as a man. Whether being a biker was a lie or not, she was his old lady who was in dire need of protection.

    He knew that she was his in this life, and he believed in the next as well, which really could be not far off as things were spiraling downward and out of his control. Floyd was likely planning his execution right now—as if he needed that hanging over his head. He carried enough guilt and burden as it was, without adding Floyd's hatred and revenge.

Do I call myself in and get yanked? Or do I find a way to end this here and now? Knox contemplated the possibilities.

Sure, he could easily make the call and those Federal agents down at the hospital could have him out of here before the end of the day. But that leaves the club knowing that he was a Federal agent. He would be looking over his shoulder for the rest of his life. Not that he would not anyway after living this lifestyle for so long…it pretty much came with the territory…someone was always wanting you dead. Rival gangs, the cops who did not know who he really was, and women he had rejected. Normal people do not go through life like this. Why he ever wanted to be anything but normal, was something he questioned now more than ever before.

He decided that he could not call himself in. He could not risk five years of living the way he had just to pack up and get picked up like he had been at Summer Camp this whole time. He was not going to punt. He had too much to lose and had come too far. He was going to finish this game. And he was going to finish Floyd!

He was not a quitter and he owed Vivienne's memory the justice she deserved. Clubs like the MCMC breed, protect, and nurture the Roosters of the world. They give them the life, and they protect them when they take life. That can not go unpunished. Elyse Goodman deserved that justice too. Just then, Knox pulled over on the side of the bridge he was crossing, got out, and hurled his FBI issued phone into the water down below. All his contacts, his lifeline to the FBI sunk to the bottom of the river in an instant and he hoped like hell that would not end up at the bottom of a river too. He thought about that scenario for a moment, but then shook it off. He could not allow himself to think about failure now, he needed to stay positive to stay alive.

Knox rolled up at the hospital and parked in the employee lot. Rod's old lady worked as an emergency room nurse. She had prepared credentials to be placed in her locker in the employee lounge. Knox was told he would have no problem securing it, as the emergency room was bottom floor, and the ICU where Cal was being held was the 8th floor. Security would not be tight there.

As promised, the credentials were there. He held them in his hand and looked down at his new fake name; apparently he was Dr. Jamison Butler today.

So many identities, so little time, he thought to himself sarcastically.

He hoisted and then lowered the lanyard with his picture on it around his neck, and then opened and closed locker doors until he found men's scrubs and a white lab coat.

He changed into the disguise. A television in the corner of the room was on and lowly chattering annoyingly, with no audience but him. As he turned on his heel to walk away, the television he was trying to tune out grabbed his attention with the force of a thousand magnets pulling him to listen.

The news anchor said, "Breaking News in Ohio today, Vivienne Taylor, the young woman abducted from Ohio, has miraculously survived her abduction and has returned to her family this week. A lot of answers have yet to be given surrounding her disappearance, but my sources tell me that due to an ongoing investigation into her abduction, there's a gag order in place by Federal Officials. We are told that this is a federal case since the victim, Vivienne Taylor, was taken across state lines and held captive in Michigan, just outside of Detroit.

Knox could not believe his ears. *She lived*? Vivienne was alive! He had never been so happy, relieved, and scared to death all at the same time.

If he was seeing this broadcast, then Floyd was seeing this too. The elated feeling was replaced by a feeling of dread. Vivienne's picture on the side of the screen, looking pretty but slightly dated, created a very dangerous and hostile situation that Knox was at the center of.

"It made national news! Vivienne's homecoming is national news! He shouted to himself. "How did the FBI let this leak to the news media? They even gave her last name! Floyd could just Google Vivienne's name to find her. She would be dead by the end of the week. She survived all of this, just to get killed for her trouble for not dying, and maybe her entire family too just for spite. I swear, the news was not in the business of reporting the news, they were in the business of getting Federal Witnesses killed!" He spat. *Those no good bastards!*

So now, with this new information, it was clear that he would have to kill the man he saved, save the girl he was supposed to have killed, and somehow, if there was time, save himself. *Nothing impossible about that scenario!*

He knew there was no escaping Floyd's wrath now. How could he explain this one? He shot her three times and she miraculously lived? He would not buy that for a second. In the eyes of his mentor, his President, he was now a traitor. If he did not kill Cal, there was no hope for him escaping Floyd. Why had he thrown his phone into the river? He had no way to call his way out of this one now. He either had to kill Cal and every agent on the 8th floor to convince Floyd of his loyalty to the club, or he had to call himself in and get taken out of here.

Since he had tossed his phone into the river, he resigned to the fact that he really only had one option, and that was to take himself upstairs and turn himself in to one of the agent's guarding Cal. With Vivienne alive, the idea of dying to see her again was not nearly as uplifting as it had been before hearing the broadcast. He wanted to see her, and he wanted to get out of here and start living his life again. If there was anything left of it after all of this time away.

His determination to see Floyd's demise fizzled the moment he realized Vivienne was home, safe and sound in Ohio with her family. To him, he felt like he had already won and beaten Floyd. Floyd may have stripped his title, his rank, and his role in the organization, but he had not stripped him of everything. He would walk out of here with one thing good from this, her life…a life for a life. Elyse Goodman's life was lost, but Vivienne's was saved. A life for a life. He could break even, in a way, if he got out now, and out is what he intended to get.

Knox walked out of the employee lounge to the elevator and once inside, he pushed the number eight. He was going up and out of here, FINALLY!

Chapter 23

VIV

Ring! Ring! went the hospital phone. *Who's calling me here?* I am supposed to be a secret, hidden from the rest of the world, while I am here on this army base. I did not know whether to answer the call or throw my phone out the window for fear of being found by another nosy reporter.

"Hello?" I said to my mystery caller.

"Vivienne, it's Detective Matthews."

"Yeah? Hey is my mom with you?"

"No Viv, she's not. I need to speak with you, it's important."

"What's up Derek?" I say in a chipper and taunting tone.

"Vivienne, I'm sorry to tell you this, but we're considering the possibility of placing you into the witness relocation program. Hopefully it will be for only a brief time, until we get things sorted out."

"No way! I am not going to be shipped off from my friends and family. I just got home, and now you want to send me away again?"

"It's better than dead isn't it?" Detective Matthews was annoyed at my obstinacy and unwillingness to "hear him out" on the subject.

"Detective, I know you're just doing your job, but I have a house, a job, a life, and family to get back to. I can't go into exile! Why would this be imposed on me, I didn't do anything wrong!"

"Vivienne, it's not about you doing something wrong, it's about keeping you alive!"

"What about Justin, does he have to go into the witness relocation program too?"

"No Vivienne, he does not. He's a highly trained Federal agent, and his identity has been concealed from the MCMC from the start. They do not know his real name or any identifying information. The FBI has a very sophisticated security system and any breach of security is taken very seriously. The club won't be able to locate Justin, but you on the other hand, are a sitting duck.

I sighed.

"Ever since that news broadcast, you would have been at great risk without the protection that we have given you here at the base. If the MCMC didn't know before, they now know where you're from, your last name…hell they now know what your mom looks like for Christ sakes! Stupid fucking media!"

Detective Matthews was obviously very upset that now my mother was put into danger. He did not like where this was heading, and he wanted to change directions fast.

"Are you going to put my mom in the witness relocation program too detective?"

"No, I wish I could make that happen, but one, she's a stubborn ass just like you, and two, she does not meet the criteria needed to get her into the program. If you were under the age of eighteen, I could send her as your guardian, but because you're not, she's excluded. I'm sorry Vivienne, but only you can be sent. I guess I'll just have to get your mom to pack up and move down here with me, for the time being of course."

"Good luck Romeo, my mom ain't going to go anywhere with you, you know that right?"

"Why do you have to point out the obvious Vivienne? Is that some kind of gift of yours?"

One could mistake the amount of sarcasm the detective was throwing out as anger and aggression. I guess he was hotter for my mom than I thought!

"Vivienne, I can't protect you if you go home, and I can't hold you hostage at Fort McNair forever either. I am giving you the opportunity of safety. Do you realize what you'd be doing if you go home? You'd be committing suicide. If you went home unprotected, you would be dead within days…*days* Vivienne! Floyd, or one of his associates will come for you. They will come because they cannot afford to let you live. This is not a game! They won't think twice about coming after your family either. Is that what you want?"

"Why does Justin get to be free to go as he pleases?"

"Vivienne, you sound like a spoiled brat right now asking questions like that! Justin's not your older brother who's allowed to stay out past curfew. This is not about me favoring him or punishing you!"

"Wow detective, so what, you're my dad now? You want to hook up with my mom, play house, including fathering her redheaded unruly daughter?"

Click. The detective hung up on me! I cannot believe he actually hung up on me. That was not very professional, even if I was having a grownup temper tantrum. I thought that all of these Federal agents were trained, groomed, and conditioned to handle the toughest situations and not break under pressure? I did not feel more at ease knowing that my fate rests in the hands of a detective who cannot handle a little verbal skirmish. Maybe I am one big gigantic pain in the ass!

"Did he hang up on you?" I heard Justin ask from the other side of our room.

"Yep, he sure did. Can you believe that? Just *click* and he was gone."

"Maybe he got disconnected?"

"Or maybe I'm a nightmare he wished he'd never gotten involved with!"

"I don't know Viv, who wouldn't want to help save you. You're a peach!" Justin said with a laugh.

"No wonder the detective compared you to being my older brother, you pick on me like one!"

Justin smiled and said, "It would have been an honor to have had you for a little sister and it would have been a lot of fun to beat up your high school suitors!"

Then Justin's phone rang.

"You're turn to get chewed out." I said to him with a fake concerned look while rolling my eyes.

"Hello?" Justin said this time.

"What, when?" He paused for a moment with a look of utter dismay on his face. "I don't believe that for a second and you shouldn't either! C'mon, you know better than to assume anything when someone's in as deep as Jude! Of course I didn't! No! Do you have any indicators other than not hearing from him? Anything from the local police? Look, I know what you are thinking, but you're wrong! You're dead wrong about this. Give him more time! Did you trace the GPS on the phone? I see. How long has he been off the radar?"

Listening to this conversation was making me sick to my stomach. Knox was in trouble. Here I was safe and sound on a damned army base, and he was out there in a war zone! I sat in my bed, resisting the urge to rip the phone out of Justin's hand and scream, "Listen here you son-of-a-bitch, Knox would never defect from the FBI for the MCMC!" But I kept my gown tightly gripped in each hand instead.

I waited for him to finish, and heard his last words of, "Keep me posted, and don't count him out. If there is one thing I know about Knox, he is not a turncoat! You don't know him like I do!" and with that, Justin hung up the phone.

"Justin, please tell me what's going on. Justin, what's wrong? What's happening with Knox?"

"He's missing Vivienne. He has scheduled check-ins with the FBI. Sometimes they are weeks apart, sometimes they are hours, but he's missed his."

"How many? How many has he missed?" I asked.

"Six. He's not been heard from by anyone at the Bureau since the night of your abduction. It's been too many days Vivienne, something's not right! They think that your death might have caused him to have some sort of break and that he doesn't want to come back to the reality of what he has outside of the MCMC. I am afraid that the lives lost during his stint with the MCMC is having a greater effect on him than we thought. When you're trained like we are Viv, saving lives is taught and ingrained in us, but when we fail, sometimes even the toughest agents can snap. Combine that with the fact that he hasn't seen his friends and family for so long, it's easy to get mixed up and lose yourself out there. But I know Jude better than most, and he's not that guy."

"I hope it wasn't my *death* that tipped the scale. I don't believe that my life's worth all that much to him. We only knew each other for a short time. I'm sure that even if I had died, it wouldn't have been the straw to break the camel's back." I said with a grimace.

"Do you really believe that Vivienne? You really believe he took you back to his room because he's trained to protect you? He could have left you in that pit and just shot the bastard that came near it to take you out. He didn't tell me to protect you because it was his job; he did it because he didn't want you to get hurt. Being intimate with people we are supposed to be protecting isn't a practice condoned by the bureau you know. It's actually more or less forbidden."

I then realized how many chances Knox took in order to have me by his side as his lady. Justin seemed to know and understand him more than anyone, so I could not help but listen intently. And so, he continued.

"He took you back to his room and gave you his vest because he wanted to. Because he is a man and you are a woman...a woman he couldn't seem to keep any kind of real separation from. I asked him once what exactly he was doing with you, and he didn't answer. I saw the way he was around you and I noticed the change. I saw the way he'd smile when you walked into the room and the way he was practically frantic when you weren't where he could see you. He told me that meeting you gave him direction and new meaning in his life. He never saw himself as a guy who would some day have a family, but he saw that with you. He saw you as something special, rare, and priceless."

Justin stopped to take a breath.

"Oh, and he did say you were the most stubborn ass he'd ever met. To which he followed with, "She's worse than I am!" which I'm pretty sure surprised him."

Justin confessed all of this to me like it was supposed to help put me at ease, but it worked quite the opposite. It only softened me more and caused my worry to soar.

"Yeah, and now he's going to die! I said, "What a great story to tell me right before they murder him, Justin! What good is it for me to believe in love, in him, when he's not likely to survive this?"

Chapter 24

KNOX
AKA: Agent Jude West

The elevator doors open, as the electronic panel indicated the arrival on the eighth floor. Knox walked out into the corridor feeling more optimistic than before, and he looked on the board to find his way to Room 8-45B. Not much farther to go now...

He turned several corners and began weaving his way toward Cal's room. When he turned the last corner, he expected to find a crowded hallway, full of guys in suits with bad cologne and meticulously groomed mustaches, but instead, he found the hall empty and desolate. Where was everyone, the other agents, the tense looking badge carriers who he would give himself over to? *Do I have the wrong room number?* "Perhaps he's been moved to another room?"

He said out loud before peeking into the room to see if Cal was there.

"No, he's not been moved to another room Sir," a voice called from behind him. "They moved him right out of here all together. Out of the hospital, from what I hear, out of the State. Guess Detroit's finest medical personnel weren't good enough for that guy. They took him by helicopter this morning. You didn't miss him by much. Took his entourage with him too, although I was glad to see them clear out, they were really causing havoc on the entire floor. You would've thought they were security guards for Bono or something! Humph!" She snorted, flipped her hair over her shoulder, and marched away leaving Knox standing in the hallway wishing he would have came up with a "Plan C".

Since Cal's room was empty, he took the liberty of using it for his own personal use. He sat on the sanitary bed and picked up the phone and dialed the one number he knew to call.

"It's Agent West for Agent Michaels. Yes, it's urgent, he should be expecting my call…I'm late in getting back to him…as I'm sure he's very aware."

An old familiar voice came on the line, "Jude? Jude, it's Jim, are you there?"

"It's me Jim, I'm here." Jude responded.

"Where the hell have you been? Everyone here thinks you've crossed over to the dark side! Are you alright? Where are you?"

"Yes, I'm fine, although I'm in a bit of a jam Jim. Shit's gone all wrong up here. Floyd sent me to the hospital to assassinate Davis and if I don't return with some evidence of his blood on my hands, I'm going to pay for it with my life! He thinks because I got Davis associated with the club that I must be a rat too. If I don't do this, he's going to make an example of me. He's testing me Jim, and I'm having trouble figuring out what I'm supposed to do here. Davis has already left the hospital, as I'm sure you know…Hell I'm sitting in his room right now!"

"Can you go back and tell them he's been moved? We really need you to stick it out up there until he's got the shipment ready to go out."

"You really think he's going to let me be involved with anything while he's suspicious of me Jim? C'mon, you're smarter than that! You know it's only a matter of time before I'm made and they decide to shoot me! Your "wanting me to stick it out here" is like saying you want me dead. Is that what you want? Do I have to prove my loyalty with my life for everyone these days! You're as bad as fucking Floyd!"

"Look, I know you're in a spot, but our investigation hinges on the MCMC carrying out the delivery. We need to bring them down completely and not a minute before this last shipment. If we take them too soon, our entire investigation falls apart!"

"You've got the girl they kidnapped. You have Detective Davis' statement…is that not enough? Jesus, you're killing me here!"

"The girl doesn't help us, other than being good for a kidnapping, rape, and attempted murder charge. She doesn't know anything of the drug trade. They kept her in a pit and raped her, but that doesn't help our drug investigation!"

"Yeah, rape and kidnapping, that's what, a minor misdemeanor to you? It's not a traffic violation Jim, its rape *and* abduction!"

"Yes, yes, the bureau takes into account the seriousness of what's happened to Ms. Taylor, however, Rooster's dead. The entire club didn't abduct her, one member did. And well...the damn girl killed him, so that investigation is a dead end, as dead as Rooster! You get us more, or Floyd won't see a felony charge come near him. We need it to be tight, and we needed it goddamned YESTERDAY!"

"Jim, let's not forget that you are sending me on a suicide mission. Are you telling me the Bureau will not come get me? Are you asking me, or telling me to stay?"

"Look, I don't like to hand down assignments to my agents like a sentence from a Judge, but my hands are tied here. I have no choice in this matter. The US Government didn't pay for you to ride around on a motorcycle for five years, just to walk away with a couple slaps on the wrists for your biker buddies and for you to get some new ink on the company's dime!"

"Fuck! You do think I've crossed over don't you? It's not just people, it's you too! You think I like this life? You think I enjoy this fucking life? You wouldn't have survived for a second out there Jim, you fucking panzee!"

"Well, it's a good thing you're there and not me then isn't it Agent West! You are going to need to stick this out until the shipment goes out. That's not a request, it's an order! If you come in now, you will not be protected…and your career as you know it will be over! I'll have you riding a desk and pushing a pencil until retirement. I know you think I'm a dick right now, but I'm doing you a favor, I'm saving your career here. You'll thank me one day buddy!"

"You're not my buddy. You're not God, a judge, or a jury either! All you proved to be today is an executioner! At my funeral, I want you to hand the folded flag to my mother. I want you to look her in the eye and tell her you're sorry and that you are the reason I'm dead! Because that's all you did here today you fucking prick! And if I do live through this, you can bet your ass Jim that

I'm coming to see you, and we aren't going to be setting up our next tee time!"

Knox hung up the phone with a deafening slam of the receiver to the base.

Now what? He thought to himself.

He then picked up the phone again and dialed.

"They moved him, he's not here, what would you like for me to do?"

Then Floyd ordered him to come back…back to the clubhouse. Knox knew this could be it for him, but he figured, *why prolong it?* He might as well face it with a shred of dignity, if he even had a shred left. He'd practically begged to be pulled off assignment and was denied. Jim was right, he would end up at a desk for this if he failed. A desk job for an agent was worse than death. Sure he'd be painted a hero for his service, should he die during the course of this, but he was no hero in his own mind. He was just a man who wanted to go home.

Chapter 25

VIV

"I want to come home!" I cried to my mother on the telephone.

"Why can't I? I'm sure the army has better things to do than protect a carved up girl like me!"

Justin watched me argue my case. He knew as well as I did, that I would not make much headway.

When I hung up, I said, "They can't keep me here against my will you know! Can't I sign an AMA form or something and get out of here?"

"What's the rush Viv? Got a hot date waiting for you back home or what? Wait, hold that thought…" Justin said as he flipped open his phone.

"Agent Davis" he said as he answered. "When? What's his status? When's he coming in? What? Why not? Under whose orders? Jim's going to get him killed! I can't fucking believe the incompetence of suits in offices sometimes! I don't care if I'm being insubordinate, I'd say it to his face. He's a moron! I just love how we're told we're going to save the world, but the very organization that blows that sunshine up our asses doesn't give a shit about saving one of their own! When did the FBI get in the business of contract killing their agents? If he gets killed, that ones on the Bureau! The agent asked to come in. How can they just leave him there to rot? I'm lying in a hospital bed with stab wounds, Vivienne has been stabbed, tortured, and raped, and yet we are not pulling the plug. This isn't the lollipop gang we're dealing with here! Where does this end, and how many lives have to be ruined for it to ever be enough?"

Justin looked defeated as he snapped his phone shut. He sat there in total silence and absolute disbelief.

I hated to interrupt his silence, but I wanted to know what was happening. It sounded like Knox was alive, and the Bureau had confirmation that he was not a traitor, but they were sending him off to die anyway. Why was it always the case that good news had to be followed by worse news?

Good news: You lived. *Bad News*: You've been beaten, raped, stabbed, and you can't have kids.

Good news: Knox is alive. *Bad News*: But not for long!

Why couldn't good news just come on its own, without it being an opening line for something horrible?

"Justin?" I whispered in his direction.

It took a minute for him to register my voice, and when he did, he looked at me with sad eyes. It was a sadness I had not seen in him before. He had always seemed like a glass-half-full smart ass like me, even with stab wounds, but now, now he looked as if he had aged ten years. He looked like he was an adult, about to tell me that Santa Claus was not real.

"Is he ok Justin?" I blinked back the tears that were creeping up on me.

"Well, he checked in, but it's not good Viv. He wanted be pulled out, and he requested leave from his assignment, but they denied him. They kept him in place and ordered him to complete his mission there. They…they may have just killed him. He doesn't have a choice from what I'm being told."

"How can they do that? How can they just leave him there? Isn't there some whole "no man left behind" code of honor you law types swear to or something?"

"Right now Viv, I'd say our government believes more in the "no child left behind act" and you know how well that policy has worked out for Education. What are we now ranked 28th out of 33 Nations in education?" Justin muttered.

Chapter 26

KNOX
AKA: Agent Jude West
AKA: Dead man walking

After a long, thoughtful drive from the hospital while heading back to the MCMC Clubhouse, Knox had conceived a couple notions. Several of those notions had him going out guns blazing killing every last leather-clad biker that stood around him, while others had him sneaking in and cutting Floyd's throat in his sleep. He even contemplated burning the damn place to the ground to make sure no one escaped, but that seemed a bit extreme, although they were rather appealing to him. He also did not want to just walk in there like some kind of prisoner, bow his head, and take a bullet to the brain.

One thing he knew, he was not going to figure this out sitting in the driveway looking like a scared kid, afraid of the bully waiting for him inside. He got out of his truck and walked toward the front door just like he had hundreds of times before. He went inside and immediately started walking in the direction of Floyd's office. Several members said hello, obviously wary of the atmosphere surrounding these last few days. Nonetheless, he made his way to Floyd, his mentor, President, and soon to be executioner. Knox knocked on Floyd's office door, and he heard Floyd say, "Come in"…

Knox walked in slowly and cautiously, while Floyd remained seated at the leather upholstered booth seat affixed to the wall in the far corner of the room. A burning cigarette in the ashtray, Floyd's hair, slicked back meticulously into his rubber banded ponytail at the base of his neck, and eyes that were slightly squinted from the smoke in the air made it hard for Knox to read his expression.

"So you're back huh?" Floyd offered to break the silence between them.

"Did you expect me not to return?" Knox inquired.

"No, it's not that. I always know that when someone leaves, there is the possibility they won't return, especially in our way of life. You know that Knox."

"Well, I'm only sorry to return here with your wishes left unfulfilled." Knox said while trying to do his best to lie through his teeth.

There was a time when the lines between being a biker and an FBI agent had gotten fuzzy, and on occasion there had been a twinge of satisfaction upon pleasing his mentor. But now, standing here in front of Floyd, any trace of that fuzziness had since been made crystal clear in Knox's eyes. There was now a line, a bold and definitive line that would never be fuzzy to him again.

"So what's the word down at the hospital? Did you get any information on where they transferred him to?" Floyd stated very on-task.

"They didn't take his medical chart when they left, must have had it faxed or took a copy of it with him, because his chart was still at the nurse's station. I took the liberty to take a look before I left. It said transfer location unknown, but it did say that any information pertaining to Agent Davis' treatment should be forwarded to the United States Army Base in Washington DC. There was a contact number to which I was unable to retrieve. I was interrupted and had to return the chart to avoid being noticed."

Knox knew he would have to come back with something to have the appearance of being a calculated hit man for Floyd.

"Maybe you're right Knox, perhaps Cal doesn't know enough to cause any real trouble for the club, but the girl, the girl is damaging. We could get brought up on murder charges out there in Reno on top of what went down in Chicago! Sure that was Rooster's doing, but we all knew of his appetite for destruction. We are all accessories, if not more. And you know as well as I do Knox, there were others, many, many others along the way. Rooster's been a part of this club for a long time, and he was hardly a saint while he was here. I should have buried him years ago. His brain was a mess from all the meth and blow he was skimming from me, the son-of-a-bitch.

I've thought a lot about this, and I think you were right to suggest Rosey. We need someone infallible, and someone not directly related to the club. We need someone who can tie up our loose ends while we quietly continue to conduct our business here at home. I have big plans for tomorrow night. We need to put our good public image into play while we take care of some club business that's a bit illicit. While half the club smiles for the public and enjoys a lovely poker run, carnival, rides, the whole fucking deal, you and I will take care of business.

Our distributor will be meeting us at the Warehouse in the Industrial Park on Lincoln Avenue. We get our distributor's supplied, get the girl snuffed out, and then we take this Club in a new direction. Something more secure—a plan the Fed's won't know how to begin to infiltrate. We are going to send a message to those fucking pigs, one they won't soon forget! They'll think very carefully before sending one of their good ole boys into the lion's den again. Because if they get in, Knox, they aren't getting out. I'm counting on you to help deliver that message. We need to strike back, and strike back hard. It needs to happen soon.

Knox tried to listen, but all of his attention was focused on how he could turn this around to save Viv.

"Oh and by the way, I called Rosey. He'll be in here within the hour. I'm going to need you to brief him on your girl, the redhead. I had to offer him stock in our meth lab over on the east side to pique his interest in doing a job this close to his last one. Apparently, he took out an entire family up in Vermont, a real mess from the sound of things, no witnesses though. The bodies had to be identified by their dental records. I'd say he's our man, wouldn't you? He's definitely got a unique talent. He's a good man to know, I have a feeling, so let's make sure our new business partner is happy with as much information as he needs. You said he had never botched a job, now only if he could deliver in fifteen minutes or less, then we'd have a real asset on our hands!"

"Sounds like a plan boss." Knox said with an ache growing in his stomach.

"Be ready for tomorrow night, we leave here at seven-thirty. Let's plan on meeting at the warehouse at 8:00 p.m."

"I'll be ready" Knox said, nodded, and made his exit from Floyd's office.

Ready by tomorrow night? There was no way he was going to be able to tip off anyone between now and tomorrow night. How would he have time when Rosey, the contract killer extraordinaire, would be here in less than an hour to be given information, by me, to plan his hit on Cal and Vivienne! If it was not for bad luck, he swore he would not have any luck at all!

"Knox, hey, long time no see…" a voice called from behind. "Rosey, hey man, what's it been a year now?"

"Well, in my line of work, the less you see me, the better one's doing right?" said Rosey as he came up and grabbed Knox's hand and gave it a grip and a shake.

"Yeah, guess you're right there Rosey. The less I see of you the better!"

"So what have we got here anyway? Floyd called me in, but he was pretty vague on the job. Where's Rooster? I thought for sure the ole bastard would be here to greet me as soon as I pulled in the driveway!"

"Rooster's dead. He was killed last week just outside Chicago." Knox said wishing he could smile as he did.

"Dead? How? WHO?" Rosey asked with a growing and violent temper that became ever more evident as he waited for a reply. "Who cut down Rooster? If that's why I've been called, to return the favor to whoever killed my brother, I will return it tenfold! Who was it Knox? If they ain't dead yet, I assure you, they will be." Rosey vowed.

"Rosey, remember the girl out in Reno?"

"You mean that blonde bitch that Rooster cut up?"

"Yeah, that's the one. Well, Rooster took one like her from Ohio, except she didn't end up dead, Rooster did."

"So you're saying some little twat killed Rooster? How does that even happen? How does some little cock-sucking whore get the best of Rooster? Was she an undercover?"

Knox thought about the idea of Vivienne being an agent and how frightening and great that would be all at the same time. He had wished that she were trained for the mental and physical abuse that was forced on her through all of this. She would have been better prepared if she were taught to fight back and trained to kill. She sure fit the bill by his standards. She killed Rooster against all odds, and yet nothing seemed to kill her, well, except now that Rosey was preparing to.

He knew it was up to him to get her out of that one, but still, Knox liked the idea that Vivienne was not a damsel in distress, or some fragile girl he had to save. He looked to her as his comrade or his associate, and even though she did not likely know it, it was exactly how he felt about her. He knew that from the start, they were in this together.

He wondered now how one innocent girl could throw such a wrench into things. The only thing that made sense to him was that it had to be fate. One way or another, he was destined to keep her alive. Knox jerked out of his own head, realizing that he had been thinking about things longer than he should have, while Rosey was waiting for an answer.

"Oh, shit, sorry Rosey, I've got a lot on my mind. As far as I know, she's just some girl from Ohio. I don't know much about her background. She's pretty young. I'd guess only a year or two out of high school. How she got the best of Rooster, is anyone's guess. Rooster must've made a misstep somewhere along the way. He suffered a very deadly lapse in judgment Rosey."

Knox took massive joy in Rooster's misfortune. What a happy, twisted fate to find its way to a soul that could not have deserved it more!

"Where is Floyd? Let's get this ball rolling. I'm itching to kill this bitch!" Rosey said, while cracking his knuckles and clenching his jaw in anger.

Knox studied him and realized that Rooster and Rosey were stunningly similar to one another. Their resemblance was striking really. Same height, same build, same eyes, could Rosey be Rooster's biological brother? Knox wondered. They always called each other brothers, but hell, so did all the members of the club. Now, Knox wasn't sure.

Rosey's demeanor was now all business and no longer the jovial long lost brother of the club. It was chilling to think that he might possibly be the actual blood brother of the recently deceased Rooster. This information would only confirm just how much of a cold-blooded killer he was, to be of relation to Rooster. The thought of him being unleashed upon society to hunt down, attack, slaughter, and disembowel his prey made him believe more and more that Rosey was indeed Rooster's relation.

Knox was kicking himself for ever bringing up Rosey to Floyd! He did not think that Rosey would get past the FBI and get to Cal in the hospital, but Vivienne, he had no idea if she was even in police custody anymore. Rosey might find her sitting at home on her porch swing reading Glamour Magazine. She might as well be sitting there wearing a sign that says "Kill me now please!" Knowing Rosey's disposition and new found hatred for Vivienne, Knox knew that Rosey would do things to her that would have her begging for death. He had to find a way to get to her before Rosey did.

Knox unfortunately could not be two places at once, and he could not avoid going with Floyd tomorrow night to the distribution deal. It was a well-known fact that once Rosey left the clubhouse, there was no undoing the deal. Once he accepted, which it was very evident he was already on board with avenging Rooster's death, there was no stopping him. He would keep going until his record was, once again, reaffirmed and made perfect. Rosey was not like the cable guy who called and said he would be over between noon and four, and would give up and move onto the next job when you did not answer the door when he showed up. No, he just kept coming and coming, until he did what was asked of him. He was a relentless, ruthless criminal, and once again, Knox was at fault.

It was like everything he did backfired and somehow put Vivienne in more danger. He was starting to think that she would be better off if she had never met him. At least then he could not keep putting her in the way of the Rosey's, Rooster's, and Floyd's of the world! *Jesus, is there anybody in the world who wanted to see this girl reach her 22'nd birthday besides me?* News reporters were trying to get her killed, and Agent Davis almost died trying to keep her from getting killed. It was like a gigantic black cloud followed her wherever she went, complete with deadly lightning bolts!

I hoped she was on that army base with Justin, because it would take the United States Army to keep a girl like Vivienne out of harm's way! Knox thought to himself as he followed Rosey into the conference room to give him the details Floyd expected him to offer. The details that would give Rosey the intelligence he needed to successfully hunt down and kill Vivienne Taylor!

Chapter 27

VIV

"Justin, I'm getting outta here!"

"Like hell you are missy!" Justin argued.

"No really, I am. My mom spoke to Detective Matthews and told him that it was imperative to my recovery to be home, instead of sitting on an army base, surrounded by soldiers and people I don't know. I'm a Taylor for Christ sakes, and my cousin's a police detective in town, I'll be fine! Why would they come after me now? If anything happens to me, they know they'll be the first suspects. Anyways, I don't know squat about the club really. I know where it is, and I know who the players are, but so does the FBI. I'm only a witness to Rooster's murderous ways, and it's been made perfectly clear that the FBI's only interested in the drug dealings with the club. Therefore, I feel like I'm off the hook, and damnit Justin, I'm done feeling like a science experiment. No more relentless nurses, needle pokes in the night, and monitors beeping into my brain! I can't take anymore! I just need to get the hell out of here!"

"Why do I get the feeling that this is the last time I'm going to see you alive?" Justin asked. "Do you have any idea what will happen to you if they know you're unattended, even for a second Vivienne?"

"Well then let them. Shit Justin, I can't spend the rest of my life running. I don't want to live like you and Knox, constantly looking over my shoulder and pretending to be someone else. I mean, I get it. I know why you do it, it's your job, but it's not mine. I am just a girl, an average small-town, nobody girl who just wants to go back to being my small-town, nobody self."

"In nursery rhymes and fairytales people have that option, but in the real world, where you and I coexist, sometimes happily ever after just isn't an option!"

"Justin, don't talk to me like I'm a child. Did it ever occur to you that maybe I just don't care if I live or die anymore? Maybe meeting my maker isn't nearly as scary as living the rest of my life in fear of dying? If the MCMC wants me, then they can come and get me. I am not going to let them control the rest of my life!"

"What about your family, Vivienne? It's not just about you! Think about your mom, your sisters, your cute little niece and nephew...don't you realize that it's not just you they will come after? The MCMC considers their group as a family, and if you fuck with their family, they will come after yours! They will burn your world to the ground if they can. Are you ready to put your entire family, your friends, and loved ones at risk just because you're stubborn? Jude was right about you, easy to love, but Jesus you're a stubborn-ass!"

"I'm not God Justin. It's not my job to control the outcome of everyone's lives. I could stay right here on this damned base and they could kill my family while I sit here perfectly protected, just to get to me. Don't you see that? Nowhere is safe, and nobody's safe. If it's me they want, I'm not going to make them go after my family to get to me. I'm going to be sitting at home right where they can find me. If they want me, I want them to know where to find me. I'm going home Justin. That's where I need to be, I'm doing this to protect my family, not to endanger them!"

"If you end up dead Vivienne, I'm going to kill you!" Justin said with a sad smile, realizing that I was right.

If they wanted me and could not get to me first, they would go after my family in order to flush me out.

Justin sat quietly, then looked at Vivienne and realized that she did not always let people know she was smart. Sometimes her stubbornness seemed to overshadow her intellect, but the girl was not stupid. She did not want to go home because she was a spoiled brat, she wanted to go home to protect her family...even if that meant dying. He could respect a person for that, and could not help but wonder where she got that from...maybe her mom or her estranged father who she hated to talk about.

Who was it that instilled this in her, to put others before herself, and to protect the ones she loved no matter the cost? He had so many questions, and he knew that if she died, the answers to his questions would die with her. So he said the only thing that made sense in all of this, "Well then, I'm coming with you!"

"What? Are you crazy Agent Davis?"

"Don't call me Agent Davis Vivienne! And I mean it, if you go, I go! Where is it you're from again? Dooofus?"

"Ha, ha, very funny! It's pronounced *DEL- FUS*! I live in Delphos, Ohio. But you can't come Justin, you're not even well enough to go anywhere yet. I didn't sign up to be your live-in-caregiver Justin Davis! Besides, what will the neighbors think if I go wheeling you into my house after I've been National News? They'll think we're shacking up! Not to mention, your old lady will kill you!"

"Yeah, uh, Viv, best if you don't call her my old lady when you meet her. She really hates it when people call her old. She's a lawyer, and I learned a long time ago, not to cross her. She's entirely too smart to ever win an argument against. Not to mention, she does kickboxing down at the YMCA, and I tell you, that shit's not just for cardio. If we ever found ourselves in a physical fight, I'm not entirely sure I could take her. She looks like a sweetheart, until she has you on the floor with your head in a chokehold between her thighs!"

Justin laughed as he spoke lovingly of his wife. He never really talked about his personal life before now, and I wondered if it was because he thought our paths were not likely to cross in the future. I knew the Bureau would not release him to watch over me, and I knew his wife would not let him go on his own free will either. So, before they came for me, I crawled into bed with Justin and laid my head on his chest. We watched an episode of Law and Order SVU together while he held me like a big brother would shelter a baby sister. It was the first man, besides the doctors, I allowed to get close to me after that night with Rooster. While I knew Justin would never hurt me, I felt the subtle change grow inside of me. There was a very distrustful bone in my body that was suspicious of the motives of mankind.

Two hours later, I was on a plane for home, courtesy of the United States military. Forty-five minutes later, my sister Bridget picked me up at the Wright-Patterson Air Force Base in Dayton, Ohio. She needed special clearance to get me, and I was so thankful that it was her who greeted me at the gate. It felt like years since I saw her hazel eyes, so much like my own, peering back at me.

"Oh my God Vivienne! Have you lost weight? You look so skinny! Did they feed you at all? What have they done to you? You look like you've lost twenty pounds. If it weren't for those bruises, you wouldn't have any color at all!" Bridget commented.

"Well, I haven't exactly been on vacation the last month. As it turns out, there are no beaches, sun, surf, or exotic drinks in hell! Shocking I know." I looked at her sarcastically.

Leave it to my sister to tell me I look skinny and pale. That was one thing I had always liked about her, even when I looked like I had been hit by a truck, she would somehow find the upside to it. So while the rest of me was in shambles, the good news was that my hourglass figure was looking more like one of the Olsen twins and less like Marilyn Monroe. *Super*!

Bridget helped load all of my things into her vehicle, and she headed up I-75 for my return home.

"Mom's got your house all set up for you Vivienne. She worked all day yesterday getting it ready for your big homecoming. She also mentioned that your house was a disaster, and she didn't raise you to be such a slob!"

Bridget laughed to herself, as I am sure it felt nice to talk to me like old times, picking on each other and joking like we had always done in the past. It was easier to fall into our usual banter, than to talk about my haunting past few weeks. I greatly appreciated her just trying to be "normal", as normal as us Taylor girls get anyways.

"Bridget, please tell me she's not throwing me a welcome home party? Bridget, talk to me. She didn't, did she?"

Bridget kept her eyes on the road ahead. "Bridget, look at me when you lie to me! Did she?"

"She might have invited just a few people for a small get together. You know, it's a really big deal having you home Vivienne. People actually thought you were dead! Dead! If it weren't for mom's constant candlelight vigils for your safe return, I think they would've just had a funeral for you and moved on!"

"Gee thanks Bridg, that's great to know!"

"I didn't mean it like that Vivienne; I just mean you're not the only one who went through something here. The entire town hung up posters and searched ditches, woods, and fields for you. They feel as though you're not just coming home to your family, but to all of them as well!"

"She better not of invited them all to my house. Lord knows I don't have enough parking for a search and rescue team of twenty five."

"Try one hundred and twenty five, at least."

"What! One hundred and twenty five people volunteered to look for me?"

"There were more, but there were at least one hundred and twenty five at one time. In all, there were approximately five hundred people who volunteered over the two week period that we were searching for you."

"You've got to be shitting me!" I said surprisingly.

"Well I can see that your time spent with the dirty biker clan didn't improve your language any. For the life of me, I'll never know why you find the need to curse like you do." She retorted.

She was always pleading with me to not curse. Bridget and I, while we shared the red hair, pale skin, and hazel eyes, we did not share our very different personalities. While she did not drink, smoke, curse, or pop an occasional Vicodin before going out for pancakes with her girlfriends, I did. She went to church and not just on Christmas and

Easter. She wanted to get married, have children, grow up in a happy world, and I never really knew what I wanted in life. To say we were not exactly alike was an understatement.

But she was my sister, and I loved her. I insisted on her not picking me up at the air force base, however my mother gave her the order to come and get me. The one thing you did not do, was argue with Josie. They did not call her "The Warden" for nothing! What she said really *did* go.

I did not want to face the hoopla that was waiting for me at home, but I figured it was the least I could do for the people who helped search for me. The least I could do would be to go, smile, and say thank you. I was not a cretin. While they did not find me, it meant a tremendous amount to me that anyone had looked for me in the first place. Here this whole time I thought my poor mom was the lone ranger in looking for me, but as it turns out, she was the general of an army of people who wanted to see me safely returned home.

All that crap Justin said before I left started creeping in…how could I go home and tempt fate by letting people celebrate my survival, knowing that it could be only a matter of days before they would wind up attending my funeral? Seemed kind of awful on my part to do that to them. Perhaps, I should consider letting Detective Matthews put me in that witness relocation program after all.

Bridget chattered on as the miles flew by, and while I wished I could focus on what she was saying, I could not help but to think about Knox. I sat in the passenger seat, wondering if he were still alive and if he ever thought about me the way I so often thought of him.

Chapter 28

KNOX

After spending an entire evening strategizing Vivienne's death with Rosey, Knox felt confident that he mislead him enough to buy him some time. Currently, there was not a lot of information available to the whereabouts of Vivienne Taylor. Not by local police and not by the hospital officials who discharged her. She had somewhat vanished as far as the average person could ascertain. The last time she had been on civilian radar was when she was at St. Rita's Hospital, and from there, she was discharged into thin air. At least whoever had her was doing a good job of keeping it quiet! Knox thought that it was about damn time something went their way. He hoped she was with Justin, on that army base in DC. He knew that Rosey would not touch her while she was there. He knew Rosey was good, but he was not that good!

So with Rosey preparing to depart, Knox had to shift his focus to Floyd, by giving the FBI what they wanted. He hoped that by giving them what they were after, he would get what he wanted…the hell out of here! So he began preparing for tonight's scheduled business trip. He reminded himself that a person can not walk without putting one foot in front of the other. Now it was time to put this ride with Floyd in front of the foot that would have him running to stop Rosey, before Rosey could put a stop to Vivienne.

Seven o'clock came not soon enough, and Knox was trying to hide the fact that he was chomping at the bit to head out. He had not left the clubhouse all day, and all ears and eyes were on him. There was no way to give the FBI their big raid so long as Floyd and all of his so-called brothers were all around. He had to think of something else. The only way he was getting a message out of here, was for it to be tied to a leg of a pigeon, or rolled up in a bottle and tossed in the creek that ran behind the clubhouse. Neither method was very effective for getting an immediate call for help.

By the time seven thirty rolled around, Knox was absolutely amazed when Floyd walked out of the clubhouse to meet him alone. The usual bodyguards, Ace and Rod, were not at his side. No muscle, just Floyd. Knox was immediately suspicious up to this point, Floyd would not take a ride with him alone, not after he was ever so clear about his suspicions regarding Knox's loyalty to the club. Knox kept looking at the door for more men, more man power to file out, but the door stood unmoved.

"Just us? Where's Floyd and Ace?" Knox asked.

"They are already there. They left early to get things rolling, so when we show up, there's nothing left to do but make the exchange." Floyd said, "They'll text me if anything looks suspicious, but I'm not anticipating any trouble. After tonight, once we finish our business, we'll have something to celebrate for a change."

Floyd swung his leg over his bike and pushed the starter button to bring it to life. His bike was beautiful, custom paint, ape hanger handlebars, a bold dazzling devilish woman with a forked tongue engulfed in flames sizzled on the side of his gas tank. The flames, chrome, and magnificent detail adorned the rest of the bike's body. Knox admired the skill and craft that went into creating a work of art like Floyd's bike. It would be a shame to see it locked in an impound shop someday, numbered and cataloged as federal evidence.

Knox threw his leg over his bike, started it up, and pulled his glasses down from his head and over his eyes. Floyd gave him a nod, and they both began to roll out. First Floyd, and then Knox followed dutifully behind. Floyd took back roads like he always did, but when he turned on a road that Knox knew did not lead to the Industrial Park, he knew this was it. Knox's uneasy feelings surrounding Floyd and this run were coming to fruition. This is where Floyd was going to bring him to meet his maker. Rod and Ace did not come on this particular ride, because only the President could demote the Vice President according to Club bylaws...and it was happening tonight.

The MCMC's President was in executive capacity on this narrow, darkening road. Knox knew his time was nearing an end, and he decided it was now or never. He took the lead pipe he kept secured to his bike for protection out from its holder, and speared it into the glorious spindles of Floyd's back tire. Floyd's motorcycle seized up as Floyd's body tried to cling to those ape hanger handlebars for dear life. The bike's response to Knox's preemptive strike against his leader was so violent and out of control, that Knox's bike could not fully escape the aftermath of his split second decision to attack. The two bikes veered into each other's paths and became entwined as they crashed, flipped, and hurled even more out of control than could have been expected.

Knox flew off his bike and into the grass, as Floyd skidded down the pavement with his bike on its side. His gorgeous stunner of a bike was just as glorious in its demise as it was in its creation. It threw a shower of sparks, spectacular enough to match Fourth of July fireworks over the Boston Harbor. The screeching and tearing of the metal did not sound painful, so much as poetic. Floyd's body came to rest within the twisted, intertwined cycles.

From Knox's vantage point, you could not tell where one bike began and the other ended. Knox had landed hard in the grass along the side of the road but was able to get up and limp over to where Floyd's motionless body was lying. There he was, bleeding on top of the bikes, with gasoline, oil, and blood all leaking and pooling together around the mangled up machines. Floyd's thigh was impaled by a piece of metal, and it stuck clean through him. That injury would be the death of him as quickly as the blood was pouring out. It had to of hit his femoral artery.

Floyd was lucid enough to look hard at Knox, as Knox peered down accessing the damage that was done to his former fearless leader. Knox was surprised at how fearless Floyd looked, even now as he was about to die. Knox could not imagine how after this crash, there could have been any way that Floyd could come out on top like he always did, but yet his look was unwavering. Even in a crash that would split oceans apart, he stayed on his bike. In that moment he reminded Knox of a bull rider who clung to the raging ton of muscle and bull that was trying to kill his rider dead. Floyd refused to let anyone dethrone him from his extension of his own manhood. He and his bike remained one.

Floyd did not beg or plead the way Knox had saw others plea for their lives at Floyd's feet. Instead, he was calm, even now with all the pain he must have been experiencing.

"I didn't think you had it in you. Agent West, I presume?" He asked it like a question, but it was a question he obviously knew the answer to. "Did you think I'd never find out? Do you think you can come into my club and burn it to the ground?"

Floyd laughed, exposing his bloodied teeth and then coughed causing blood and spittle to escape his lips.

"Oh, and your little girl friend, she's back in Ohio. According to my sources, she is about to attend a very large, *very* public, welcome home party. Good news always travels so fast." Floyd smiled utterly insincerely at Knox as he delivered his message. "Rosey can't wait to welcome Vivienne home and meet her friends and family. Oh what a homecoming that will be, too bad you won't be there to witness it!"

Knox looked down at his fallen leader and said, "My, my, how the mighty have fallen, eh Floyd? You're threats don't change the situation here though do they? You think killing Vivienne makes your dying of any significance? You think you are getting me, for getting you? I thought I lost her once, and I can survive if I lose her again. You know what memory will keep me warm at night in her place? Your cold, rotten, corpse, ten feet under, eaten by maggots, and rotted to the core. Which you were in life, as you will be in death! How does it feel to know that? Since we're being honest and sharing our hopes and dreams with each other now!"

     As Knox's final words sank in, along with the expression on Floyd's evil face, Knox did not blink or give himself a moment of reprieve as he pulled out his 9 mm and without saying a word, shot Floyd between the eyes. The shots he had pretended with Vivienne that night in the field, now found their intended mark. Three in all were fired, and all three landed with lethal force. Floyd's body slumped backwards and joined in death with that of the two motorcycles he was entangled with. Knox watched as the gasoline, the oil, the blood, ran together and then spread, creating a lake of mixed fluids. The rainbow coloring of the gasoline, the bright red blood, the dark black oil…he had never seen anything like it. When the lake reached his feet, he took a step back, and then another.

Frozen for only a moment by his lethal action, Knox did not waste any time mourning Floyd's death. Instead he bent down and felt around Floyd's body, and was astounded when he found Floyd's cell phone secured in its leather holder affixed to his belt. The leather case was all scratched to hell, but the phone was left unscathed. He dialed in the number, and this time he did not hesitate to say, "Agent Michaels please. It's Agent West."

"Hello, Jude?" Knox's boss replied.

"You've lost the right to first name basis with me Agent Michaels.

This is Agent West and I'd like to report a murder."

"Whose?" Agent Michaels inquired.

"Floyd Daniel Moore, President of the Motor City MC" Knox announced unwaveringly.

"Jude, what have you done? You can't just go on a murdering spree and think your badge covers all matters of sin!"

"Oh, like you would have done... had it wound up being me with my head blown off on this deserted road up here in bumfuck Michigan! Does your badge cover all matters of that sin? He was going to execute me, and I just beat him to the punch. You want your drugs? You have fifteen minutes to have a team together and be at the Lincoln Avenue Industrial Park, Building 6. The deal goes down at eight o'clock. You will have your drug deal, dealers, a dead kingpin, and that's the good news. The bad news is you have one pissed off agent who is going to go and try to stop the contract killer Floyd hired to kill Vivienne. After that, I'm coming in and the first stop I make is going to be your office!"

Agent Michaels was silent, so Knox began again... "Tick Tock Agent Michaels, glory awaits you. Go nab your bad guys, and be the hero. I'd hate for you to miss you're big shining moment you hypocrite!" and Knox terminated the call.

With Floyd's cell in hand, he began running and limping back to the main road, as he was in desperate need of new transportation!

Chapter 29

VIV

After a couple hours on the road, Bridget dutifully delivered me back to my hometown. As we drew closer, my stomach was in knots. How could I be so nervous to go back to the only place I had ever called home? For crying out loud, since I was taken, all I wanted was to go back home, and now, here I was about to do just that, and I was as nervous as a whore in church.

I saw the first stop light and the sign saying, "Welcome to Delphos, *America's Friendliest City*"…which c'mon, who are we trying to fool?

Delphos could hardly make a claim like that and take it seriously. But the sign said we were friendly, so we do not put up much of a fuss about it!

Block by block, turn by turn, we weave through and across town headed towards my house. We drove past Pizza Hut, Main Street, the video store and Speedway...getting closer to my long awaited home. It was the one I had been so proud to buy all on my own. The house was a two-story, with white vinyl siding and burgundy shutters. It had off street parking and a fenced in back yard, where my dog Chubs liked to frolic around. While I was stupidly excited to see it again, all these feelings of terror started to creep in. I was not sure if I was scared this could all be over, or scared to go home knowing it was far from over.

I started trembling, and Bridget put her hand on my arm and said, "Vivienne, oh, my, are you OK? You're shaking like crazy! What's wrong?"

"I don't know Bridge, I...I just feel really uneasy about this."

"Is it the party? Vivienne, Mom's not having it until tomorrow night. She wanted you to have time to settle in and get your bearings, so don't worry. You won't have to deal with anything except Mom and I once we get you home."

"It's not just that, it's well...I don't know. It's like I am feeling everything I should have felt, but didn't, the entire time I've been gone. I'm scared, nervous, worried, and nauseous. I feel dizzy, my hands are sweaty, and my chest is tight. It's hard to breathe Bridget! Open a window! I need some air!"

Bridget looked visibly worried and scrambled to roll down the window. Once down, I hung my head out the window and let the cool air hit me square in the face as my body convulsed uncontrollably.

Bridget reached for her phone.

"Mom! Something's wrong with Vivienne! I don't know...she's shaking and looks sick. She's white and clammy and she's... she's.... Mom, she's scaring me! I don't know what's wrong with her!"'

When Bridget pulled into the driveway at my house, my eyes were closed and I still had my head hanging out the window. I smelled my mom's perfume before I opened my eyes to find her rushing towards me.

"Vivienne, honey, what's wrong? Tell me what's the matter?"

All I could do was shake. I wanted to pull myself together, but the world around me was spinning, and I just could not collect myself.

When my mom opened the car door, I nearly fell out onto the concrete driveway. I heard my baby sister gasp at my inability to be the independent, big sister she knew me to be. I saw the ghastly look in her eyes when she saw me that way…trembling, weak, physically ill, and beaten down. I knew she wanted to just joke, smile, and pretend like I had been gallivanting around Europe these last few weeks. That would have been much easier to imagine and more pleasant to tell one's friends as opposed to, *Yeah, my sister's the girl who was abducted this summer! Cool huh?* I didn't envy Bridget in this moment any more than she likely envied me. It was ironic really.

As I lay on the cool hard ground, with my cheek on the slab of concrete in my driveway, I watched the fluffy clouds float overhead. I tried to slow my breathing while my mom frantically dialed someone. I assumed it was 911, knowing her, but I could not hear anything anymore except my heart beating in my ears. It drowned out all the other sounds...*thump, thump, thump*....fast and loud, as the corners of my eyes faded in and out of darkness, and then it all went dark.

Chapter 30

KNOX

There were no cars to be seen or heard as Knox kept loping towards civilization. He thought to himself, what the heck, maybe she is listed. He dialed 411 and waited for the operator to respond.

A lady on the other end of the phone stated, "How can I help you?"

"I need the number for Vivienne Taylor."

"City and State please?" the operator said. "Um, Ohio, but I don't know the city. Can you just see if you have any listings for a Vivienne Taylor without the city?"

Knox was huffing and puffing into the phone as he ran down the rural road in the dark. With the luck he had, the first car that came along would not see him and run him clean over!

"Sir, We have no listings for a Vivienne Taylor."

"How about a V. Taylor? Are there any with just a V.?"

"One moment sir while I check that listing for you," she said in a robotic tone.

Knox kept running. He could hear the wind blowing into the receiver making an annoying sound blare from the speaker right into his ear.

"Sir, we do have multiple listings for a V. Taylor in Cleveland, Lakewood, Springfield, Akron, Delphos, Columbus, Toledo and Cincinnati. Do you know which location sir?"

Knox knew Viv did not live in a big city, so he went with the only Ohio town that he didn't know. "Um Delphos? Please give me the number and transfer me to the Delphos number please!" He was impressed with himself for the courtesy and patience he was showing with the phone operator. He was already feeling more like his old self, more like Jude West and less like Knox the biker.

He reached into his pocket to get a pen. He stopped running momentarily while he scribbled the number that was being announced mechanically to him. "You're call is being transferred...click, click, click...TRANSFERRING CALL..." and then the phone began to ring.

Over and over it rang. Knox began running again, never losing urgency for the situation and his desire to stop Rosey before he could keep his promise to Floyd. Even dead, Floyd was still a pain in Knox's ass! He chuckled to himself thinking of how Floyd would love to hear that. It was exactly the kind of thing that would please Floyd even more; the rotten bastard thrived off of the pain of others when it served his purpose. Many people thought Floyd was a decent man, but they did not know him like Knox knew him. They did not know the talks that went on behind closed doors. They did not know the true thought process behind the dark-eyed man who surrounded himself with mystery and cigarette smoke.

"Hello, you've reached 419-555-5545. I'm not home right now, but if you please leave a message, I'll get back to you just as quick as I can! Thanks, Bye," was what Knox heard on the other end of the phone.

The fantastic news was that he had her phone number; the shitty news was that an answering machine was not going to do him any good right now. What would he say? "*Uh…Hey Viv, it's Knox. I know you hate me and likely wish I were dead for lying to you about everything…but hey—there's this sadistic killer named Rosey, about 6'2' 180 lbs., dark hair, dark eyes, around thirty five years of age, on his way to kill you. So, if you see anyone of that description, run for your life, ok? Sweetie, I'll be there as soon as I can ok, luv you, buh-bye!*"

He could not say that! He could not say anything. Instead, he kept running, while his mouth hung agape without the words to explain. He had no credibility with her at this point, and he did not know if she would even want to talk to him after everything that had happened. As the machine went beep, he reluctantly closed the phone and ended the transmission. With his luck, Rosey would have been sitting right next to the phone anyway. Maybe it was best he did not have the balls to leave a message. His good-faith efforts to keep Vivienne alive always seemed to backfire. He thought it was right to just get there and do his best to stop what he blamed himself for setting into motion. It would not benefit anyone to leave a warning on a machine that she may not ever live to get!

Into the darkness, Knox ran on without seeing a headlight in sight. His heartbeat continued a rhythm in double time with his feet slapping the pavement. He wondered how long he could run like this. While training at the academy, he was in top physical shape. He could run to the end of the earth and back, but now, after living the life that he had been living, Knox realized he no longer had the endurance that he once had.

He grimaced as he thought about being forever altered by this experience. It was not supposed to be this way. He was a bright up and comer at the bureau and had graduated at the top of his class. He was well liked and respected with career opportunities ahead of him, and now, after living among murderers and thugs, he did not remember the young man who he had been not so long ago. He had a clear vision for his future, and it was definitely not this!

As he flitted about in his mind, and tried to think of other things to block out the stinging in his lungs and burning sensation that was taking over his legs, Knox tried to think happy thoughts. *Happy thoughts Jude*, he said to himself to try and keep himself going.

The first thing that popped into his head was the color red, *Vivienne's hair.* He closed his eyes at the thought and allowed his imagination to become more vivid. Once he was in the dark and in his mind, he forgot his body aches and pains when he saw her hazel eyes looking at him. Her lips curled up in a smile, and her cheeks were pale, pink, and plump. Her face would light up when she smiled, with always a touch of mischief behind her eyes. She smiled like that when she looked at him. That very warm thought persuaded Knox's face to contort into a smile himself. Even now, Vivienne made the darkest moments brighter. It was the most painful thing in the world right now, the thought of Rosey putting that light out as quick and easy as someone snuffing a candle. It made Knox's guts twist and heart ache just thinking about it.

BEEEEEP! Knox opened his eyes and found himself running head on into a set of very bright headlights! "SHIT!" Knox yelled as he dove onto the shoulder of the road to avoid a collision.

The driver of the vehicle slammed on the breaks, tires squealed, and the smell of burnt rubber and smoke filled the air. Knox's body was like a bowling ball rolling down the shoulder of the road. As he came to a stop, so did the vehicle that nearly flattened him. Knox heard heavy footsteps approaching his way, and before he could roll over to see who it was, he heard "Hey Man, you ok?"

Knox remained face down and motionless. He felt like an idiot of course, day dreaming about a girl, and nearly getting killed in the process. It took him a moment to shake off the embarrassment before he answered.

"Um, yeah, I think so." as he tried to resume breathing. Staring down a Dodge Ram Pick-up tends to make one's life flash before his eyes!

"Sir, are you sure you're not hurt? I damn near killed you just now!" Knox looked up to see a young man with a chubby face and bright eyes. His head was clad with a camouflage ball cap that read, "I'd rather be fishin!"

"I'm Travis" he said as he extended his equally chubby fingers and hand to Knox, offering to help him to his feet.

"Knox" Knox said while being helped up.

"Knox, that's your name? From the looks of you, it looks like someone's knox'ed you around some! You're a mess! You some sort of Iron Man or something?"

"Huh?" Knox said with confusion.

"You like training for a marathon or something? You really should wear those geeky outfits with the safety reflectors if you're going to be out here running around in the dark with your eyes closed!"

"I'm not training for a marathon. I wrecked my bike a few miles back, and I'm in a bit of a pinch Travis. I need to get to Ohio, and I needed to get to Ohio...like yesterday! It's a life and death kind of need, if you can understand what I'm saying." Knox informed the cherub-faced boy standing in front of him.

Travis shifted his weight from one foot to the other, spit some chewing tobacco out the side of his mouth, onto the blacktop and said, "So you're on some sort of mission then huh?" He gripped the bill of his hat, lifted it up off his head a time or two, trying for a better position and said, "Well sir, I ain't doing nuthin. I suppose I could give you a lift. Where abouts are we going in the Buckeye State?"

"That part's tricky Travis." Knox confessed. "I'm not entirely sure...I think the town's name is Delphos?"

"Delphos, Ohio... hmmm, never heard of it. You know, for a guy who's on a mission with a life or death kicker, you'd think you'd at least know where you're going to do all this saving the day kinda stuff. Do we know who we're saving at least?"

"What's this we stuff? Travis, you're giving a guy a lift, I'm not about to get you involved in this mess too!" Knox said begrudgingly.

"Too late fella! I ain't your taxi cab. I'm your knight in fucking shining armor! Check out my white steed." Travis said smiling with an exaggerated wink, as he pointed to his big, jacked up white Dodge truck.

"You wanna ride the big white steed and get rescued by a chubby white kid from Michigan's Upper Peninsula? Then you gotta pay the toll!"

"Toll?" Knox questioned.

"Yeah, the toll is this, you don't get to treat me like a damn immigrant NYC Cabbie! Either we are saving the day, or you can keep running your happy ass down the road here."

"Look, *Kid*, you don't know what you're asking here! You don't know the dangers of what I'm about to face. This isn't Scooby Doo and Inspector Gadget kind of shit here. This is real honest to goodness get you killed kind of stuff!

"*Kid*? I ain't no kid! I'm TWENTY-TWO! If I am old enough to fight for my country, then I can fight for whatever it is you're fighting for!"

"You're in the military?" Knox asked disbelievingly.

"Hell no I'm not in the military, look at me, you think I get up and run five miles in the morning? I'm not in the military, but I can shoot the shit outta my twelve-gauge shot gun. I'm deadly as they come with a rifle. I'm a corn-fed farm kid. I aint a cabbie or a soldier, but I'm all you got right now son. So, get in the truck, or beat feet down the road and hope some other redneck don't come along and plow your ass over! Come to think of it, you're damned lucky I replaced my breaks last week or you'd be road kill right now."

Knox could not argue with his logic. Travis was right. He was the only option he had at the moment. With that in mind, Knox practically sprinted to the passenger side of Travis' truck and hopped in.

Travis was not a sprinter, but he made good time getting back to his rig and up into the driver's seat. It was only a moment before the two of them were flying down the road, going no less than seventy miles per hour, headed south and headed towards Ohio.

Knox was not as chatty as Travis, and he felt like a heel for not keeping up his end of the conversation, but he had a lot on his mind. Knox was sure Travis had some things on his own mind like, "What the hell am I doing picking up a bloodied, limping, yet running hitchhiker on a back road outside of Detroit?" Knox thought, *hell, I could be a serial killer for all he knew*! So, Knox made a note to give Travis a stern talk about picking up strangers, after this was all over. He did not want to spook him now, not when he was the only thing getting him where he needed to go.

Travis popped in a CD and began rocking out to the latest Kid Rock album.

Knox rolled his eyes and said, "Of Course, Kid Rock, the Son of Detroit turned Country Rocker!" He shook his head and said, "Kids!"

Travis said, "What? Kid Rock is classic Detroit!"

Knox laughed out loud. "You want classic Detroit, try, Bob Seger, Ted Nugent, Alice Cooper, Grand Funk Railroad, or Glenn Frey of The Eagles. Next thing you know you're going to be telling me that Eminem is the savior of modern day music!

"WHAT?" Travis threw his hands up in the air, "His lyrics are stellar! Don't even play like you don't bob your head along to his catchy riffs. You look like you're a head bobber…yeah, you are! I can see it in your eyes, *Head Bobber*!" Travis accused with a snicker.

Knox looked out the window as Kid Rock sang, "*Ahh the landlord called the rent is due I spent it all on a KISS tattoo, I rock n roll all night…*" and realized the kid did not have it all wrong. Kid Rock was not bad. Hell, under normal circumstances, he likely would have enjoyed the truck ride with a guy like Travis. He was youthful, full of all sorts of misconceptions about life, and had a love of Michigan Musicians. But then again, these were not normal circumstances.

He found it excruciating to sit there in Travis's passenger seat and do nothing, knowing all the while that with each minute that passed, he could be a minute too late.

Chapter 31

VIV

I awoke to find myself back in a hospital bed. Damnit! I wanted to go home. I did not want to be back here! Worse yet, I awoke to a room void of any family or friends. Instead, I found myself next to tedious and dull Detective Matthews!

"You again?" I said with a slight scowl on my face.

"You again!" he said back to me to return and confirm my sentiment.

"Ah, I see you're about as happy to see me as I am to see you! Great, we're finally on the same page!" I said to him.

"Yeah, Vivienne, you're not exactly my most grateful save, you know!"

"Save? Why do you continue to get this mixed up... you did not save me! I did not see you riding in on your white steed to save the day! You did not save me, I just didn't die like I was supposed to, or like I should HAVE!"

"Should have what?" My mom said as she walked in through the doorway. "What'd I miss?" she inquired of the detective.

"Oh, Vivienne was just telling me how she should have stayed in Virginia where she would have been safe and pampered by the hospital staff who were equipped to handle special patients like herself," lied Detective Matthews.

I shot him a look of disdain, and he shot one right back at me. I swear that guy's like the pain in the ass big brother I never wanted! Why couldn't he be more like Agent Justin? Justin was so pleasant and likeable, not smug and detestable like this guy! How could my mother find anything to like about this man? Sure he was handsome enough, but what an odious creature he was. With a personality like a wet blanket, I did not know how his own mother even liked him. I knew I certainly didn't! And what was he doing here anyway? He did not even like me, so why did he need to be in my room?

"What's he doing here?" I pointed at the repugnant detective with a shaky finger.

"Who, Detective Matthews?" My mom said surprised. "Why wouldn't he be Viv?"

"Um, what is he my dad now or something? I don't think the FBI pays him to sit around and annoy people do they?"

"No, he's here because he cares about you, and he doesn't want anything to happen to you."

"Cares about me? He doesn't care about ME, he cares about YOU! He'd throw himself in front of a bus for you, and for me, eh…yeah, not so much *mother*! Don't kid yourself and don't try and sweet talk me. I know people, and he definitely ain't here because he cares about me!"

The hateful words just poured out of my mouth, and frankly, I did not know what the hell was wrong with me. This was not respectful, it was not polite or courteous, and it was not ME. I did not know where all this blind rage and hatred for the detective was coming from. I bit my lip while I considered it…

Maybe all this male influence in my life here lately was throwing me off balance due to all of these male figures inserting their opinions about my choices and direction. For so long it was just me, my mom, and my sisters. Then I was taken, and it has been all about what Rooster wanted, what Knox said, what the doctors recommended, or what Detective Matthews ordered.

I was just damned tired of being told what to do, when to do it, and what not to do by a bunch of overly dominant dudes with god complexes! Who were these men to me anyway? Did I ask for any of this?

Holy crap! I could feel my blood boiling. It felt like my heart was beating in my neck, and I felt the thudding growing up and out of my chest cavity. I closed my eyes to try and calm myself, and I imagined my body convulsing and then bursting into a million pieces, like the Hulk, or some other freak of nature.

At first it was paralyzing fear, and now every fiber of my being was filled with rage. Was I finally succumbing to my injuries? Was the damage to my body finally catching up to my brain?

"Make it stop, make it stop." I said as I pulled myself into the fetal position while sitting up and rocking myself back and forth in my bed.

My mom rushed to my side and threw her little arms around me as best she could.

"Shhhhhhh…Vivienne..shhhhh, it's going to be ok." she said in a whisper into my ear. She held me until the hot hate turned into a cold and clammy chill of fear once more.

Once I calmed down and stopped acting like a rabid animal, I began shivering, and the nursing staff was told to bring me additional blankets. All of the sudden, the world seemed too scary of a place to return to. I felt more afraid than I had ever felt in my life. Afraid of who was about to burst through the door, afraid for my family, my friends, afraid of noises and smells. My mind raced, my heart beat erratically, and everything seemed off. I wondered how I could have deteriorated so quickly?

Now back at St. Rita's, the hospital staff was familiar of my case, and once more, I got to see my neurologist Dr. Bradshaw.

"Well, well, Miss Taylor, I see you returned from Virginia. Somehow you look worse than when you left! How is this possible?"

"Well Doc, I don't know what's happening, but it's like I'm shutting down. I keep having these episodes."

"Panic attacks?"

"Do panic attacks make you feel like you're about to die?"

"Some" the doctor nodded. He continued with, "I've reviewed your chart Vivienne, and your MRI was clear. There were no bleeds that I can see, so I have to conclude that these episodes were not of a physical nature. They were psychological."

"So no surgery or medication will fix me?" I said defeated.

"Well, I wouldn't say that Vivienne. We could prescribe you an antidepressant and anxiety medication to help you for now, but quite frankly, it would only serve as a Band-Aid to your psychological damage. Eventually, you will have to face these problems head on. Through the use of therapy and support groups, you would have the opportunity to work through the events following your abduction...along with medication of course." Dr. Bradshaw offered while looking at me sympathetically. His bedside manner was excellent really. He was one of the new men in my life who I did not feel the need to rip his face off, which seemed progressive based on the way things had been going lately.

Dr. Bradshaw seemed genuinely concerned with my wellbeing, and he was obviously an intelligent and educated man. I had no cause to doubt his diagnosis, regardless of how much I wished he were wrong.

"Vivienne, I can keep you here for observation if you are feeling unstable, or I can release you with some medications to alleviate the panic and mood disorders you are currently suffering from. I will get you a list of psychotherapists in the area that specialize in trauma and abuse cases. I think you could really benefit from seeing someone and getting the help you need to not only survive this event, but to live a full and healthy life, despite what has happened to you." Again, Dr. Bradshaw's tone and demeanor oozed sincerity.

"Yes sir, get me a list, and I'll see to it that I schedule something as soon as possible. Also, I'd like to go home. If you give me a sedative or something to get me through the next couple days, I think I'll survive until the crazy doctors get to take a stab at me."

My mom cringed at my use of the word stab, so I looked at her and said "pardon the pun mom". She just nodded and looked out the window as she tried to hide her teary eyes.

"Ok, Vivienne, I will get the discharge nurse up here to get you on your way and I will write up a prescription for the nurse to give to you before you leave. It was a pleasure meeting you, and I wish you all the best in your recovery dear."

He held my hand as he said his farewell, and then I watched as his white coat disappeared around the corner and out of sight.

That was the thing about the men in my life these days, they never seemed to stick around for very long! Either I killed them or someone else killed them…or they just flat out disappeared! Dr. Bradshaw was gone like all the rest of them. Detective Matthews, on the other hand, would not go away. Of course I would get stuck with him! *Luckiest girl in the world*, I said to myself as I rolled my eyes.

Within the hour, the discharge papers were signed, and an orderly wheeled me out the front door and into the parking lot. Detective Matthews was waiting in the driver's seat of my mom's PT Cruiser. My mom hopped out of the passenger seat to help me into the back.

"Where's Bridget Mom?" I asked.

"Oh, she's back at your house Viv. She was pretty upset about seeing you this sick, so she wanted to wait for you there."

"Oh," I said. "Was I really that scary to watch?"

"Viv, you're eyes rolled back into your head and you laid there unconscious. It was enough to scare anyone! Even the paramedics that brought you here seemed apprehensive about your condition."

"That good, huh?" I said embarrassed.

I buried my face in my hands, unable to visualize myself in such a state, and embarrassed to be falling apart seemingly in front of the entire world.

"Vivienne, don't worry, we're going to go to the pharmacy and get your prescription filled. The medication will help you ease back into things. I think it was all just too much that happened too fast. You were probably right, you should have stayed in Virginia a bit longer," she then trailed off in thought.

As she did, I noticed Detective Matthew's eyes looking deeply right into mine through the rearview mirror. I shot him a look as if to say, *See what you started*! He shook his head disapprovingly at me but did not say a word, and just kept driving me back to my home.

Once we arrived back at the old homestead, the first order of business was to take my medicine. I was prescribed Klonopin to help alleviate my anxiety. Apparently it is a good drug for Post-Traumatic Stress Disorder, which is what my chart was officially updated to before being released from the hospital. The chart read, "Patient suffers from PTSD," a diagnosis which would surely follow me around for the rest of my days, just like the haunting memories of Rooster. I was horribly afflicted by both the memories of my time with Rooster, and my current mental state, with each passing day. The more of Rooster I saw, the worse PTSD I suffered, and being home alone only made me feel farther away from myself. It did not make sense to say out loud, but made perfect sense to me.

There is something about being taken from the familiar life you had always known. It seemed to erase who you were before. The life I created and grew to love before my abduction suddenly seemed like it never existed in the first place. The place I had loved, my home, held no comfort for me now. The people who loved me before my abduction, did not feel like the people I had left behind. Even they were altered in my mind.

Thoughts like, "I should have just died in that field" and "I'd be better off dead than this shell of a person." kept rolling over and over in my awareness. But I could not shut them off any easier than I could un-carve Rooster's name from my stomach. This nightmare was my reality, despite my desires to go back to life before this all happened.

I popped my Klonopin in hopes that it would make all of these unwanted thoughts go away. I knew magic pills did not exist, but with my eyes squeezed shut, I wished for a simple fix. Since returning home, I was always in a state of contradiction where my body felt numb, yet my mind never felt more alive. It generated more hate, more anger, more fear, more worry, and more mental anguish than I had ever known in my life. It was just too much to bear. *Please God make it stop, please make it go away. I don't want to feel like this anymore*, I prayed.

My prayer was interrupted by my mother who barged through the door, and into my room, where I had been sitting quietly on my bed with my eyes shut.

"Which one?" she offered, as she held up two dresses in front of me.

"Which one what?" I inquired.

"Which dress do you want to wear to your party tomorrow?"

"Mom, do I really have to? I mean...I just...I'm not sure I'm up for a big thing right now. What if I freak out and scare everyone, like I did to you and Bridget today? The doctor said I'm supposed to take it easy and not bite off too much right away. You were at the hospital with me today when Dr. Bradshaw gave his instructions, don't you think a big party might be too overwhelming for me right now?"

"No Vivienne. I think it would be therapeutic for you to see...to *really* see how important you are to the people of your community, to your family, and to the world."

"Really, the *world* mom?" I said with sarcasm. "I hardly believe that the world gives a crap about me! That's a bit of an overstatement wouldn't you say?"

"No! I don't think it's an overstatement. It's a miracle you're alive, Viv! A MIRACLE! Do you know how lucky you are? Do you even know? You are a survivor! Not many people would have made it through what you endured!"

"But mom, I didn't! I didn't make it through…THIS PERSON DID!" I pounded on my chest emphatically. "I'm not me anymore! You're daughter, Vivienne Lynn Taylor, I'm convinced she's still up in Michigan in that pit, or strapped to that bed in that seedy motel room in Chicago, or maybe she died in that field! But I promise you, I don't feel her here anymore. So the world shouldn't celebrate me not dying, because despite the overwhelming feelings I have, the one thing I don't feel is me! I don't know WHO I am, or WHAT I am anymore!"

With that, the tears welled up and spilled out of my eyes.

My mom threw the dresses onto the bed and sat down next to me. Comforting me was starting to seem like it would become her full time job after the way I was constantly melting down.

"Viv, you're still in there! I know you are. Don't worry, we will get you back! First we'll take the shell, and then we'll work on filling you back up. We knew you wouldn't be the same girl that you were when you left. How could you be? After everything you've now been through, how could you be the same? But who's to say this isn't who you are destined to be? I know you probably want to curse God for letting this happen to you, but God has a plan for each and every one of us. He doesn't bring you to it if he doesn't intend to bring you through it! You know that. I know those Bible lessons had to sink in at least a little."

My mom smiled at me and wiped my tear-stained cheeks.

My mom was not a strong woman because she was born that way; it was because of her unwavering faith. Her words hit home, and found a small place in my heart. I responded by pointing to the piles of fabric on the bed.

"That one, I'll wear the blue one. I know you hate the color blue, but you know it's my favorite, so I'll wear that one."

My mom's face lit up as she realized her words infiltrated my head causing some of my hopelessness to fade away, at least for the time being.

"Good," she said as she stood up and hung the dress on my mirror. "Now, shoes!"

And she began to pile up shoe boxes determined to pick out an ensemble that would be perfect for my "*Welcome Home, we're-glad-you-didn't-die party*".

Wow, I can hardly wait, I thought to myself mockingly. Then, I wondered if thinking to myself sarcastically was something I did before I was abducted, or something I just started doing?

Once all of the clothes had been selected and the pep talks and prayers subsided, I was finally left alone. Both doors to my bedroom were closed and I sat there peering at myself in my mirror which sat atop my dresser. *What a mess!* I thought.

I could hear voices outside my room, my mom, Detective Matthews, and Bridget. They were all likely discussing me now that I was out of earshot, planning my lengthy mental impairment and hopefully recovery. I wonder, while sitting here alone in my room, if a recovery was even possible?

My Klonopin began working its magic, or the exhaustion from the stress to my body began to kick in, because I could feel my eyes getting heavy and my face felt kind of numb. My eyes blinked slower, my heart beat slower, even swallowing seemed like it took longer than normal as I could feel my saliva make its way down my throat.

I felt the need to lie down, so I allowed myself to collapse backwards onto my navy blue fluffy pillows. The fall back even felt like it was in slow motion. *So this is why people do drugs?* I thought. It was such a welcomed relief to have a mind that was not racing. I tried to think about things, but instead, it felt like a warm bath had been poured into my soul and it began to soothe me from the inside out. The only word that came to mind then was, *Ahhhh*. I closed my eyes and allowed myself to drift off peacefully into unconsciousness. The world, my brain, and my body went quiet, and I smiled at the pleasure it gave me to feel a small version of peace.

When I awoke, I was in the dark and completely panicked! I sat straight up in bed realizing that I had no idea where I was, until I felt my old familiar comforter between my fingers. I reached to my right grasping the air, trying to find my lamp's chain. I felt the little metal ball hit my fingertips, and I grabbed hold and pulled down as fast as I could.

Suddenly I could not stand the vast darkness that filled my room. I needed to be able to see immediately, or I was certain I would die! My chest was tight, my hands were wet with perspiration, and my head felt as if it was spinning. When the light finally came on and shooed away the evil darkness, once more, I found myself peering at my disheveled reflection in the mirror. It scared me to see myself.

I looked at my cell phone and saw that six hours had passed since I had laid down.

It was 11:30 p.m. Outside my window was dark. *Why did I paint my walls such a dark navy!* I leaned to my left and switched on the overhead light. Two, one-hundred watt, light bulbs lit up and illuminated the room. This was better than the light from my bedside lamp. I instantly felt better, reassured by the light. The reassurance was short lived as I nearly jumped out of my skin when I heard the knock at my door.

"Who, who is it?" I hooted like an owl.

"It's Detective Matthews, may I come in? I thought when you woke up you might be hungry, so I took the liberty of picking up one of your favorite meals, two Cheesy Gordita crunch tacos and a very large mountain dew."

"With extra ice?" I asked.

"Yes, extra ice. I just returned when I heard you fumbling in your room to turn on the light."

"Come on in." I grumbled, despite the delicious smelling tacos.

"Hi Vivienne. Here, help yourself. I didn't know if you wanted sauce, so I grabbed a handful of everything. After I stopped at Taco Bell, I sent your mom home for the night. I told her not to worry, and that I'd stay and watch over you. Your sister's upstairs asleep in the spare room. I can take up a spot on the couch. I hope that's ok?"

"Why are you being so nice?" I asked him as I crunched into the taco and took a big slurp of the dew.

"Am I not normally?" He said as if I had hurt his feelings.

"No, well, I don't know, you just seem overly polite all the sudden. Did my mom tell you to be nice to me or something?"

"Vivienne, I'm not the villain in your story you've created. I didn't try to steal your mother away from you or your family. Hell, I never even made it to second base with your mom!"

"Ewwwww! Seriously detective, I cannot think about you rounding the bases with my mom, I might just lose my appetite over here! Please don't ever mention the word base and my mom in the same sentence again." gesturing a finger in my throat to throw up.

The detective laughed out loud at my attempt at humor.

"You know Vivienne, you're a real piece of work. If we hadn't gotten off on such a rotten start with one another, perhaps we might have liked each other."

"Let's not get crazy detective!" I said with a smile.

For the moment, a truce was forming between us, and it was a welcomed change of pace. I did not have it in me to hate him at the moment. Hate required a lot of energy, and energy was something I did not have.

"Nightmare?" he asked as he pointed around the room at all of the lit light bulbs.

"Um, no, just an irrational fear of darkness at the moment." I answered.

"It's not irrational. It's only natural that you'd have some new phobias and quirks about you after your ordeal."

"Quirks, is that what we're calling them now'a'days? It's not like I have a crooked toe, or a stutter."

"Oh, well, trust me when I tell you Vivienne, I wish your only quirks were a crooked toe and a stutter. You'd be a lot easier to talk to, and it would take you fuh-fuh-fuh-ever to interrupt me with your sassy mouth then wouldn't it!"

Detective Matthews again laughed wholeheartedly at his little poke at my expense.

"Oh, c'mon Viv, that was funny! Laugh already would ya!"

I gave him what he wanted, and I chuckled a bit. Of course he was right, I was as big as a pain in the ass as I thought him to be, which is probably why we butted heads the way we did. I grew up knowing that two hard heads do not do much but clash into one another, never giving each other an inch.

"Alright Quirky" Detective Matthews said, "I'll give you some privacy. I just wanted you to know you weren't alone here tonight. Detective Matthews, reporting for duty."

He gave me the salute as he stood up from his seat on the foot of my bed.

As he headed for the door he said, "G'night Viv," and he shut the door behind him. *Damnit*, I was just resigned to the idea that I hated Detective Matthews, and then he had to go and get me Taco Bell! Now that he decided to be all human and decent, I had to reconsider being his sworn enemy. Hating him had come easy and now to stop hating him might be a little more difficult, but it surprisingly was not.

He did not deserve all of the blind hatred I directed at him since our first introductions, even though it sure felt good to unleash it. He was the type that would not show it if something I said was offensive, or hurt him in any way. Detective Matthews really was the perfect scapegoat for my inability to contain my emotions, but he did not deserve the brunt of my frustration and anger. I thought I would have gotten it out of my system when I killed Rooster in cold blood! Most people would assume that was all the revenge a girl would need, but I unfortunately was never an easy fix kind of girl. This whole ordeal was turning me into one of those "high maintenance" kinds of girls, a type of girl I spent my whole life trying to avoid.

"Hello, my name is Vivienne, and I'm emotionally high maintenance." I said aloud to my imaginary support group.

"Hi Vivienne" they imaginarily said back.

Just then I heard my door begin to open, "Did you forget something? If it's food you're after, there's none left!" I started to say to Detective Matthews, only to be stopped short when I saw a man slowly and methodically opening my door.

It was not Detective Matthews. It was evil with a face, a face that slightly resembled Rooster.

"Hello" the man said to me in a deep voice.

I had never seen this man before, but his eyes looked frighteningly familiar. They were damned near identical to ones I had seen before. Irises so dark, you could not tell where the pupil stopped and the iris began.

"Do you know who I am?" the man inquired.

"No, I do not know you." I replied.

"Yet." He clarified. "You do not know me yet, but Vivienne, you will. I've come to collect a debt, and before I kill you, I'm going to introduce you to some things." He held up one finger and said "Pain." He flicked another finger and said, "Suffering." And rose the last one and said, "Misery." "Oh yeah, and don't forget…DEATH," he clarified as his fourth finger flicked up with the other three. "You're going to receive a very slow suffering, miserable, and painful death courtesy of Floyd and Knox, on behalf of the dearly, yet departed, Rooster."

"You look just like him." I could not help but point out.

"Our mom used to say the same thing…she called us her little Irish twins. He was my baby brother. Only ten months younger than me."

"Who are you?" I asked.

"I'm Rosey, and I'm going to take from you what you took from me…a life for a life!"

"Your brother all but killed me anyway, so go ahead and kill me!

You'll be doing me a favor!" I said as I looked down, waiting for death.

"Don't you fucking say that! Don't you dare act like you've just been happily waiting for me to appear and finish what Rooster started!"

"But I have been. I should have died in that field, but your amateur brother was too weak to finish the job!" I said boldly as I could feel myself not being overwhelmed with fear, but with hate again.

I was so full of it, that I was indifferent with my own fate. If I was going to die, I wanted to make sure Rooster's brother did not find my homicide nearly as enjoyable as he likely fantasized it would be. Detective Matthews would say that I needed one last shot at using my sassy mouth. I smiled then at the thought.

"Is that a *smile* I see? Well, how about we go upstairs and take care of that little sister of yours, Bridget. That is her name, right? I doubt you'll be smiling when I cut the life right out of her. In case you're contemplating screaming for your little FBI boy toy in the front room, don't bother, he won't be coming. I took care of him first so I could spend some quality time with the Taylor sisters. Well actually, I had only intended on spending some quality time killing you, but your sister, wow, now that's an added bonus I didn't plan! What luck I must have, two redheads for the price of one! Not that I'm getting paid, no, no…I offered to do this one for free since you took something from me. Now I'm going to take *everything* from you!"

"BRIDGET RUN! He's going to kill us both! RUN! Don't come downstairs!" I screamed.

Bridget was asleep in the room directly above mine, and while my walls were not paper thin, they were not thick enough that she would not hear my screaming. She was known to be a very light sleeper, and for once, it was a quality I liked!

I heard footsteps stirring above right before Rosey clobbered me on the head, knocking me clean off the bed. He was on top of me, and my head was pinned up in a very unnatural way against my dresser. In one quick move, it felt like he ripped my ear off. Instantly I felt heat start to radiate from that side of my head, face, and neck. Rosey covered my mouth before I could scream any more, but I knew my message had been delivered to Bridget.

Rosey pulled out a knife and said, "One more peep out of you, and I'll cut you!" He then he got up and pulled me to my feet. He shoved a knife's tip into my back as he forced me up the stairs to my sister's room. She had not come down the stairs, so I was worried sick that I would swing open the door, and find her there blinking and rubbing her eyes saying, "Viv, what's going on?" I had shared a room with Bridget for nearly her entire life. I have seen her, several times, wake up and repeat those exact words.

I could just hear that little curly-headed, strawberry-blonde saying, "Vivey, what's going on?"

She was the only person to ever call me, "Vivey", and it really was the most adorable thing ever. Why had my mom told her to pick me up? Why couldn't she be safe and sound in Dayton, over a hundred miles away from here? Why was fate trying to take away everything I loved in my once grand life? Bridget never hurt anyone her entire life. She was practically a Saint! God would not let something happen to Bridget; it goes against everything that was right and good in the world.

When we made it up the steps and to her room, Rosey kicked the door wide open. The sheets were turned back and there was no sign of Bridget in the room. There was however an open window, which was never open any other time. Both Rosey and I knew that she had gotten out of the house.

How did she get off of the roof? The roof was very steep, and I knew that Bridget was deathly afraid of heights. She must be absolutely terrified out there! It pained me to think of her all alone, clinging to the dew-soaked asphalt shingles, knowing that her only chance at survival was to jump. I hoped and prayed Bridget was brave enough to jump from the roof and risk a broken ankle or leg to avoid a severed jugular, crushed skull, or whatever it was Rosey had in store for her, or for us both.

Rosey let go of me momentarily to survey the situation. In that brief moment, I made a run for it, but not before he grabbed my foot tripping me at the stop step and causing me to fall down the entire flight of stairs. Crashing, twisting, turning, and falling. Before I even knew what had happened, I was lying in a pile of skin and disorganized bones at the bottom of the steps. Amazingly, I managed to get to my feet and dart off towards the kitchen. Rosey descended the stairs three or four at a time. From the sound of things, it was not long before he was once more right on my heels and within his reach.

I was afraid to look behind me and see how close he was, but I could hear a set of dangling keys clanging together on one of his belt loops. I heard it *chinging* and *chiming*, as it rose and fell at his waist. I could not turn around to look, but I could hear those keys getting louder and LOUDER… closer and CLOSER.

CHING! CHANG! Went the keys.

The sound became so piercing it hurt my ears. I was nearly out the front door when I felt his hand grab my hair. He yanked me back with such force that my head went one way and my feet actually flew out from under me. I looked like a sling shot recoiling as Rosey's big hand was tangled in my hair. I felt like a moth in a spider's web, caught in Rosey's trap.

When he got me under his control, he threw me to the ground, face first. My cheekbone bounced off my hard wood floor and I landed with a thud. My eyes welled up with instant tears due to the pain bursting through my cheek and into the rest of my face. At first my tears made it hard to see, but as they found their way out, sight found its way back in.

Then, all I saw was red…BLOOD! Blonde hair, wavy blonde boyish hair, soaked in blood. I did not have to see his face to know it was Detective Matthew's limp body lying in a pool of blood on my living room floor. I wanted to cry out for him, but it was too late, my former sworn enemy, turned ally, had been slain.

My mother's future lover, quite possibly my one day step-father, was lying dead on the floor, and I was about to join him. The guilt over seeing someone like him, someone so young and so strong, shook me to my core. If Detective Matthews could not survive Rosey, how would I? I did not have a prayer! I did not dare move. My body was as still as the dead body five feet into the living room. I heard Rosey catching his breath, and then he kicked me in the ribs so hard, it left me gasping for air. I clutched my side in agony.

"Fuck! Bitch, you trying to kill me!" he said as an afterthought. "Lay there and soak that in for a second, and understand that me breaking your ribs is the nicest thing I'll be doing for you this evening."

He knew I would not be going anywhere for the moment due to my debilitating pain, so he took the liberty of going back upstairs to find Bridget.

I heard him crawl out on the roof, and then I heard his footsteps pounding this way and that way, searching for my little sister.

"Oh, please have jumped! Please have jumped Bridget." I chanted quietly to myself.

For the first time, I really thought it would be ok that I died now. Sure, I was thinking those things before my encounter with Rosey, but they were not this real until relief washed over me thinking about the end. No more pain, no more worry, and no more drama, just eternal rest and peace. The idea eased the sting of broken ribs, and released my lungs little by little allowing them to breathe in and out. My breathing was shallow, but it was providing my body with oxygen...oxygen I desperately needed.

As I regained my ability to breathe, I half crawled out the front door. It was dark, and my motion sensor light on the front porch was removed. I knew there was no way anyone was going to see me until I made it to the street. I desperately needed a car to drive up without running me over.

So I crawled toward the street, but not fast enough. Before I even got past the sidewalk, Rosey was back, once more wrapping his man hands into my mane and dragging me to my feet. We went up the steps, across the porch, and into the house again.

"You're sister flew the coop. So I've got a decision to make. Do I kill you now quick and easy so that I can snuff your sister? Or do I let you live knowing that I'm coming back for you? Sure, you'll try to get into witness relocation or something, but I've infiltrated that system before. Having you disguised and relocated wouldn't do much except to challenge me. Hmmmm, what's a man to do?"

I stood there in shock while Rosey contemplated the options of my death.

"On second thought, maybe I'll let you live and just kill your entire family. Then, I will come looking for you. You killed my family, so it's only fair that I kill yours. I saw the pictures of your momma in the newspaper.

"*We just want our Vivienne back*," he said in a mocked mother's voice. Do you suppose she'll be happy to get you back in pieces? I could take you with me and send her an ear here, or a toe there, and continue until I ran out of parts! Now that would be quite the irony wouldn't it!

I imaged my mother's sullen and haunted face, as my body came via the United States Postal Service, bit by bit…piece by piece. I imagined what that would do to her and to everyone I love. I felt my heart breaking, just like my ribs had, at the thought.

Rosey really took contract killing seriously. As much time as he devoted to the in's and out's of killing, he seemed to have a poetic-ness about it. It was clear killing was his life's work. My guess is that he probably never had a paper route or flipped hamburgers in his early years. I am sure he went straight from torturing neighborhood pets and strays, to killing for hire.

Detective Matthew's voice then popped into my head saying, "You should of stayed in Virginia where they are equipped to take care of special patients like you!" *Damn him*! He was dead and still he was right! The only way I was going to save my family was to die. If I was dead, the death would stop with me. He would not punish me by killing my entire family if I was not alive to know what he had done. So I did the only thing I knew might work, I begged for my life.

"Please, please, please don't kill me! I'm only twenty-one! I'm too young to die! I haven't even had babies yet!" I then had a genius idea, and before I knew how it would be received, it flew out of my mouth. "I'm having your brother's baby!"

Rosey stopped dead in his tracks. He tilted his head and looked at me skeptically.

"Look, why do you think he carved this into me, he knew! Do you know how many times your brother came inside of me? Do you know how many times he raped me? I'm twenty-one and I'm fertile as they come!"

"Then why did he try to kill you? You're telling me my brother wanted to kill his unborn child?" Rosey said disbelievingly.

"He knew I'd be ruined. He wanted to whore me out, and he was looking at leaving the club and venturing out on his own. Once he knew I was knocked up, he knew I'd be worthless to him. He couldn't stay riding with the club with a bambino bouncing around the place. So he took me to Chicago to kill me.

He was going to cut the baby out of me so they couldn't trace his DNA back to him through the fetus. I killed him before he had the chance to kill our baby! A mother protects her young, even when they are a product of rape!"

Rosey was in a quandary. "I hope you don't think that I'm above killing a woman with her unborn child. I'd kill the pope if it suited my will. So if you think your little heartfelt plea will touch me in my love for babies place, I should warn you. Such a place does not exist!"

There was a pause.

"However, my brother's legacy could live on in his stead. You give me something to consider. How do I know you're not lying to save your own sorry ass?"

"Kill me and find out!" I dared him.

"I'll do you one better, how bout I feel up inside there and see if I can't feel my brother's off spring."

"As long as you don't hurt the baby!" I said cautiously.

"I fucked a pregnant chick once. She told me it was perfectly safe and I wouldn't harm the fetus. She just felt different inside. So, this is what I'm going to do."

I stood there trying to hold a calm and steady face.

"I'm going to fuck you before your sister can get the police down here to test your theory. If I feel my brother's blood in you, I'll let you live until the baby's born. If you're barren, I'm going to cut your empty uterus out and make you swallow it."

He spun me around and pinned me up against the wall in my foyer. The lights were dim, but I could see what was about to happen before he even told me his plan. He smashed me against the wall with his forearm across my shoulder blades. My cheek smooshed onto the cold plastered wall, and I felt him tugging at the zipper on my jeans. After he had my pants around my ankles, he began tugging at his own until they were dangling around his legs awkwardly. It was the only time Rosey did not look deadly to me.

At this point, I began to once more wish I were dead. The idea of getting raped again was more than my brain could comprehend and more than my body could bear. Tears streamed down my cheeks as I braced myself for him to penetrate me. I bit my lip to distract myself from the awful pain it would cause. I felt him prodding me, looking for his entrance. He rammed his fingers into me, and I knew the rest of him was next.

I saw headlights on the street and thought to myself, I'm right here! Someone, please, please... someone come and help me!

Then, out of nowhere, the loudest bang I had ever heard pierced through my ear drums. I did not know what happened until I felt Rosey's forearm leave my back. I was no longer pinned by him. I heard a thud and when I turned around, I could not believe my eyes! There stood Bridget, all 5'6" of her with a shotgun still in her hands. I was covered in blood, Bridget was covered in blood, and so were the walls behind me. We were all splattered and speckled with the red droplets. I looked at my feet and saw Rosey's head. He was absolutely and unequivocally dead. He did not twitch. He did not whisper any dying words. He was just dead.

Bridget was pale as a ghost. She swung the fire arm down and leaned it up against the wall. She looked to be in an absolute state of shock. I was afraid she would start to sob at what she just had done, but instead, she looked me hard in the eye and said, "I jumped off a roof! I'm scared of heights, and I jumped off a roof!"

She walked over to the kitchen table, slowly pulled out a chair, and sat down.

"I killed that guy!" she looked at her trembling hands disbelievingly. "Vivienne, I killed someone!"

I walked over to Bridget and said, "So did I."

We both looked into each other's faces for some sort of recognition, or maybe some sort of forgiveness. The girl looking at me now was not the same Bridget she had been before tonight, just like I was no longer the same Vivienne. She then nodded, looked towards the corpse at the door, and said, "Raped by brothers, killed by sisters!" She put her hand on my shoulder. "We really ought to call someone."

"Bridget?" I stopped her before she got out of the room. "Why didn't you run for help? Why did you risk your life to sneak back in the house and into my closet to get my gun? You could have just gotten the police and saved yourself first!"

"I didn't want him arrested Vivienne. I wanted him dead! It's not the Christian thing for me to ignore the Thou shall not kill of the Ten Commandments, but he was going to kill my sister. He was going to kill you! I couldn't let him get sent away for fifteen years for attempted murder, only to get out in ten for having good behavior, then come back here and kill you, me, mom, and the dog! No, no! He would have come back and eventually killed us all, one by one."

I expected my little fragile sister to be hysterical, but I also expected her to be too afraid to jump off the roof. Instead, she was calm and steady. She was ten times the girl I thought she was. She was a strong and brave woman. A woman you did not want to mess with! I spent my whole life protecting this little girl from others, and here she was, now protecting me! I am in awe of her in this moment.

She sees the look of amazement on my face and says, "What? Did you think I wasn't capable of this?"

"Did *you* think you were capable of killing someone Bridget? Because honestly, I didn't know that I was until the anger took over. One day I was just a girl, like you, and in an instant I was completely transformed into someone who wanted to take the life of another. It was like there was this switch, and Rooster flipped it on."

"Our blood's the same Vivienne. We are Taylors! Redheaded Taylor's! I felt that same blood boiling as I watched that sorry excuse for a man trying to hurt you. You've been hurt enough, and I wasn't going to run away and let you get hurt more. I knew you had the gun in your closet. Mom told me you killed that Rooster guy when he tried to kill you in Chicago. So I knew that if you could do it, I could do it too. I've spent my whole life looking up to you Vivienne. You were always so gutsy and brazen. You seemed fearless to me, and I've always wished that I could be more like you. How could I continue to look up to you if you were buried six feet under me? Killing him was easy, but losing my sister would be unbearable. Our family would never recover. Let's call the cops now."

"Shit! Detective Matthews! Oh my God, Mom's going to be devastated!" I exclaimed.

We both got up and ran toward the living room. I flipped on the overhead light to find the detective not where Rosey had left him. There was blood smeared all across the living room floor, and Detective Matthews had moved closer to the door.

"He's alive?" Bridget said looking wide-eyed at me.

I fell to the ground next to the detective. "Detective Matthews, oh my God, Detective Matthews, please don't die. My mom will kill me if I let you die! Please don't die!" I chanted as I held his head in my lap.

His pretty blonde hair was as red as mine, stained with his own blood, but he was alive. Bridget ran for the phone and called 911. Within two minutes, two Delphos Police

Cruisers were in front of the house. Within twelve minutes, two Ohio State Highway Patrols, one Van Wert County Sheriff, two ambulances, and a fire truck were parked all around my home. My neighbors stood on their front porches in their pajamas, curious and concerned about what was going on in the neighborhood. The EMS personnel came in and began working on the detective, who I was cradling in my arms.

They shooed me away as another EMT swooped in to attend to my wounds. Rosey left a nice gash on the side of my head, the cast on my leg was broken, my cheek was swelled up pretty good, and the pressure in my ribcage was making it hard to breathe. They moved without hesitation to get me to the hospital to evaluate my new injuries. I would not let them take me, at least not yet anyways. I just sat quietly and watched as they worked on the detective, hoping and praying that he would pull through this. If Justin survived Rooster, surely Detective Matthews could survive Rosey! He had to! Just then, my mom burst through the door.

"Where is he?" she said to Bridget with tears in her eyes. She knew right away when she saw me sitting next to the huddled mass of medical people. She literally sprinted to him. She immediately pumped the staff for answers. "How bad is it? What are you doing exactly? Is he going to make it? Would somebody answer me and tell me something!" she demanded.

The detective was unconscious, and the room's mood was ominous. They lifted his body and loaded him onto a stretcher. He was rushed out the door and into the back of one of the ambulances. My mom was running behind them, and when they tried to tell her she could not go to the hospital with them, I thought she was going to claw their eyes out. If she would have had a gun, I think she may have shot someone so she could ride along. Eventually after some words were said, my cousin, Delphos Police Officer Ryan Carlisle, flashed his badge and got my mom admittance into the ambulance. The sirens blared, and they tore off into the night.

I will never forget the haunting sound of those sirens, and the gut wrenching feeling of uncertainty about Detective Matthew's fate.

Bridget and I were taken out of the house and put into cruisers. They said it was for our own protection. It seemed fitting that here we both were, in the back of a squad car, murderers in our own right. Now if only my older sister would knock somebody off, then we would be quite the trio of deadly sisters. I was glad she was not here for all of this. I am glad one of us would not be forever scarred by this experience. She would be safe where she was, safely away from all the danger my life seemed to bring on my family.

Sitting in the cruiser, I could not shake the look on my mom's face as she was frightened to the core at the idea of losing Detective Matthews. She loved him. I could see it written all over her face that she truly loved the guy.

I watched through the big bay windows in the living room as they drew chalk lines around Rosey, bagged him up, and removed his body. I watched them place their little evidence cards around shell casings and struggle indicators. The whole scene played out with red and blue lights flashing through the landscape. I laid my head on the window, pressing the cold of the glass onto my searing hot cheek bone.

When I opened my eyes, the landscape had changed. There was a big jacked up white pickup truck parked in the middle of the two police cars. I saw a young guy with round features jump down from the cab and stand just outside the perimeter of my house. He watched as another figure went running onto my front porch. The State Highway Patrolmen tackled him to the ground. Then I saw them yank him to his feet, and as they did, he escaped their grasp as he ran and peered into the front window.

Then I saw the man hang his head and look down defeated as the State Troopers pulled their weapons and pointed them at him. They were yelling at him and commanding him to put his hands on his head and turn around to face them. He turned, and I immediately recognized him. It was Knox. "KNOX!" I yelled as I beat my hands frantically on the windows. Nobody paid attention to me. I looked to the other cruiser where Bridget sat and saw me freaking out. I saw her mouth to me "What's wrong?"

I kept yelling his name, "KNOX! KNOX!" but nobody could hear me. Knox still had not put his hands on his head. He appeared to be unresponsive. The officers called for backup and the Sheriff approached with his gun drawn. One of the Delphos officers tackled the round-faced kid standing by the white truck to the ground. He was holding him at gunpoint telling him to be still.

I could not wait, so I lifted up my good leg and I kicked at the window trying to break it free. It would not budge. So, I hoisted my broken leg and broken cast up to meet my good leg, and kicked with both until the window broke out of the cruiser. Glass shattered everywhere, and in that moment, all of the officers looked away from Knox and over to me.

"Knox!" I screamed.

Knox's head shot up and he looked right at me. He did not need to search, for he looked right at me! It took a moment for him to show a reaction, but it registered as I crawled out of the broken window. I fell into the street and then began hobbling towards him.

"VIVIENNE!" He said out loud. He put his hands on his head, "Viv? Is it really you?"

The officers tried to stop me as I went running toward the house, but I screamed in their faces, "He's one of you! Get your guns off of him! He's FBI! I know this man, put your guns down!"

I stood there impatiently as they threw Knox on the ground and patted him down. He had no identification, and I was distracting. They took Knox into the house and held me at the street. I stood there anxiously, and then let my sister out of the back of the police cruiser. She again said, "Vivienne, what is going on? Who are those guys?"

"Bridget, there are some parts about my abduction you don't know about. Like the fact that I wasn't held captive the entire time by Rooster. I was semi-rescued for a time. The man they have in that house, he's the one who rescued me!"

"What's he doing here?" Bridget questioned.

"I don't know exactly, but I'm sure he was aware of Rosey coming down here to pay me a visit. Before you blew his head off, he mentioned something about Knox."

"That's Knox!" Bridget asked wide-eyed.

"You act like you know him Bridge. I never told you about him." I said to her.

"Oh, you didn't have to. Mom told me. She said that when you were unconscious, you constantly talked in your sleep, and Knox was your favorite subject. Mom said all you would talk about was Knox, but nobody really knew what you were saying."

I blushed at the thought of what I might have said during my time spent in the hospital. My cousin, Officer Carslile, interrupted my thoughts and said to Bridget and I, "You can go inside now. There are officers set up to take your statements, and then get you over to the hospital. Just don't touch anything, as everything is evidence in there until we say it isn't! Got it kiddos?"

"Yes sir", Bridget and I said in unison.

"Oh don't either of you wash up or change clothes. We need to photograph the blood spatter patterns on both of you."

I had completely forgotten that I was covered with blood from Rosey. Bridget must have as well, as we both put our hands to our faces to feel the dried droplets. God, I must look horrid! Why does this always happen to me? Every time I see Knox, I look like death! I'm probably the freaking bride of Frankenstein in his eyes!

Bridget and I went into the house. I saw the crime scene all layed out, but I did not see Knox anywhere, until I heard his voice. An officer said, "You can have a seat here Vivienne. I need to take your statement about the events here tonight."

"Wait, just a sec, I just have to..." And then I turned the corner and there he was, sitting on my kitchen countertop. His head popped up as he saw me enter the room.

The uniformed officers he was speaking with said, "Well, we'll step out for a second and let you guys um, catch up."

They filed out and there we were, Knox and I in a room, with neither of us about to die. He looked at me for a long time, and then he looked down and said, "I'm so sorry Vivienne. I'm sorry I was late! I'm sorry I lied to you about who I am, and I'm sorry…I'm just sorry for everything!"

"Sorry? You're sorry? You came for me!" I said.

"Well yeah, why else would I come to Delphos, Ohio? I'd never even heard of the place until now. I had to make sure you were alright. I somehow feel like my entire existence now seems to gravitate around whether you're alright or not!"

"Why?" I said without even thinking.

"Why?" He asked me back.

"The last time I saw you, you were pointing a gun at me! You left me for dead in that field in Chicago. I thought…I thought you hated me! I thought maybe you wanted me dead too, like everyone else."

"Are you kidding me? Vivienne, I love you."

As soon as he said it, his eyes got wide at the urgency of his own confession.

"I…I…well, yeah, I love you! Besides, if I wanted you dead, you would be! Trust me on that point, I'm trained to kill. I had to point my gun at you, and I had to shoot to make the others believe you were dead. If I wouldn't do it, Floyd would have done it himself! They had to think you were dead in order for you to have any shot at getting out of this alive. I wanted to come back for you Viv. I planned to, but then my job got in the way, and I wasn't able to save you! I know it sounds like excuses, but please forgive me, forgive me for letting you down!"

"You didn't let me down." I said not knowing what I was doing as I made my way across the kitchen. I placed my pale, white hand against his scruffy unshaven face, looked into his eyes, and said, "I just made my own way is all. I do that sometimes. If what you say is true, then you didn't let me down Knox. You saved me like you always do!"

He slid off the counter, put his hands on my face, and kissed me so softly and warmly that my knees went weak. He picked me up and sat me on the countertop and then kissed me more deeply. I wrapped my good leg around him to pull him closer, and his hands clung to my face as if they too were afraid to let go.

"Get a room you two!" I heard Bridget say as she walked into the kitchen. "Your turn Viv, they need your statement. Oh, and stop it before you wipe all the blood spatter pattern from her face! You're a cop aren't you? You should know better than to touch evidence at a crime scene!"

I blushed at my sister catching me making out with a virtual stranger to her, so I thought I would rectify the situation. "Bridget, this is Knox, err, I mean Agent Jude West from the FBI."

Bridget shot me a look and said, "You didn't tell me he was a good guy! I thought you went and fell in love with one of those dirty, tattooed, biker types that you always seem to pick!"

"I did!" I said to Bridget while looking at Knox.

Knox smiled and mumbled quietly to himself, "She loves me too." He nodded and looked down bashfully at his shoes as I went into the dining room to give my statement to the cops.

I heard him start to say to Bridget as I left the room "So, I hear you're handy with a twelve-gauge..." And I smiled so big my puffy and wounded cheek throbbed with pain. Not too often in life you get to smile so big it hurts!

Chapter 32

Due to the circumstances surrounding the events that transpired the night Rosey was killed, they postponed my welcome home party. Knox took a leave of absence from the Bureau, and Bridget and I both enrolled in counseling sessions with a certified professional. My mom sat vigil by Detective Matthew's bedside for two weeks before he came out of his coma. They told her there was little to no hope that he would recover from his injuries, but when he opened his eyes and saw my mom there next to him, I guess he decided he was going to go ahead and defy modern medicine.

It was a common joke around my house that we were a family compiled of people who should not be alive.

On the night of my rescheduled party, everyone showed up like my mom had promised. Even Detective Matthews got out of the hospital in time to attend. He has a nasty scar on his neck and up the right side of his head, but he was still handsome and even more attractive when his face lights up the way it does when he looks at my mom. It was really hard to hate the guy these days, even though, we still pretend we do sometimes just for kicks.

I wore the blue dress my mom bought for me, and my bruises had all but faded away. So I looked rather presentable. I wore heels that had me eye to eye with Jude. I stopped calling him Knox after the night he saved me for the last time. In my heels, I actually liked being as tall as him. Something about everything matching up without anyone having to bend down to someone's level is kind of sexy! He helped me zip up the back of my dress, and we headed off to the VFW down the street for the big party.

The first person I saw was Justin, Agent Davis. I hopped up and down with glee. "You came!" I nearly squealed.

"Viv! Don't jump. Remember, your leg is still broken! And of course I came. Someone's got to keep you out of trouble!"

He shot a big grin at Jude who said, "Oh yeah, buddy, I remember you winding up in a hospital bed trying to do just that!"

"Yeah, well if you weren't shoving your girlfriend off on me all the time, we wouldn't have these problems would we?" Justin shot back.

I interjected with, "Well what about poor Detective Matthews! Look at that guy. All he did was sleep on my couch, and look what happened to him! Ya'll should get hazard pay to be within one hundred yards of me!"

"I do!" Justin said with a snort.

Justin and Jude both laughed at my self-satire, but it was Justin who scooped me up in his arms and lifted me right off the ground.

He said, "Viv, I've missed you!"

I hugged him wholeheartedly back and said, "Me too Justin, me too!"

"Ehmmm…am I interrupting something?" I heard a female voice say.

"Oh, sorry darling," Justin said. "Vivienne Taylor, please meet Mrs. Davis."

"I hate when you call me that, you make me sound like your great aunt or something. You can just call me Kate." She stuck out her hand for me to shake.

"A great pleasure to meet you Kate, Justin has told me so much about you!"

"Did he tell you that crap about how I beat him up and practice my kickboxing moves on him?"

I looked nervously at Justin and said, "If I lie to protect him, will you use your kickboxing moves on me too?"

She laughed out loud and said, "Buster, you better stop telling people I abuse you, or I'm going to start!"

Justin and Kate were amazing, and I was thrilled that they were able to make it to my party. The party I initially did not want to attend, but now was such a breath of fresh air.

I was told shortly before the party that they were to include an honorary moment for Jude. Some FBI big wigs thought my very public and very American hero-esque party would be a great time to honor one of their own for his years of dutiful service to the Bureau.

I told Jude it was grandstanding. He nodded and said that he personally felt it was unnecessary for him to get recognition for saving the girl he loved. He was always saying things like that to me, always reminding me that we almost lost each other in the midst of all that happened.

There were reporters and all of the big news channels represented. It was not often that a small town like Delphos received such recognition. *CNN, Fox News*, they were all present, and crammed into the VFW hall.

The group from the FBI gathered near a podium and announced that they were about to begin their scheduled presentation.

Camera men readied themselves as Jude asked, "Is my tie on straight?" I smiled and adjusted it to be perfect.

"There's my boss, Jim." Jude pointed out one of the suits on the stage. Jim was your typical six foot, mid 40's white male, with evident hair loss and a bad tie. Jude squeezed my hand before heading onto the stage to join the others and accept his recognition.

When Jim started his speech about Jude's duty, honor, and courage during his time with the Bureau, I was beaming with pride. I could not believe I had gotten so lucky to have a man of his caliber by my side. Jude looked regal standing there in his navy blue suit in the spotlight...well, until Jim started talking about me. He talked about my bravery and how the Bureau coordinated every step of the way in my safe return.

That was right about when Jude's face went dark. When Jim finally wrapped up and motioned for Jude to come and accept his plaque, Jude walked up to accept Jim's open hand for a handshake, but instead of accepting the plaque, he took his left fist and bounced it off of Jim's face. Then Jude smiled. He ignored the crowds audible response as he bent down to a horizontal Jim and said, "I warned you, you son of a bitch, you had one coming!" Jude laughed, and then stepped over Jim to address the crowd. This time, setting the record straight, "Vivienne Taylor is alive today, not because of the FBI, not because of me, or because of any one person; she's alive because someone upstairs must be looking out for her. She fought hard to be here today, and to get the chance to spend more time here on earth with her family and friends. So honor me by honoring her."

The crowd gave him a collective *Awww*.

He then continued with, "I thank you for all that you've done, the time volunteering, and the prayers that you've prayed." Then Jude asked Vivienne in front of the crowd, "Well Miss Vivienne, the entire room wants to know, what's next for you? Where do you go from here?"

I bit my lip and offered my answer, "Quantico."

Knox looked at me like I had just punched him in the stomach, successfully knocking the wind out of him.

He paused and then said into the microphone, "And do you want to tell the nice people of Delphos what Quantico, Virginia holds in store for you?"

"FBI Training Academy...if they'll have me..."

I smiled obstinately while Knox tried not to roll his eyes.

If there was one thing I knew, it was that this ordeal had quite literally kicked my ass. With one dead guy's blood on my hands, and one on Bridget's, I knew my life and my family's life would never be the same. If there was one thing I learned it was that, *when the going gets tough, the tough get going*, and I was not the type of girl who would lie in any ditch and just accept death. With that in mind, I could not help but feel that now was the time for me to keep going. I needed to make a fresh start where this ordeal had seemingly ended. Life is just too damn short not to. And besides, what could go wrong?

~THE END~

ABOUT THE AUTHOR:

Heather Lynn Osting is no stranger to disaster, born in the Blizzard of 1978 in rural Ohio, she knew being taken to the emergency room in her mother's womb on a snowmobile would make for a great first story for her life.

A paralegal by profession, a writer by passion, writing was something that was always within her. Be in legal research and writing, or writing poetry as a child, or her very first start in fiction, Heather Lynn was always going to write '*something*'.

It all started one day after she had finished reading a particularly fantastic novel and wanted desperately to find something else to read that she would enjoy as much. She went to the Library searching for something that would snag her attention, but grew disheartened in leaving the library empty handed. So then and there, as she walked to her car she said, "Well, If I can't find a good book to read, then I'll just write my own!" and she did. Later that afternoon Dead in a Ditch had its start.

Heather Lynn is a long time resident of Delphos, Ohio with her collection of vintage books and her adopted dog "Chubs". She continues to work within the local legal community.

Made in the USA
Columbia, SC
04 June 2020